# A FLASH IN THE PAN

# A FLASH IN THE PAN

## A NOVEL

## Ralph Williams

QUOIN PRESS

First published 2001


ISBN 1-877163-27-9

Published by Quoin Press
P.O. Box 2151, Christchurch, New Zealand
Production and design by Orca Publishing Services Ltd

Text printed and bound by Deadline, Christchurch
Cover printed by Rainbow Print Ltd, Christchurch

*The contents of a book, the secrets of a man's soul, the yolk of an egg,*
*forever remain locked, hidden, until*
*like a nutshell, they are finally cracked open and revealed to all.*

Rough translation of a Chinese inscription on a very old brass-bound wooden box displayed in the Otago Early Settlers Museum in Dunedin. The box contains a small ivory abacus, a miniature painting of a beautiful young woman, a lock of black hair, a gold ring and a steamship ticket to Kowloon. The accompanying label reads: *Kindly loaned by Mr. George Mann who discovered it while prospecting in Gabriel's Gully, Central Otago.*

# PROLOGUE

*The dreadful thing had smashed into his soul the first time without prior warning. It was evil. It was malevolent. It scared the living Christ out of him. He could tell no one. If the ever-inquiring doctors gained so much as an inkling that he had this awful thing inside his mind he knew he would be locked up. He had eventually named it 'The Crush'. He had seen other men admit to things like this and they were now incarcerated in strait-jackets. 'Shell-shock' was a well-used word that had its beginnings in the First World War but no one seemed to know just what it was that changed a man's attitude and habits, sometimes in a split second. It had meant that many men had been court-martialled and shot for cowardice, others treated like outcasts for the rest of their lives. Not him. He was going to escape this thing. Its ingress into his brain was insidious. It sometimes lay dormant like an evil snake in the grass but he alone knew it was waiting to escape and take control. There was nobody with whom he could burden this dark secret. He would have to not only conceal it but treat it with cunning before it got the better of him. Some times he could recognise the warning signs and brace himself to withstand its wicked onslaught. Sometimes not. He had a sickening feeling that it could be gaining the upper hand. He would be cunning and defeat it. He called it Crush. Crush was his enemy and he would fight Crush. He would overcome Crush… or perish.*

The large brown trout was lurking in the shade provided by the low overhanging rock, its tail slowly moving in order to retain it in position. It was just clear of the influence created by the faster moving current and it felt safe from the attention of the numerous shags which frequented that part of the stream. Its attention was fixed on a mixture of muddy water being stirred up next to the bank. A small, yellow-striped bumblebee, which had inadvertently become crushed in the dirt, floated away, feet up, on top of the water. Dead. It's colour signaling that perhaps it was edible. With a quick flick of its tail the trout with lightning speed darted out from its hiding place and swallowed it with one swift gulp, returning almost immediately to resume its vigil for any more such offerings.

The cause of the muddy water was hunkered down on the bank of the stream. A young man, both white knees poking through his tightly drawn trousers, was holding a shiny tin-metal dish in both hands.

It was a totally different type of metal that glittered brightly in the bottom of the pan. Gold. There was more than a thimble full. The pan's owner's eyes glittered almost as much as the residue in the pan. This was the third wash in a row that had revealed this much to his gaze. His heart pounded uncontrollably in his chest. Try as he might he just wasn't able to stop his hands from trembling. This was it. He had fossicked here in the Three O'clock Stream – a tributary that flowed into the grey and sometimes muddy waters of the Taieri River – for almost a month now.. His gut instincts had finally paid off. Admittedly he was only a very amateur gold-miner, but with a smattering of geology obtained from an intensive pressure-cooker course self-taught by browsing through the local library, and some shrewd lateral thinking, he had finally tracked the source of this ever-increasing trickle of gold he had been panning. He had found signs at irritatingly irregular intervals for the past few days before ultimately tracking its tenuous path to this point. Other scavengers of the precious metal had fossicked in the area but had tired or had finally been put off the scent. Did gold have a scent? he laughingly thought. Of course it did. He picked up the pan and held it to his nose. Yes, he thought again. Of course it has. I can smell it!

Others were put off the trail by the mere fact that there had been a fault-line in the hill and the source of the vein was at least fifty yards to one side of the fault. There must have been a gigantic upheaval of earth and rocks thousands of years ago. It hadn't struck him till that day, when he had rested, splay-legged, on the hill opposite for a cigarette and had noticed the difference in the lay of the land. He had sat bolt upright. There was certainly a difference in the vegetation growing on the fault, no doubt due to the water-retention qualities of the lower rift.

He wouldn't perhaps have seen it then, but for the fact that a wild pig, rooting amongst the abundant Nassella tussock grass growing there, had diverted his attention. The young man had squatted there on his haunches enjoying the view and the antics of the pig that was quite unaware its porcine eating habits were being closely watched, when he noticed the anomaly in the hillside. Perhaps it was the angle of the sun that had accentuated the faultline and brought it to his attention. He climbed up to the shelf of rock which had the appearance of a chimney in the cliff face, looked carefully for the point where it joined the other outcrop and with his small shovel dug energetically at the base of it. Somebody surely must have fossicked here, he thought. The whole area had been worked over many times by goldminers in the early days, especially the itinerant Chinese. A large contingent of these people had moved across the Tasman when the Australian diggings at Kalgoorlie and Coolgardie had started to peter out, and were eyed with suspicion by the other goldminers here. Life indeed was not pleasant for these so-called intruders.

Forget about history, he had thought. Today's today!

He carried the heaped pan carefully down the slope. It was only a small distance down to the fast-flowing creek where he divided his heap and left a small portion of the spoil in the pan. Immersing it in the stream he sloshed the water into the pan and swirled it round, quite vigorously at first, then more slowly as he dispensed with the larger residual pieces. With increasing caution he became gentler in his panning efforts until finally he had a cupful of residue remaining in the vessel. He scrutinised the bottom intently and saw to his satisfaction that the results of his efforts were beginning to bear fruit. Another minute and he sat on his haunches staring in amazement at the bottom of the pan. The results were astonishing.

He had hit paydirt, as they would say in America. As they would say anywhere.

He had been in the district on and off for the last four years or so. The war had played havoc with his visits unfortunately. But after a long two-year absence overseas he was here for good now. To hell with the war. He was finished with that nonsense. Practically every weekend he had managed to come out here. Sometimes even during the week. It was good therapy. Those of the local pub crowd who had come to know him had liked him in spite of him being somewhat a loner, and had thrust upon him the title of 'The Panhandler'. He didn't actually object to this sobriquet and indeed was secretly pleased with it. He was only twenty-seven years of age and looked much younger. He was quite popular with the locals and they treated him with good-natured tolerance. They, too, had seen gold-hunters come and go. Never before as young as this though.

They were used to such well-known fossickers as Gumboot Jim, Next-Time Taylor, Nugget Barber and Swagger Stickle. All of these gentlemen had for years followed their noses and their instincts to no avail. They all to a man 'knew 'where it was but hadn't quite succeeded in their quest for 'the big one'.

'The Panhandler' bought the occasional drink for the older locals and listened to their tales with interest, trying at times to sort the 'shit from the clay', as he succinctly put it. He possessed an unusual and prominent scar, which started on the hairline of his forehead and finished behind his left ear. It looked as though he'd had a major operation at one time. The locals were curious but never found out what it was. Some of the tall tales that were handed to him were obviously fabrications especially concocted for his benefit but others were well worth investigating. And investigate them he did. The town had seen many incursions dating back to about 1860 when Tuapeka became the Mecca of thousands of gold seekers from across the other side of the world. Many had perished through sickness, drunkenness and other types of mayhem that had been rampant at that time. The mere mention of gold was enough to warrant a throat being cut. Early photographs had depicted the myriad rude huts and tents dotted around the hills and he had read all the necessary books on that period. It held a fascination all of its own for him and he was totally immersed in the lore of the district. Lawrence was his favourite area and he was fully conversant with all the creeks and streams around from Waitahuna to the south and Evans Flat to the northwest.

The area he was in now, however, was totally different. Just opposite the little railway settlement of Hindon and above the Christmas Creek whistle-stop. Christmas Creek was the only entrance to the Silver Peaks and Lambhill sheep stations.

He'd had a hunch and it now looked as though it had paid off.

He felt an empathy with the early diggers and wondered if he had lived in that era whether he would have had the guts to follow it through to the bitter end as many had tried. And failed.

But here he was. Triumphant. He had found it. Was it the mother lode? It had been talked about at length and never been discovered. He climbed back to where he had obtained the original spoil and sat down, exultant. What to do next was the big question.

*Was Crush going to intrude on this moment of triumph? He could feel the warning signs: heart starting to pound… sweating palms… a feeling of a vice gripping in his chest. The sky was going to fall on him. He wondered if these were the first signs of a heart attack. Why does it have to be me? Sit still George and breathe deep. Deep. Deeper. Don't let it do this to you. You are the boss of your own destiny. Lower your pulse rate. Steady, steady now. It can't touch you when you're in control, can it? No, of course not! He was starting to accept the fact that it had assumed a personality now. What the hell was he thinking? Things like this don't have personalities! It's all in your mind, George. Steady the Buffs. You can beat it. Breathing in long, measured intakes of air he remained poised till the oxygen had a somewhat calming effect on him. The feeling slowly but gradually dissipated. He relaxed cautiously. One up to him, this time anyway.*

As he looked at the cliff he could see that at its base was the site of an early stone hut, typical of the Chinamen's rock dwellings that abounded in the area. The easiest method of construction was to obtain flat rocks and place them across a chimney such as this, packing the spaces with moss and mud. It would provide cover from the biting Central Otago winds that could kill during the wintertime. He had seen some of the huts and imagined that to the average goldminer of that period they would have seemed quite opulent. He could still make out the very faint smoke-blackened area that the fireplace had occupied. The previous occupant surely must have known he was sitting overlooking a fortune. He wondered if the owner had been favoured enough to discover this. After all these years he thought it still had soot attached to its inner walls. He idly scratched the luxuriant growth of moss on the back of the rock-face with his little fossicking pick. His efforts uncovered a rock dissimilar to the rest of the face. Quartz. It didn't belong there. A stranger to the rockface. His curiosity getting the better of him, he scratched harder using the point as a jemmy and inserting it further. The rock parted company with its perch where it had been jammed in and fell onto the ground.

There was quite a cavity behind the rock's resting-place. He could see something sitting faintly visible in the gloom of the hole. Reaching in, his groping fingers touched a square object the size of a little tea chest. He carefully drew it out into the light and gazed at it. He estimated it to be about eight inches square. It was an old and mouldy, but surprisingly not at all rotten, box made of wood, bound with brass and with Chinese writing on the lid. Obviously a miner's ditty-box that would probably have contained his most personal items. Surprised by its weight he hefted it with both hands. He placed it gently on the ground and lifted the tightly seized lid. Inside the box lay gold. Packed to the brim almost. Gold. It was filled with the stuff. There was another box just like it in the cavity. This one, however, was much lighter than the first and opened readily. No gold in this one. Only some scraps of paper, a picture and some kind of object made of bone. He closed the lid and went back to the first box.

He sat there for what seemed an eternity and breathed deeply to try to contain the immense surge of excitement which had once more taken control of his shaking body. Slowly he calmed down. He had to think more constructively. He was behaving like a child. He laughed out loud. 'So bloody what if I am?'

*A pang of 'The Crush' hit him. Brutal forces at work once again. Waves of depression enveloped him like a grey cloud of fog. It was similar to the cloying smell of death, which he had encountered many times while at the war. One would know when entering a so-called deserted building that its occupants were still present. Their souls were long departed but their earthly presence was very much in existence. As a lad on the farm it had been one of his jobs to pluck the wool from dead sheep. At times their flesh had taken on a bluey-greenish tinge and stank to high heaven, but a human body had a smell all of its own. Indescribable. It stayed with you. The crush was indescribable.*

*He felt better now. It had lifted. But for how long?*

He had to get out of here. He felt guilty, as if committing a crime, and could feel unseen eyes watching him. With trembling hands he placed both boxes carefully in his knapsack, then without checking the area any further he rose and walked the mile down the creek bed to the railbridge where his vehicle was parked on the Hindon side. His shoulders felt quite sore from the weight by the time he reached his car. He carefully stowed the knapsack in the back seat. It was only then that he realised that in his excitement and haste he had left behind his prospecting hammer together with his little shovel and gold-panning dish. It was lucky he had made a spare pick.

At that moment he heard voices along the road leading down to the bridge. He glanced up furtively and saw seven Girl Guides marching along the path towards him. The Guide leader looked rather horsy and was authoritatively issuing orders to the laggard at the rear to 'Get a wriggle on'. This one was wearing a sulky look and carrying the pack's flag tied to a manuka stick. As they passed the young man they were chattering away noisily. The leader said a brief 'Oh, hello' as though she had just noticed him and the rear one gave him a surly stare. The leader bellowed 'C'mon, Cynthia' to the fractious banner bearer and swinging her arms vigorously strode off in the direction of the railway bridge.

A footbridge, just wide enough to accommodate a horse, ran alongside the railway bridge. He had seen three musterers leading their beasts over it that morning and had idly wondered what would happen if a train was to exit from the tunnel which was but about fifty yards along the track. Somebody would no doubt get one hell of a fright. The Guides by this time had left the bridge and were heading upstream in the direction he had just come from, their flag fluttering a defiant salute.

The young man climbed into his Chevrolet and drove off. No one saw him leave. Except maybe the pig.

*He drove slowly and carefully up the grassy incline from the railway siding and onto the gravel road, trying to restrain the mounting surge of excitement. This is it. I've done it. I've found it!*

*Then, in the midst of his exultation he dismayed to feel a sense of uneasiness growing in his stomach as he recognised once more the warning signs. He pulled over to the side of the road, switched off the Chevy's engine and sat there with his face buried in his hands, waiting. Crush was coming. He braced for the first excruciating pain to strike in his brain. He stiffened in anticipation of the malignant thing's onslaught. Crush was here. He stifled the first sob welling in his guts. 'God!' he screamed silently. 'Why me?' The pain spikes increased in bursts of swelling intensity until finally peaking in a blinding flash. He lost consciousness and slumped on the car's front seat. Forty minutes later he opened his eyes and stared at the mass of wires under the dashboard. He sat up straight and pulled the starter switch. Five minutes later found him driving down the road as though nothing had happened. Crush had once more vacated his tortured being.*

# CHAPTER ONE

The little cemetery spilled out and down from the trees surrounding the consecrated area. The tiny chapel overlooked the panorama of lichen-covered headstones, some, dating back over eighty years to the goldrush days. The age of each grave was reflected in its degree of neglect. Some, however, were of much more recent origin and of these, there were small, sad plots consisting of only little mounds of earth awaiting the arrival of a more formal means of identification. The setting of this hallowed place was complimented by the lovely sunny afternoon and all was still. Even the silence sounded reverent.

Someone long ago had, with kind forethought, decided that the dead also deserved the opportunity to satisfy an aesthetic desire to face the warmth of the north and had designed the area to be situated on a gently sloped hillside. Not too steep to make any elderly person afflicted with a trembling walk fearful in their efforts to pay last respects to a loved one in that area, but with fall enough to provide a generous run of any surplus water that might be found there. It most probably had been the choice of a man who had some previous experience of gold mining. A man who was determined that when he too departed this cruel world, he was not going to be up to his neck in freezing water, as he most probably had been through much of his working life.

To an observer with a minimum amount of imagination, the place could have been likened to an ancient Roman amphitheatre, it's fifty or so grey, sombre tombstones standing like members of the senate, idly chatting to each other and perhaps awaiting the arrival of a furiously galloping courier from the war-torn north bringing some news to cause a ripple of excitement to an otherwise boring day. Having conjured up all manner of fantasies the observer would not have been disappointed by the arrival of, not as he had expected, a Roman courier, but three very out-of-breath children who had legged it all the way from the church to make it to the impending funeral of one of the town's old identities.

The three had started their run from the service as the cortege left the church situated in the middle of the town. The idea was to see if one of the runners could get to the grave-site by the time the hearse arrived at the cemetery. To do this, a fairly high degree of fitness was required by the participants. It was an age-old ritual, apparently initiated to overcome a shortage of seats on the accompanying funeral vehicles, and it became a race of honour over the years. To be 'in at the kill' as it was irreverently described, put one up on the school social scale until another funeral eventuated.

Practically all the able-bodied school children in Thexton had taken part in 'the coffin run' over the years and this funeral of course was no exception. The local bookie had tried to cash in on it one year but after allegations of fixing the race he had been asked to desist from his dealings with the departed. It just didn't seem nice.

The winner on this sad occasion was a young lass by the name of Yvette. It was not known by anyone on that day that she would go on to represent New Zealand at the Olympic games years later. From such competitions are the means by which dreams come to fruition. The two puffing boys who accompanied her made grudging acknowledgment that she had indeed made it to the winning-post first and one even patted her on the back. An accolade indeed! The three then climbed up a neighbouring tree and idly swung their legs as they awaited the arrival of the procession. Now and then their chests heaved in unison.

The sombre black hearse turned into the graveyard and drew to a halt at the end of the second to last row. As soon as the following vehicle had parked behind it the funeral director and his companion got out and moved to the rear of the hearse. There was a slight delay while a fair-headed young man climbed out of the rear car and helped a sobbing woman to alight. He was obviously trying his best to console her but to no avail. The watching bystanders could see by his sagging shoulders that he too was in a state of grief.

Harry's mother had maintained a calm attitude towards the proceedings but it looked at this stage as though her composure had completely evaporated. Two women hurried to help her up to this, the final hurdle. They stood beside her, each holding an arm in undeclared support. Meanwhile Harry, who by now had assumed a certain amount of authority, calmly stood at the head of the coffin while the other five pallbearers lined themselves up and the coffin slid out of the vehicle. The funeral director moved the pallbearers into position as unobtrusively as possible then stood back, hands clasped, as funeral directors are wont to do. He gave a nod to the group.

The coffin and its bearers moved slowly into the aisle and proceeded at a sombre pace along the grassy strip. They placed the casket onto the two wooden bearers straddling the hole and stood to one side. Harry rejoined his mother and put his arm around her.

The priest intoned the burial service readings. These seemed to be interminable, but to everybody's relief eventually came to a halt. Another nod from the funeral director and the coffin was slowly lowered.

The flowers on top of the coffin were Nana's favourites. Harry had picked them especially from her garden that very morning. Masses of sweet peas. He had helped to prepare the bed for them last winter. He had built the trellis to grow them on and they had joked about the terrific amount of cow manure Harry had insisted on putting in the trench. Nana reckoned the lot would rot rather than sprout and he was secretly pleased when they grew strong and healthy. A colossal crop. A tremendous heaping of colours to deluge her coffin with.

She would have liked that touch. It would have tickled her sense of humour. She always said he was a bit heavy-handed when it came to dishing out anything for her in the way of gifts. Not that he could ever afford anything expensive.

When the priest had finished his ritual all the mourners filed past, pausing for a moment to pay their last respects. They were handed a little flower each and in turn dropped it into the hole, no doubt hoping it would serve as a small but tangible acknowledgement of their farewell and gesture of their grief. This done, they stood for a while at the edge of the grave and silently said their goodbyes. Some wandered off in the direction of the parked vehicles. Others gathered in little groups and spoke in undertones. Every now and again someone would break off and approach Harry's mother with an expression of their condolence.

Harry still had a small bunch of flowers in his hand. He moved away from the main group and carried on walking until he stood at the foot of a small mound of earth three aisles away. The small, white, temporary cross bore the simple lettering, 'Kathleen Hicks'. Harry leaned forward and placed the small bunch of assorted flowers on the bare earth. He then stood back and straightened up to his full height. An observer would have seen his lips moving, but would have heard no words spoken. A message when delivered from the heart has no sound in a case like this.

Harry was saying farewell to a very dear childhood friend. It hurt him like hell. His lips trembled and it was with some difficulty that he managed to stem the imminent tide of tears. For him the moment was doubly sad.

Abruptly he turned away and went to rejoin the other mourning group. His mind was still with the plot he had just left and with the person that lay deep in that plot.

He would never forget Kathy. His first love. First loves are always the hardest to eradicate from one's memory. They create the deepest impressions somehow.

Harry clicked the gate behind him, paused, and took one final look back up the flower-fringed path. Last look. Last time. Regretfully he turned on his heel and with both arms weighed down by suitcases he strode up the gravel drive. An onlooker would have perceived by his body language that his heart wasn't really in his actions. About the time Harry took his twentieth step, however, the watcher would have noticed something change in his demeanour. He suddenly squared his shoulders as though having made up his mind to face whatever it was in front of him. Five minutes later found him standing at the end of the long driveway up from his nana's little farmlet, at the spot where the New Zealand Railways bus would stop to pick him up. The spot that for the past nine years or so had been his school bus pick-up point.

This would be the last time. He tried to shake off a feeling of self-pity. He had about twenty minutes to wait. As he gazed around a flood of memories enveloped him and for a short period he wallowed in a throat-lumping blanket of nostalgia.

There was the massive macrocarpa stump where he would sit waiting for the school bus to arrive. Other school children, largely thanks to the efforts of their fathers, were fortunate enough to have had bus shelters erected for protection from the elements. Harry's only recourse when inclement weather loomed was to take cover under the main trunk of the tree which still lay half-attached to the stump. It had never been properly cleared away after the Electric Power Board gang had taken to it with a large crosscut saw five years ago. A half-hearted attempt by Harry and several local kids to commandeer it and construct their own treehut of sorts was doomed to failure as the cows in the paddock had decided to make it a shelter for themselves. End of building programme. It didn't worry Harry much – the place was always full of cowshit and besides, a treehut is supposed be up a tree not underneath it.

The tree stood in the corner of an old orchard that backed onto the main road. The orchard itself had been quite well maintained by dint of sheer hard work by his nana. She had religiously kept up a prune-and-spray programme. The orchard next door, however, was a completely different kettle of fish.

Old Dinny Croyden owned it and to be quite frank he was not to be considered the world's greatest exponent for anything remotely agricultural. His apples were full of codling moth grubs and other things that went bump in the night.

The ground would be thick with windfalls of apples that were left to rot there. One year, in a spurt of enthusiasm, Dinny had decided to make an attempt at brewing cider but it really hadn't come to anything. He was highly suspicious of anyone being in his orchard and as a consequence the local kids seemed to think that because they were forbidden then it naturally followed that his apples tasted much better than anyone else's. Dinny became fair game to their poaching forays. There were holes in his fence that could be 'snuck' through and to hear Dinny in full cry as he caught sight of someone pinching his apples was a wonderful thing.

'When I ketch holder you young bestids I'll give you such a tonguing you'll not sit down fer months!' And he'd wave his stick around like a Zulu warrior and thump it down on the barbed wire in frustration. The more he swore, the tastier the apples seemed to be. Something to do with forbidden fruits, Harry supposed.

He remembered his mother telling him about being driven home from Sunday church as a young girl with the old Catholic priest, Father Casey, at the reins. The priest was on his way to visit his sick mother and had kindly offered her a lift home to her gate. He was very proud of his gig, which was kept in tiptop condition.

The horse was a fancy high-stepper given to him by an affluent parishioner who, being not only a horse lover and a bettor, had covered his chances of getting through the pearly gates to heaven with a two-way gift pack bet. Hence the horse. Some of his other parishioners wondered why the horse had been christened 'Sinner'. They were never enlightened. Big Ernie Wilson reckoned that the Reverend Father heard the horse's confession once a month prior to a race meeting. Reckoned the horse supplied him with a few winners. Old Father Casey liked his pint and he certainly enjoyed the occasional punt.

'Senga, m'dear,' said the Reverend Father as he drew the gig to a halt beside the gate to Alby Cousin's orchard. 'Now wouldn't that be a great idea to maybe hop over the fence and get two of those shiny apples. They're just waiting to be plucked from that tree over there. I'll just be waiting for you here while you do it.'

'But Father,' replied Harry's mother, 'won't that be stealing now?'

'Oh, tush girl! Of course it wouldn't be. Not since you've been told to now.'

After hearing this story and many others from his mother Harry was inclined to view religions and what they purported to stand for with some suspicion. It seemed rather strange for quite a few so-called staunch churchgoers to get drunk, beat their wives, swear, curse and bet, then on Sunday arrive at church all spruced up in their finery and be forgiven all their sins. Monday morning and it was all on again. Like flicking a radio on and off according to the needs of the occasion. His nana went to church whenever possible, a rather reluctant Harry being dragged along behind, simply, it seemed, so that she could pray for divine intervention to ensure that he grew up to be a boy she 'could be proud of'. Harry was unaware of any spirit on high aiding him and decided at quite an early age that you make your own luck. His nana was pretty straight in all her dealings with people and advocated that one was 'To fear God, look people straight in the eye, and carry a big stick at the same time as you're looking.'

A small group of objects travelling across the horizon diverted his attention from the stump. Young Doug Macbeth and his team of Clydesdales were moving obliquely across the hillside pulling a set of discs. By the colour change which had taken place across the ploughed paddock it could be seen that Doug had been at it for some time already that morning. His father Ted owned the farm and operated it with Doug's help. Doug had not been able to go overseas to the war with his mates as he was prone to bad attacks of asthma and even though it wasn't his fault he somehow felt inadequate because of this. As a consequence he worked like a Trojan as if this was one way he could show people what he was made of. There was really no need to go to these great lengths as he was well known as a worker and was well thought of by the community as a whole. But work he did. Hard.

Ted preferred Clydesdales to tractors and was often heard to say that a horse was always pulling in top gear, whereas a tractor had to change gear to get the same results. To argue with Ted about the merits of this hypothesis was a waste of time, as Ted would never listen to anyone who held a different view on the subject. In the end it was better to simply agree with him then forget about it. His front room was festooned with ribbons, cups, and medals. On his 'skite wall' there were photographs of Clydesdales facing left,. Clydesdales facing right; Clydesdales pulling wagons, pulling ploughs, discs, harrows, logs and loghaulers. Row upon row of ribbons. Photos of parades, plodding ponies, processions, prizegivings, proud ploughmen. Certificates, cups... clusters of more bloody Clydesdales than you could count. When young Douglas was born it was said by many that it was only with the greatest difficulty that Mrs Macbeth prevented him from being christened Clyde.

For some strange reason people had the impression that Ted Macbeth was rather fond of Clydesdale horses.

Over the door of the stables was a horseshoe measuring eighteen inches across. Ted, when asked, always said it fell off a sickly foal he once had. Only those who glimpsed the twinkle in his eye knew that their leg was being pulled.

Ted had been brought up on a farm in Hawkesbury where he learned his trade as a ploughman. In those days a working day was termed 'eight hours tight chains'. In other words, the horses did eight hours' work. The ploughman's time was taken up with catching, feeding and grooming the horses. His boss had been an ex-cavalry officer and the horses' comfort and well-being took precedence over the man's. It was a tough life and he wouldn't have swapped places with anyone. His father had been a goldminer in the early days. A mine cave-in killed him when Ted was only three years old. Fortunately for Ted his mother married a farmer who was also a keen horse lover and introduced Ted into the mysteries of mucking out in the stables. Ted took to this like a duck takes to water. Thus a life devoted to things four legged was formed.

A deep reverberation down the road indicated that the New Zealand Railways bus was approaching. The rumble was being caused by the multitude of corrugations in the gravel road. Where the corrugations ended the potholes commenced. Because of the war the road maintenance programme was sadly in arrears. The roads in that area had cut up rather badly and the ditches at the sides were slowly and inexorably decaying despite the valiant efforts of the two ancient county council surface men, Georgie Beaumont and Shorty Dix, who should have been put out to pasture years ago. They were aided in their efforts by Percy Coleman who drove the decrepit council Bedford truck carting gravel from the local creek bed. Out of Georgie, Shorty, Percy and the Bedford it was decided that of the four of them the truck was the one with the worst case of arthritis.

Everyone knew that creek-bed gravel was not the best to use on a highway because the pebbles were inclined to roll off the road faster than a kid's marbles on a sloping playground, but it was better than nothing.

The bus came to a halt accompanied by the screeching sound of protesting brake drums most reluctant to carry out their duty. The wheel closest to Harry locked up prematurely and created a skid mark about six feet long in the loose gravel. A cloud of dust arose and enveloped Harry so that when the door opened and he boarded the bus, he was accompanied by a barrow load of dried silt, the consistency of talcum powder, and half the local riverbed. The driver quickly shut the door, though far too slowly and far too late as far as old Mrs Cain was concerned. She was a crotchety old biddy who had boarded the bus just up the road by the bridge. She stared coughing like a woman possessed. Harry reckoned half of it was a put on.

'Why couldn't you wait till the dust had settled, Driver?' she angrily snorted, tapping her stick on the floor. The driver, knowing her of old, said nothing. She knew his name quite well but always insisted on calling him 'Driver'. It annoyed the hell out of him. Start an argument with her and you could be here till doomsday.

Harry placed his two suitcases in the space up the front next to the driver and proffered a ten-shilling note. He did have the correct change but it looked better if you flashed a note. He hoped most of the passengers were watching. If you've got it, flaunt it. He moved back along the bus which immediately took off with a jerk and made his passage rearward more undignified than he would have wished. He hoped most of the passengers weren't watching.

Spying an empty seat about two-thirds of the way down the bus he made for it, just as the vehicle rounded the first bend. Caught once more off balance Harry made a vain effort to swivel his frame and sit down at the same moment.

A young lady wearing horn-rimmed glasses was seated next to the window. Harry, carried sideways by the force of gravity, thought for an agonizing moment he was going to punch her in the face. He altered the position of his right hand and pushed her heavily on the shoulder. His left hand travelled past her face and dangerously near her left breast, finally coming to a halt on the window ledge. He managed to get one knee onto the seat and keep it there. Meanwhile, his nose was about two inches away from being buried in the girl's left ear. Amongst all this carry on he noticed that she smelled of fresh soap. Nice.

Fortunately at this point the bus straightened out and the pressure Harry was under was eased somewhat. With a Herculean effort he completed his half-turn and flopped into the seat.

'I'm awfully sorry,' he stammered. 'I hope I haven't hurt you.'

She smiled. 'Nice save. Bit of a rough driver today. I think the old dear's upset him. You all right?' Her sentences were clipped and concise.

Harry was relieved. He hadn't made exactly the entrance he was supposed to but it didn't seem to have fazed his companion.

'Yeah. No problem. I did think I was going to land in your lap for a moment.' They both chuckled as if sharing a secret. Eye contact was established for a brief moment.

Harry decided she was nice. Sort of comfortable.

'You going far?'

Harry was about to ask that question himself but she beat him to the punch. 'To the stars and beyond,' he replied. He hadn't quite meant to say that but he and his friend Maggot used the phrase quite a lot and it came out automatically. He hoped it didn't sound too high and mighty.

She smiled again. 'Nothing like aiming high, eh?'

'I'm off to Dunedin actually. I've got an interview for a job as an apprentice motor mechanic. So I guess I'm a little excited. Y'know – working in the big smoke and all that.'

'Oh, I wouldn't say it's that exciting. I've been in Dunedin now for three years and to me it's a lot of hard work.'

'What sort of work do you do?'

'Not very exciting, I'm afraid. I work as a seamstress at Bagleys. I've just managed to get three days off so I could go up to Alexandra to see my mother who's got tuberculosis. She's not very well I'm afraid and I just had to go and see her. The doctor said she's not going to be with us much longer.' Her bottom lip trembled as she spoke.

'I'm sorry to hear that,' replied Harry. 'Just lost my nana and that was a bit hard to take.'

'I'm Leda Lamb, and what's your name?' she asked. Straight out. Just like that. No mucking around.

'Harry. Harry Evans.' He had been going to say something facetious when he discovered her name but decided not to. Most probably she had heard about 'leading a lamb to the slaughter' a thousand times already. There was a time to be humorous and this was definitely not it.

The bus pulled into the Thexton stop.

'Ten minutes for refreshments and your comfort stop,' announced the bus driver.

Initially only three passengers climbed out. One of these immediately entered the back alleyway that bore the sign 'MEN' above it and emerged a few minutes later with a relieved look on his face. It was unfortunate that he had omitted to button up his fly. Harry wondered whether he should tell him and decided not to. Let someone else do it. Didn't want to make the poor fellow feel like a fool.

It was at this point that Mrs Cain decided it was about to alight. She kept muttering to herself, but loud enough to let everyone know that 'the service was disgraceful and the company should seriously think about employing a different driver.'

The driver ignored her once more and busied himself shifting Harry's two suitcases into the rear compartment of the bus. He, too, was doing a bit of muttering and the word 'bitch' was to be clearly heard amongst his mouthings. Mrs Cain wandered off down the street, ostensibly to do her weekly shopping. The driver knew she would be waiting for him at five o'clock that evening to vent her feelings in no uncertain manner when he did the return trip.

Harry stood up. 'I think I'll just pop in to get some chutty,' he said to his travelling companion. 'Coming?'

'Right with you,' she replied. She certainly didn't mince her words, he thought.

She followed him out of the bus.

'Always strikes me as a bit of a hick town,' she uttered. It seemed to come out as a statement of fact rather than an attempt to sound malicious.

'Aw, I guess it's not that bad,' said Harry. He didn't want to appear parochial in his outlook by defending his old home town too vigorously, yet by the mere mention of 'hick' he felt that she was inferring that he too might possess a degree of 'hickness'. And this coming from a total stranger. Definitely not on.

'At least everybody's pretty friendly,' he submitted lamely.

To his relief she didn't pursue the subject further so he left it at that.

Having bought a couple of sticks of chewing gum, he offered her one. She shook her head and instead bought a small bar of milk chocolate. Snapping a piece off she held the remainder out. Almost as a peace offering, he thought. It was his turn to shake. Disappointingly, it seemed they had dissimilar tastes. He wished he'd bought chocolate instead though.

Harry gazed around the little tearooms that served as a bus-ticket sellers, gossip centre and a provider to the passing public. They had a reputation for making fantastic Cornish pasties. Harry had drawn the line at their mince pies after retrieving a thumbtack from one. He was lucky it only pricked his gum. It wasn't till later that he wondered what would have been the result if it had gone the way all good food was supposed to go. His mate Maggot laughed his head off when Harry had told him and said it could have been worse as he might have finished up having a 'fart-a-tack'. Harry thought Maggot could have shown a slightly more sympathetic attitude but they both finally had a laugh at it.

Harry and Leda observed the driver getting into the bus and resumed their seats. Harry wondered how long it would be before he returned to see his old friends. He settled back on his hard green leather seat and wriggled his bum to get more comfortable. He could feel a renegade spring trying to free itself from the confines of the seat and wondered if it could be waiting to inflict some terrible damage on his private parts. He supposed he could sue the bus company but it would be embarrassing all the same. He shifted to one side as far as he could. No use tempting fate.

'And away we go once more, Leda,' Harry said, trying desperately to think of something to say that might sound intelligent.

'Would you mind not calling me Leda?' she said.

'I thought that was what you said your name was,' apologised Harry. There, he'd mucked up again.

'No. I'm afraid that was my fault. You see my name really *is* Leda but I prefer to be called Lee. I guess it's just one of those names your parents give you without thinking of the consequences. All my life I've heard nothing but Leda better life, Leda little love in occasionally, you can Leda horse to water but you can't make him drink follow my Leda, and so on and so on. It really gets my goat. To be quite frank I hate it. So if you don't mind... ' She left the rest of the sentence hanging in the air.

'No, I can certainly see what you mean Lee,' said Harry, mentally patting himself on the back for not saying what he was going to blurt out previously. That was a bit close.

With a hiss of air the door closed and the bus pulled out into the main street. There was no traffic. Harry always said everyone called Thexton a one-horse town.

Everybody, that is, except the street cleaner.

It had been a fraught couple of weeks for Harry. The funeral arrangements had gone fairly well, all things considered. He had tried to support and comfort his mother as much as possible, but he had the strangest feeling that he knew his nana better than her own daughter did. He had been cared for by Nana since he had turned seven years of age and she had succeeded in placing her stamp fairly and squarely on him.

Harry's mother had made it patently clear that he would not be able to continue at school even though it had been his original ambition to become a surgeon. The night before his nana's funeral both of them had sat down and in what could be termed a family council of war they had quietly and dispassionately discussed his future. She could not now afford to keep him at the local school. His father was no help. He would just have to go and seek employment. Fortunately for him there was no shortage of jobs around and it would prove easy to obtain a position. The question was, what did Harry want to do?

Strathmore Baines provided the answer. Harry's big cousin. Strath wasn't a close cousin by any means but he had a heart as big as one of Ted Macbeth's Clydesdales. He was about forty years of age and had been in partnership with his brother in a small goldmining concern in Central Otago. Trying to scratch a living out of a job that had him in water all day long hadn't done his health any good and he had had to give it up because of the effect it was having on him. It looked as though he was already suffering from an early onslaught of arthritis. He and his wife had sold the small goldmining claim and their property and with this money they had invested in a small dairy in South Dunedin. Harry was welcome to stay with them for a while anyway, till something turned up. It was laid down that it definitely would not be on a permanent basis – Strath and his family still had their own lives to lead. Nonetheless, Harry was assured of a warm welcome.

All this had come about the evening after they had laid the old lady's worn out body to rest. So the decision to go to the big city was made. Strath suggested Harry should obtain an apprenticeship.

Although disappointed in more ways than one Harry was of the opinion that you make your own luck and devil take the hindmost. He would deeply miss his friends but to hell with it. You gotta get going sometime.

Harry and Leda had seated themselves on the opposite side of the vehicle in order to get a better view of the lake as they passed it and were chatting about ferrets, of all things. This was a subject dear to Harry's heart. He'd had his pet ferret for three years and had made quite a bit of money out of it before its untimely demise. It was its own fault, he had decided later. A ferret's duty to its master, after the necessary nets had been placed over all the outlets where the rabbits might escape, was to get down along the burrow and chase the rabbit out of the warren. While this was great in theory it also happened to be a fact that if the ferret hadn't been sufficiently well fed that day he would decide that the time was right to dally in the hole, kill the rabbit and partake of a nice morsel of the furry animal. On the other hand, if it had just been fed it might also be of a mind to sleep it off while down in the burrow. It was very exasperating for the owner to have to dig the offending hunter from its hiding place. It also looked rather ridiculous when one of your friends came along at the precise moment you were down on your knees earnestly beseeching something hidden deep in the bowels of the earth to surrender itself to your tender care, while trying desperately to restrain your voice in order not to tell the furry little creature how much you'd love to wring its neck.

The upshot of the last episode concerning Harry's ferret was that, after coming to an end of ideas on how to persuade the reluctant animal to surface, Harry had decided to dig it out with his rabbiting adze. Adzes are supposed to be used for trimming timber and are usually kept in a sharp condition. Rather unfortunately it was the keen edge that came down on the poor animal's neck just as it emerged from the entrance to the nether regions. A French guillotine could not have been more efficient.

Harry grieved over the decapitated body for only a short period before considering the fact that, if nothing else, the pelt was undamaged. He went ahead and skinned, stretched, dried and sold the pelt before his friend Maggot got hold of it and made it into a Davy Crockett hat.

Maggot had originally sold the animal to Harry in exchange for a Hikers One crystal radio set complete with headphones and Maggot held firm to a belief that Harry had diddled him. It had stated in the accompanying brochure that all one had to do was to connect the aerial up to a fence and you could listen in to radio stations all over the world. It hadn't mentioned the fact that this did not include electric fences, which maybe could have been the trouble with the set. It was the last time it had worked. Maggot had loftily stated that he could fix it, no trouble. He was, however, not informed of the little puff of smoke Harry had spotted coming out of the set the day it died. When thinking about it much later he was kind of glad he hadn't been wearing the headphones. Harry wondered if he would have ended up like the fellows in death row and found himself fried up. Them's the breaks, he decided.

Leda empathised with Harry regarding the sorry departure of his ferret. She had regaled him with the sad story of her goldfish that she absolutely adored. An admirer had given it to her. The fish, in a moment of piscine exhilaration, had flipped itself out of the bowl and when she let herself into her lodging room after work she found the piscatorial piece of putrefying flesh under the piano. Not everybody should be asked to suffer a loss of that magnitude on their very own. It established a rapport between them that was hard to describe.

The two felt even closer. Sort of nice and fuzzy.

At that precise moment there was a loud report from the front offside of the bus. The vehicle gave a horrifying lurch to the left. For a moment it seemed as though it was going to leave the road altogether but with consummate skill the driver brought it to a more or less smooth halt at the side of the road.

'Bloody blowout,' he somewhat overzealously informed his quite startled passengers. All were well aware that something smelled in the State of Denmark. They all piled out onto the verge and viewed the damaged tyre, or what was left of it. For about a hundred yards to the rear of the vehicle they could see the shredded portions of the tyre which had decided in no mild manner to give up the ghost. The path of the rubberless rims, which had cut deeply into the road, was very plain, and gave one some indication of the seriousness of the incident.

'Could've bloody killed us,' muttered the driver again. He was not usually given to swearing in front of his passengers but the adrenalin rush in his veins had not at this stage abated and he was still riding somewhat of a high. The passengers didn't seem to notice too much as they were as relieved as he. Harry pushed his way to the front. 'Do you want a hand?' he offered.

'Nah,' replied the driver. 'I'll just pop in to Partridge's place and ring Thexton Motors. They can make short work of this. Right up their alley. Save me busting a gut. We'll be a little late over this, folks. Make yourselves comfortable in the meantime.' With those words he marched or rather limped up the short drive to the farmhouse.

Lee suggested to Harry that they could both perhaps walk up through the fence and inspect the view from the little hill above the bus. There was a small outcrop of rocks from which they could view everything that was going on. It was a lovely morning and the rocks were about fifty yards up from the road.

Harry helped her through the fence. She caught her coat on the wire and for a fleeting moment Harry had a flashback to the day that Jake had been shot while climbing through a similar opening. A small tingle ran down his spine for a split second. He quickly freed her from her entanglement and recovered himself promptly. Nasty feeling. Lee climbed up onto the ledge and sat down.

'Wow!' she exclaimed. 'Masters of all we survey. What a lovely view.'

The rest of the passengers had spread themselves out in the shade and didn't seem too fussed about their fate. Just as well Mrs Cain wasn't there, thought Harry. Talk about 'raising Cain'!

They watched the driver come out of the farmhouse and then

remove some tools from the luggage compartment which ran the length of the bus. Even from where they were perched they could see that he kept up a continuous muttering under his breath. He finally sat down on the step and lit a cigarette. Harry had a fair idea he'd received a real old fright and was doing his damnedest not to show it.

'When do you start your apprenticeship?' enquired Leda.

'Oh, I haven't been interviewed yet. I might not even get it,' replied Harry. 'I've got to see the boss at eleven o clock tomorrow. My cousin Strath arranged it. Well, he's not my cousin really. It's his wife I'm related to. They've got a couple of little kids and I'm going to stay with them for a while. He's a good stick and it's all taken place rather in a hurry due to Nana passing away. So I'm off to make my fame and fortune just like old Dick Whittington.'

'I think you're a bit of a romantic at heart, Harry,' Leda laughed. 'It's not so easy as you might think.'

'Well, I guess I'll never know till I get there,' said Harry. 'I guess you've got to at least give it your best shot. My Uncle Jack said something once about climbing the ladder of success – "If you scorn the bottom rungs, my lad, you'll never reach the top." It was in a poem he used to recite.'

'Do you know many people in Dunedin?' Leda asked.

'Not really,' replied Harry. 'Only a couple of old great-aunts and of course my cousin, but no doubt I'll make a few friends. I guess that will be the least of my problems. I like making friends. To be quite honest I find it an easy thing to do."

'I can see that,' replied Leda. On impulse she said, 'Look, Harry, I'll give you the address where I stay and if you would like to you can contact me there. How's that?'

'Great,' replied Harry. 'And I'll give you Strath's home address. You got many friends?'

'Not really. I read a lot and I belong to a good library. I have an uncle – my dad's younger brother who has been invalided home from Egypt. He's in the Rannerdale Home for War-Wounded and that's where I go a fair bit, to visit him. He had his leg blown off in an explosion in the desert. He was with the Long Range Desert Group in Egypt somewhere. Doesn't talk about it much but I believe he had two other soldiers with him and one was wounded badly. He only knew of them by their first names – George and Len. He remembers them well as he reckons he owes his life to them getting him safely back to base. They were engineers apparently and had gone out to fix a truck my uncle's troop had abandoned in the desert. When they got back to it it had been booby-trapped or something. Must have been awful. If they hadn't had a medic with them... '

*Len and George were working back at the base and were rather surprised to see their commanding officer drive up in the battered Mercedes-Benz which he had commandeered from a captured German supply dump some weeks before. He had persuaded the other units (and higher authority) that it was in such a state of disrepair that it wouldn't last very long. With typical Kiwi ingenuity it had been kept in as scruffy a state as possible to deter any member of officialdom from taking it for use by headquarters, and no senior-ranking eyebrows were raised as he raced around in it. Both Len and George knew that the Merc, underneath its decrepit exterior, was in pristine condition.*

*Next to the driver sat a rather filthy looking person wearing a turban and shorts, no rank showing.*

*'Corporal Rowley, I've got a job for you and Mann. This is Sergeant Lamb and he's got a vehicle that he wants to recover. It's about an hour's drive from here and just within limits as far as those Jerries out there are concerned. The rest of the mechanics are tied up, but take Bertha and go with him. Take rations and all the rest of the necessaries and watch your step. I'll brief you all before you leave .Okay?'*

*As they were to leave on dusk they had plenty of time to collect and check their gear. It wasn't usual for the engineers to do vehicle recovery as this was a function of a separate unit altogether, but Len and George didn't mind as it was a fairly monotonous job at base. In fact both of them admitted to a slight feeling of excitement as they worked in preparation for their night exercise. All going well they would be back by dawn.*

*Five minutes later the adjutant walked into the workshop followed by a soldier wearing the caduceus insignia of a medical orderly.*

*'This is Jack Armstrong .He's just been posted out to join us . I want you to take him with you. He's new and he might as well get blooded.' He smiled at his own bit of wit. 'Get it fellows? Blooded?'*

*Little did he realise how prophetic his statement would turn out to be.*

'I've got an uncle also but he's up in the Islands. I think he's still in one piece. He's just gone back up there after being on leave. He's pretty annoyed about all these slackers back here getting out of the fighting. There seem to be an awful amount of draft dodgers in good jobs.'

He tried another tack. This was getting pretty dull.

'Do you like dancing?'

'Oh yes.' she said. 'I go to a church social once a fortnight and it's good fun. Do you?'

Not much fun there, thought Harry, but there again, she looks a bit of the bookworm type. Then he kicked himself. I shouldn't be thinking like that. I read everything I can get my hands on. Here she was trying to be nice to him and it was a bit ungrateful to be thinking about her like that. Think big, Harry!

'Yes. It's a lot of fun. Have you tried the jitterbug yet? The Yanks are pretty good at it. I'm just learning it.'

'They don't go that far at the social hall. I can't imagine the vicar allowing that sort of goings-on. You'll have to teach me.'

'I'm not that good. But I'm slowly getting there.' It was a little white lie really. The only jitterbugging he'd done had been when he and Kathy were fooling around in the woolshed after seeing an American film the night before at the Palladium, the local bughouse in Thexton.

Harry and Leda sat there that day in the sun and a warm friendship was slowly developing. They discussed innumerable things and were still hard at it when the bus horn sounded to warn them that the repair had been completed by the mechanic summoned from Thexton and they were on their way once more.

Leda's cheeks were flushed with excitement. She had really enjoyed her talk with Harry and she realised that though she was older than him by at least three years she had found his conversation stimulating. It could have been something to do with his good looks and his blue eyes. A momentary naughty thought made her blush inwardly. She was somewhat diffident and rather naive regarding the opposite sex. She was also very surprised at her unbidden reaction to Harry.

They exchanged addresses and when the bus finally arrived at the terminal they both alighted to the noise and cacophony of the main Dunedin bus station. They waited for their luggage to be located, both of them feeling rather sorry in a way that the trip had ended.

Strath's wife Tracy was waiting for Harry and it was with a slight touch of embarrassment that he introduced Lee to her.

As they went to go their separate ways Lee impulsively leaned over and kissed Harry on the cheek. 'Best of luck tomorrow, Harry,' she whispered. Harry had been about to shake her hand and found himself groping in mid air for a split second. He recovered to find himself looking at his cousin.

Tracy stifled a chuckle. She hadn't missed a thing. 'How long have you known her, Harry?' she asked.

'Only since we got on the bus.'

'Fast work.' Tracy had a lot of time for Harry and teased him unmercifully whenever she could. His faced reddened to her remark. He knew she was pulling his leg in the nicest way possible.

They took the tram out to Anderson's Bay and when they reached Strath's place they went into the spare room and Tracy made Harry welcome once more. She made herself at home on his bed.

'You realise this is only until you get on your feet, Harry. I promised your mum I would help out. It's really Strath's idea and he doesn't mind a bit but we think we've got to be realistic about this. Don't you?'

Harry felt slightly uncomfortable. The welcome was genuine enough and it was good of these two to go out of their way to take him in. It was quite embarrassing to say the least. He determined he would seek alternative accommodation as soon as possible. He would have to put his thinking cap on but first thing to deal with was the forthcoming interview.

Strath arrived home from work and they all sat around the table. After the meal Harry and Strath did the dishes while Tracy bathed the two little girls and put them to bed. Harry of course had to tell them a bedtime story. He had a happy knack of telling stories at the drop of a hat and was getting to the scary stage of one when Tracy walked in. By the look of her round-eyed children she could tell immediately that he had gone far enough. 'I said no horror stories now, Harry.'

Harry grinned rather shamefacedly, toned down the finish of the tale and finally joined the parents in the lounge.

'All set for tomorrow, Harry?' asked Strath.

'As right as I'll ever be. I've got all my papers ready and a couple of character references. Just have to keep my fingers crossed, I guess.'

'Right then, feel like a game of crib? Might help to keep your mind off things.'

'Great,' replied Harry. 'I sort of miss the game Nana and I used to play.'

Strath brought the cribbage set out from the sideboard and arranged it. He shuffled the cards and for the next two hours both of them were engrossed in the game while Tracy did the pile of ironing.

Finally Harry rose and said, 'Bout time I hit the sack. Big day tomorrow.'

Tracy came over to him to kiss him good night. She rolled back her lips in a tightly clenched style and said in her best Humphrey Bogart voice, 'Give 'em hell, kiddo. You knock 'em in the aisles, babe.' Then she blew the smoke from her two outstretched 'pistol' fingers.

Harry went and cleaned his teeth and retired to his room. Later as he lay in his bed he heard the muffled tones of Tracy and Strath talking in the bedroom next door.

Even though he had done nothing but dry a sink full of dishes it seemed to have been a long day. Leda Lamb. Funny name. Nice smile though. He rolled over and in a few minutes was fast asleep.

# CHAPTER TWO

The first indication he had that something was terribly wrong was when he felt the searing pain in his eye.

Something was interfering with his eyelid. He tried to open it but it was jammed shut. He felt more slight pain, then pressure on the lid itself. The eyelid was lifted up and he found himself involuntarily staring into another eye about three inches away and peering intently into his.

A small voice alive with satisfaction exclaimed, 'There, Nancy. I told you he was awake!' It was Theresa, the younger of the two girls, and owner of the offending digit.

Harry's eye was watering profusely. He blinked furiously.

'What do you kids think you're up to?'

Both jumped in unison.

'We thought we'd see if you were awake.', said Nancy.

'And you were too,' added Theresa smugly, wearing an 'I told you so' look on her little face. 'Are you getting up for breakfast?'

'Be right there,' he answered.

They stood there as if something was about to happen. Harry paused in his reaching for his trousers hanging on the chair beside his bed.

'Well, what are you waiting for? Can't you see I've got to get dressed?' he growled.

The two girls ran out of the room giggling. This was good fun having cousin Harry staying with them.

Harry appeared at the table washed and decent. Tracy already had the table laid and the two girls were tucking in. Strath was about to leave.

'Hope the interview goes all right. See you tonight.'

With a peck on his wife's cheek and a big hug for the kids he was on his bike and away.

'Why didn't you call me earlier, Tracy?' Harry asked. 'I could have given you a hand.'

'Oh, don't worry. I thought one little lie-in wouldn't come amiss on your first day. You seemed pretty tired last night.'

'Thanks, Trace,' Harry replied. She was a little beaut. She *was* little too. She came up to Strath's shoulders. And she almost had to skip beside him like a little girl while they were out walking.

Strath was of Irish descent and had a bit of a twang, which he had most probably caught from his father. He worked as boilerman in the local gasworks and although it was good steady work and wages the conditions didn't treat his oncoming arthritis too kindly. He would have to find more sedentary employment sooner or later and it worried him not a little. For all that he was a large, kindly man with a heart as big as an ox – to suit his frame – and he didn't really let the worry show too much.

The appointment at the place where Harry hoped to obtain an apprenticeship was a ten-minute tram ride away and Tracy made sure he was correctly dressed for the occasion.

As he was leaving she gave him a big-sisterly peck on the cheek and wished him luck. He only had to wait three minutes till the correct tram hove into view and he was on his way. Bouncing and grinding, the tram made its journey, wheels squealing steel against protesting steel on the sharp corners, bell clanging its warning. God help the unwary cyclist who was foolish enough to put his wheel in the groove. Although all town dwellers were aware of the danger there always seemed to be somebody that tried it on, with dire results.

Tracy had given him one of the kid's little suitcases to carry his papers in. He didn't think the number of papers (there were only six of them) warranted all this fuss but she insisted and that was that. The suitcase it was.

Five minutes prior to the allotted time found Harry standing in front of the reception counter. He had stopped outside the big showroom windows and checked that his hair was slicked down before approaching the receptionist.

He stood pretending to earnestly examine a large poster depicting the merits of the latest car that would be in the showroom "early this year". In reality, however, Harry was listening to the girl on the phone explaining that the manager, Mr Brooks, was away that morning and would not be back in his office till the afternoon. Harry's heart sank. Mr Brooks was the person that he had the appointment with and it now looked as though he might have to arrange another meeting. He'd been all fired up for this and now things were going to have to change. He wondered how he had been forgotten. If I ever get to a manager's position, he thought to himself, I definitely will not forget the poor bloody apprentices.

'May I help you?' The voice belonging to the frizzy-blonde receptionist intruded on his thoughts.

'Yes, I have appointment with Mr. Brooks in… ' He looked at the clock. 'In two minutes' time. Harold Evans is the name.' Harry wondered what sort of excuse she would make for Mr Brooks forgetting to see him. He waited for her reply with interest.

'Certainly, Mr Evans. I'll just see if I can contact him for you.'

She picked up the phone. She's bloody bluffing, Harry thought.

'Mr Brooks? There's a Mr Harold Evans here to see you. Right, Mr Brooks, I'll show him in.'

With a curt 'follow me', she minced down the passage and knocked on the door. Without waiting for an answer she turned the handle, leaned in and having announced Harry then left, closing the door behind her.

Harry was slightly bewildered at this turn of events having mentally prepared himself to be disappointed by the non-arrival of Mr Brooks. Here he was now standing in front of the gentleman.

'So, you're Harry Evans. Well now, take a seat, Harry Evans, and we'll have a look at you.' Before Harry could sit down Mr Brooks had shot out of his seat and shaken Harry's hand. He returned to his seat, half-hidden behind a pile of paperwork.

'So you want to be mechanic, Harry Evans.' He paused for what seemed an eternity, then to Harry's complete surprise leapt to his feet and almost shouted, 'And, may I ask why?'

Harry was rather hesitant to answer straight away because he thought he might stutter his reply.

'Well, Harry Evans, I'm waiting.'

Harry wondered if this was the manner in which interviews were supposed to be carried out. Strath had offered to go along with him and Harry rather regretted not taking up his offer, but he'd certainly burned his bridges now. Here he was on his Pat Malone. The name Horatio and a picture of a bridge flashed through his brain.

'Mr. Brooks, sir," Harry began. He thought he would put in the 'sir' bit as it sounded respectful and he needed all the help he could get just now. 'The best reason I can think of for wanting to be a mechanic is that my Uncle Jack used to say that although any fool can drive a car, it takes brains to fix one.'

Even Harry had to admit it sounded pretty trite and he wished to hell he had prepared a suitable answer to a question of that nature being fired at him. Too late now to start thinking straight. Might as well do an Ernie Wilson and bulldoze right on through.

Mr Brooks beamed. 'I rather like that statement, Harry Evans. I happened to be a mechanic once myself, though I must say I don't get my hands dirty much these days.' His smile was rather self-deprecating.

He continued. 'Your cousin, Mr Baines, whom I happen to have met, is a good friend of my service manager and apparently speaks rather highly of you. I understand that because of the death of your grandmother you have to find work. Well, Harry Evans, I'm going to take you on and we'll just see how you shape up. How does that strike you now?'

Harry was flabbergasted. By the sounds of things Mr Brooks had decided to hire him before he had even reached the point of being interviewed. Strath must have really impressed the foreman – a person he still had to meet.

Mr Brooks stood up and held out his hand. 'You start here tomorrow morning. Three month's trial probation period as laid down by the Department of Labour, then we'll see about the technical details of the apprenticeship. I've got five other apprentices working here and they all get on pretty well. Now, I'll just get Christine to take you down to see Jim Schultz, our service manager. He'll show you round.'

He picked up the phone and next minute the receptionist reappeared.

'Take our Harry here down to Jim's office, Christine, then come back here. I've got some more letters to dictate.' With that remark Harry felt himself dismissed.

He followed the girl down to the main workshop area to a small office situated next to the pits. A prematurely white-haired person in a matching dustcoat sat at a desk with a telephone pressed to his ear. He looked up, waved Harry in with his finger towards the chair opposite and with the same finger indicated to Christine that she was dismissed. Economy of effort, thought Harry. 'Okay, Mr Brooks,' Harry heard him say. Obviously the manager had wasted no time ringing through. He hoped it didn't bode ill.

'Sit down, lad. My name's Jim Schultz and I'm the service manager here. I'm the boss. Apprentices call me Mr Schultz until I tell them otherwise. Your cousin is a good friend of mine. He's spoken highly of you and I'm well aware of your circumstances. That doesn't mean to say we're employing you because of that though. You'll have to prove to me what you're worth. You'll start here at eight o'clock tomorrow morning and that means start, not arrive. You'll be on trial for one month from tomorrow and we'll see how you shape up. Got any friends here in Dunedin? No? Well, no doubt you'll soon find some. Don't fall in with the wrong lot. I run a tight ship. I'm ex-Navy and don't take crap from any-one. Understand? If you've got any problems come and see me before they get too big. That'll be all for now.' He stood up and walked to the door of his office. Harry noticed he limped slightly.

A young fellow Harry's age was passing just at that moment carrying a rather rusty old exhaust pipe over his shoulder. Jim signalled him.

'Fred. Get Frank to report to me on the double. Frank is our senior apprentice. He'll show you some of the ropes.'

Frank turned out to be a rather tall, open-faced fellow of about nineteen. Jim introduced them, then said, 'Frank, you've got thirty minutes to show Harry around the shop. I've got work to do. Thirty minutes only, Frank. Then kick him out.' He smiled as he said it. 'I'll see you tomorrow, Harry. Eight. Sharp.'

He retreated to his office and closed the door behind him.

'So you're the new dogsbody, Harry?' Frank asked, in a rather disarming fashion. 'Dinky will be pleased to see you, I bet.'

'Who's Dinky?' asked Harry.

'Dinky is the last apprentice the firm took on, and the junior apprentice, as you will find out, has to do most of the shitty jobs around the place. I went through the whole lot and I've just about finished my time before I become a qualified tradesman. Poor old Dinky has been our junior gofer for nine months and was starting to think that he would be at the bottom of the ladder for the rest of his life. So I guess he'll welcome you with open arms.'

'What's a gofer?' asked Harry.

'Don't tell me you don't know what a gofer is?' Frank said with disbelief written over his face. 'A gofer is an apprentice you send to go fer this and go fer that. The bottom of the scale. The lowest thing on earth, according to some of the journeymen mechanics around here.'

'So I won't be fixing motors straight away?' asked an alarmed Harry.

'Hell no, you'll be bottom of the pile for a while. The idea is to keep your head down and show them you can work. Above all, don't give the older mechanics too much cheek. If they get a down on you they can make your life pretty miserable. You'll be put under the wing of a journeyman who will teach you the ropes. You'll be shifted around a bit to get a fair grounding on each and every aspect of the job. You'll have to go to night school and sit exams too. Say, didn't you know about all this?'

'No, but I'm learning fast. How long do I do at the bottom of the heap?'

'Until such time as they employ another apprentice. Here's

Dinky now.' A freckle-faced lad about Harry's age approached the pair with a somewhat jaunty step. He was wearing filthy overalls. They matched his face – covered in oil splotches.

'Hey Dinky, come and meet your new boy. Harry Evans, Dinky.'

Dinky shook hands with Harry. Harry felt something soft in the palm of his hand as Dinky's closed on it.

He looked at his hand. It was covered in black sticky grease.

Dinky grinned. He had seen Harry being shown around and guessed this was the new boy. A quick application in the palm of his hand and the fun had begun.

'Oops!' said Dinky. 'Sorry about that.'

With a wry smile Frank handed Harry a piece of rag. 'Graphite grease is inclined to stick a bit.' He was quite aware of what the score was. He'd been through the mill himself. Apprentices were the same world over, he supposed.

Harry mentally chalked up a score he would settle on Dinky when the time was appropriate. It could wait. He smiled and passed it off lightly. 'Oh, I guess I'll be into plenty of this stuff soon without your help, Dinky.'

Dinky had a box in his hand and a notebook. 'What d'ya want for smoko, Frank?'

'Just a mince pie today,' answered Frank, handing Dinky the correct amount of change.

Dinky placed the money in the box and scribbled something in the notebook. He winked at Harry and said with a smirk, 'This'll be your job soon, Harry, and good luck to you.'

With great difficulty Harry swallowed and said, 'I guess you'll enjoy the break from that.'

'Yeah, and a few other grotty jobs too.' Dinky couldn't contain his relief.

He moved off and Frank showed Harry a few areas of the big garage.

Okay, Harry, time's up,' Frank said, looking at his watch. I'll see you here tomorrow. Just wait outside Jim's door and he'll deal with you as soon as he has allocated jobs for the morning. Don't get in his hair until he wants you. He's a bit on the scratchy side until things are running smoothly. The important thing is to keep your head low.'

To Harry it sounded as though he was going to work in a war zone.

He walked outside into the fresh air and watched the traffic roll by. He had all the afternoon to play with and decided that as he was going to start in the morning maybe the pictures were the answer. Accordingly he took a tram into the city and after strolling around the shops went to a matinee of *The Shores of Tripoli* which was showing at the Strand. He would have to watch his money from now on as an apprentice's wages weren't the highest. He might have to get an extra job to supplement his meagre income. That was no worry to Harry. He was sure he would get by somehow.

Living by your wits could be a challenge. He looked forward to it.

It was just on five o'clock as he stepped inside the gate. Tracy was in the kitchen cooking tea.

'I was wondering where you might have got to,' she said. Harry didn't think she was checking on him. Tracy wasn't like that.

'Can I help at all?' Harry asked.

'Just a bit of kindling for the front fire and the woodbin needs filling. You can peel some spuds for me too if you like. As a matter of fact I'm running a bit late. Had to give the next door neighbour a hand. She's getting too old to be on her own and as for that useless son of hers… ' She left the sentence unfinished.

Harry sped out the door and it took only a little time to do the chores as requested. As he was peeling the potatoes Strath came through the door and was immediately pounced upon by the girls. Harry saw some fast work going on between Strath and Tracy and wondered what it was all about. The girls were clamouring to get at his lunch bag which he had swiftly passed to his wife. She had taken it into the other room and reappeared with it almost immediately. The girls opened their father's tin and found two pieces of fruitcake wrapped in silver paper. The girls squealed with delight and started to eat. Tracy explained: 'This started ages ago when they discovered Strath's lunch was more exciting than just ordinary baking out of the tin in the cupboard. So I wrap two slices up and slip it into his lunch when he gets home. I haven't been caught out yet but I don't know how long I can keep this sort of thing up,' she laughed.

'That certainly explains a lot,' chuckled Harry, rather relieved.

'How did things go today, Harry?' asked Strath, but Tracy wouldn't let Harry say anything until they were sitting down at the tea table. 'I don't want to miss anything. Not one tiniest bit,' she said.

They were on to the dessert before Harry had told the whole story of the day. This also included a fairly large slice of *The Shores of Tripoli*.

'I hope I haven't spoilt the movie for you,' said Harry.

'Not at all,' said Tracy. 'But seeing you've watched it now you might care to babysit the girls for us while we see it.'

'Fair enough. Only too happy to oblige,' replied Harry.

They cleaned up after tea and Tracy made sure he had the correct clothes to wear to work for the next day.

On Strath's advice he had spent some hard-earned rabbit skin money and bought some decent working trousers and a couple of hardwearing shirts. His money was running out fast. He'd have to watch it closely.

Bit of nuisance, this work business.

He awoke next morning without the aid of having his eyeballs extricated from their sockets. Obviously the girls were still asleep. He leaped out of bed and managed to reach the toilet as Strath was emerging.

'Wouldn't go in there yet,' said his big cousin. 'It's still a bit choice.'

Harry just had to endure it. He decided that he would have to be like the little pig and get to the market earlier before the smelly wolf beat him.

He had a quick wash and sat down with Strath for breakfast.

Tracy, after a quick good morning peck, informed Harry she had packed a lunch for him.

'Try and avoid buying your smoko, Harry,' she said. 'I've put an extra sandwich in for your play lunch.' She smiled.

'Gee, thanks a million, Tracy,' replied Harry.

'She's bloody spoiling you, Harry. I don't get a play lunch,' groaned Strath in mock reproach.

'You don't actually look too starved to me, big boy.' Tracy gave her husband a playful cuff over his head. Harry liked the way they related to each other. It made the house feel full of good vibes.

Strath scraped his chair back from the table and stood up.

'I gotta get going. Give 'em hell, Harry. Remember everything I've told you.'

A peck on Tracy's cheek and he was out the door. His whistle could be heard down the short path leading to the right of way behind the shop.

Harry finished off his piece of toast. This was the big moment. Putting his lunch into his old school bag he slung it over his shoulder. Tracy put her arms around him and gave him a nice hug. 'Harry, this is a big day in your life. I know things will go well for you. All the best, kiddo.'

He boarded the tram and sat watching the passing traffic. The tramstop was opposite the garage. He waited till there was a break in the vehicles and walked across the road. He could feel his gut muscles tightening. He told himself to relax. People start new jobs every day. So what's the big deal? he asked himself.

It was about ten minutes to eight when Harry positioned himself outside Mr Schultz's office. He could hear Jim Schultz shouting at someone on the phone and he didn't seem to be in such a good mood. Harry hoped it wouldn't rub off too easily.

He was heartened to see Frank go past. As he did so he winked at Harry. 'Sounds like a hot one this morning Harry. Be ready to duck.' And he rolled his eyes back into his head.

Harry just stood there. Only cowards flee.

It was going on for ten minutes past the hour when Jim finally got around to doing something about him. He came out of his office and said, 'Right, Harry, let's see what we can rake up for you. Now where's that bloody Dinky hiding? I told him to wait here only a few minutes ago.'

Dinky's head, grinning broadly, appeared around the corner as if on command. 'You shouted, sir?' He couldn't contain his delight.

Jim ignored the cheek. 'Right, Dinky. I want you to show Harry what your job is and what you're supposed to do during the day. I want him fully up with the play by tonight. He's yours for the day. I warn you though Dinky, get up to any tricks and you'll wear my boot in a sacred spot. Now along with you.'

Dinky was rearing to go. Here was his big chance to relinquish the hated position of the junior apprentice, the lowest in the mechanical pecking order. He was reveling in the thought that he was on his way up the ladder of success.

First things first.

He took Harry along to the time clock outside Jim's office and explained the system of clocking on and off jobs. Harry was interested to learn that each job's commencement and cessation had to be recorded and that each job had a number and that each customer was charged by the minute. Dinky clocked him in. It made a horrible clunking sound.

'That tells the boss if anyone's trying to start late.'

'But that means I'm already fifteen minutes late,' protested Harry.

'Don't worry. The service chief or the foreman checks the time sheets before they go upstairs to the girls. If they notice any errors they'll be down on you like a ton of bricks. Your main job number will be 104. That number will stick in your head.'

'What's 104?'

'Sweeping and cleaning, and running errands.'

'Oh.'

Overalls. That was the next thing. He took Harry to the parts store and introduced him to the parts manager. Jack O'Hanlin. Jack had just arrived out of the army where he had been an equipment officer. His obsession with numbers was ridiculous. Even if you wanted a piece of number-eight wire seven inches long Jack would want the engine and chassis number before he would give it to you. It really made one mad at times. But he was the parts manager. Even God himself would have to supply the requested numbers. He wrote out an order for Harry and then Dinky took Harry down to the clothing store in the firm's van. He received three pairs of overalls and they drove back to work.

'You got a driver's licence yet, Harry?' asked Dinky.

'No. Do I need one?'

'Course you do. That's part of the job. A fair bit of my time is spent running customers back and forwards after they've had their cars serviced. It's a bit of a perk. You get to drive some decent cars once old German Jim gets to trust you.'

'German Jim?'

'Schultzy. Don't bloody call him that though – he'll kill you. Still thinks he's in the Navy at times. Bit of a slave driver but fair as. We'd better get back – got to collect the smoko orders.'

'Have you fixed many cars yet?'

'Shit no. You'll be lucky if you even touch a spanner for the first six months. No Harry. I'm afraid you're dogsbody till we get a new apprentice. Then you'll feel like I do now. Real bloody good.'

Harry swallowed hard. This was going to be a lot different to the job that he had previously envisaged. Either that or Dinky was pulling his leg. Quite frankly he was of the opinion that Dinky would put something across him as soon as look at him. In the meantime he'd just go along with whatever crap Dinky wanted to feed him. As Nana used to tell him, 'Walk softly and carry a big stick.'

'Righto, Dinky. What's next on the agenda?'

'We gotta clean up the smoko room. It's got to be scrubbed clean – and make sure everything's tidy. I've got to go downtown on a message for a while. I'll see you at smoko. Make sure the water heater is hot for it. Don't worry about the fellows' lunch orders. I'll do it today. The cleaning gear's in this cupboard.'

Harry changed into his overalls and hung his gear in the allocated locker. He'd have to get his own key for it. He looked around the smoko room. It was in a mess. Cigarette butts all over the floor and a large area around the tea-making bench was covered in stains and leftover food. The rubbish container stank to high heaven. He rolled up his sleeves and set to work with a will. Work of this nature didn't trouble him as he had been raised on a farm. A cowshed and a pigsty were worse than this. Or were they? He wondered just how the room had been allowed to get into this mess. He would sort out Dinky by showing him up. With this plan of action in mind there seemed to be a purpose to all this non-technical work. He got stuck in.

Every now and again one of the mechanics would come into the room and either take out or put something into his locker. A couple of them introduced themselves to the new boy but the rest didn't bother.

Frank came in and stood for a moment, watching. 'Nice going, Harry. 'Bout time this pigsty was cleaned up. Your idea or Dinky's?'

'Dinky said it had to be done.'

'Yeah, he's supposed to do it every day but he hasn't lifted a finger for ages. You'll do.' With that slight attempt at praise he went out.

Harry went like a cut cat and by the time the staff filed into the room for their break the whole area had been tidied up.

Dinky returned and placed a box with pies, cakes and sausages on the table and stood there checking everybody's orders off his list. Harry hadn't brought a mug to work but he found one that somebody wasn't using, gave it a good scrub and sat down with Frank. Frank offered him a big dollop of condensed milk to go into his cup. He found out later that Frank was a condensed milk addict. He even had his sandwiches filled with the stuff – he said it was something to do with a prenatal fixation. Harry noticed his locker was covered with pictures of amply proportioned naked women. But so was everyone else's. The rest of the mechanics were all busy talking flat tack, and apart from the odd glance Harry was mainly ignored. Friendly bunch, he thought.

Smoko over, the men all vacated the room and Harry was once

again on his own surveying the mess. He wondered what sort of homes they came from. He also wondered whether the mess was deliberate because he was a new boy. Dinky had disappeared. Harry put everything into it for the next hour and finally the room was pristine. He had even cleaned the windows.

He decided it was time to obtain some instructions from the chief.

He knocked on Mr Schultz's open door. 'What's up, Harry?'

'I've just been cleaning up the smoko room and there's a lot of filthy overalls and other rubbish on top of the lockers. They stink to high heaven. How do they get washed?'

'Well, every Thursday everyone changes their overalls and puts them in that drum, then they take the laundered ones out of that cupboard. Dinky should have already told you this – it'll be your job to bundle them up and have them ready for the Chinese laundryman who comes around. If they're up there obviously nobody wants them. I'd chuck them out. Good idea. The room needs a bloody good clean out. Go to it.'

Harry thought he wouldn't get a better chance to get ahead of the dirt. He took all the stuff he could from the top of the lockers and carted it out to an incinerator that was burning at the back. It had a high chimney on it and Harry dumped the lot in.

It wasn't till the lunch period that the trouble started.

The men came into the lunchroom and were visibly impressed with the new boy's handiwork. Some, however, were visibly unimpressed as soon as they saw that their prized possessions were missing from the tops of the lockers. Old jackets, girlie magazines, bits and pieces of stuff they had thrown up out of sight 'just in case it's wanted sometime'. Treasures that would stay there till doomsday.

A few of them did their blocks.

'What the bloody hell do you think you're doing chucking all our stuff out?' one asked Harry.

Harry had already figured out that this move would be unpopular and was set to cover himself. 'Dinky showed me what to do.,' he said blandly.

'Where's that bloody Dinky? I'll fix the little basket.'

Dinky entered the room and copped the lot. A few of the boys had gone out to see what they could retrieve from the incinerator but to no avail. All their treasured items of greasy apparel had gone up in smoke, together with their sleazy magazines. Harry was going to shove some of the more interesting stuff into his locker but thought better of it. There would be more later no doubt.

Frank grinned at Harry. 'The place sparkles. Haven't seen it as clean as this in ages.'

Dinky had finally managed to convince some of the mechanics that he wasn't responsible for telling Harry to clean the room so vigorously. They came back to stand over Harry, who by this time was starting to enjoy himself. Bill Pugh, the tallest of the apprentices and next in line to Dinky seniority wise, was a fellow who liked shoving his weight around. He was a bit thick but got around that problem by bullying the more junior and smaller apprentices.

'Well,' Bill said, 'Dinky says he didn't tell you to clear it all up so it was your idea to burn all our stuff.' He glowered. 'What have you got to say for yourself? You a smart arse or something?'

Harry stood up and faced his accuser squarely. He thought to himself, this is my first day and I'm in the bloody gun already.

He cleared his throat. The others were standing there plainly interested to hear what the new chum was going to say to get himself out of the cart. Most of them were of the opinion that Dinky was a lazy little sod and they had to secretly admit that the tea room looked great after Harry's efforts.

He spoke clearly and quietly. 'I don't really know why you're getting all fired up about this. Dinky showed me what to do and I did it.'

Dinky interrupted. 'But I didn't tell you to burn all that stuff though.'

'No, you didn't, Dinky.'

Pug, as was his wont, really bulldozed in. He was a mate of Dinky's and now was the time to show it while he had the upper hand. To show this new boy on the block a thing or two.

'So who bloody told you then?'

'I bloody told him,' said a voice. 'And what do you intend to do about it, Billy Pugh?'

The cavalry had arrived in the nick of time. There stood German Jim (God bless his soul) right behind Pug's back. He swung around and was at a loss for words.

'Mr. Schultz,' Pug whined, 'all our gear we had on top of the lockers has been burned.'

Before he could say anything further Jim interrupted and said, 'How many of you fellows were here about three months ago when I said that all the gear up top of the lockers had to be stowed away, otherwise I'd have it ditched? Bloody near the lot of you. Well, I gave everyone fair warning and now it's gone. So hard bloody luck. Maybe you might listen next time.'

With that remark he turned and went back to his office. He was a man not to be trifled with. Harry wondered if he had an ulcer. Old Tim Riley had an ulcer and he behaved just like that.

Frank sat down with Harry. 'Bit of a near squeak that time, eh Harry?'

'Aw, not really, Frank. I just played on the fact that Mr Schultz had okayed it. Otherwise I wouldn't have touched that stuff. I was told by my cousin about not pinching anyone's chair when you start a new job. That's why I waited till everyone was sitting down before I did. I'd like to think that I'm not thick enough to be caught by these tricks that are played on new boys. I can keep my eye peeled.

'Well, Harry,' said Frank, 'just keep your eyes on Pugh. He's not nicknamed "Thug" for nothing.'

'Thanks,' replied Harry. 'Sounds as though I've got to watch my back. Great way to start a job.'

'Don't worry, you'll do all right. I think old Schultzy's quite pleased you hoed into the room. As I said before, it looks great, Harry.'

The bell went and they went out to where Dinky was waiting.

'Righto, Harry, next job.' He was enjoying himself immensely.

He felt like a boss even if he did have only one slave. He took Harry across the street to where he bought the lunches for the men and introduced Harry to the owner. 'This is Harry Evans who will be doing the smoko buying from tomorrow. Harry, Tom Breckon. I've been promoted,' he added somewhat unnecessarily.

Harry shook Tom's hand. It felt like a wet fish.

'Good to do business with you, Harry. I've always treated Dinky all right, haven't I Dinky?'

Smarmy bastard, thought Harry. Wonder what he's up to?

'Too right, Tom. You give us all a fair go,' said Dinky with a broad wink.

As they returned to the garage Frank called out, 'Hey, Harry the boss's looking for you. Better shake it up.'

Harry walked into Jim's office. The ex-Navy chief looked up. 'Sit down, Harry. What was all that about today in the smoko room?'

'Aw, nothing really, Mr Schultz. I just thought that if my job is to keep the place clean, it'd be a darn sight easier if I attacked it right from the start. Sorry if I caused a bit of trouble. I didn't mean it to turn out like that.'

Jim Schultz smiled. His sole reason for calling Harry in to explain was to see if the boy was going to try to slide out of the situation and lay the blame on someone else. The explanation wasn't unreasonable and confirmed his evaluation of Harry from when they first met.

'Don't think I didn't notice the good job you've done. Keep it up. Don't worry about what happened today. Call it part of the learning curve.'

Harry relaxed a little. He wasn't in the gun after all.

Jim continued. 'Here are a couple of papers to sign regarding your apprenticeship. Take them home and read them and if you're happy with them, sign them, get them witnessed, and bring them in tomorrow morning. That's all for now. See you tomorrow.'

As Harry left the office Dinky came past, snickering.

'Get your arse chewed out?'

Harry stopped in mid stride.

'Just a sec, Dinky.'

'What d'ya want?' He'd gone all defensive.

'Just to tell you something. Listen carefully.'

'Okay, shoot,' said a somewhat defiant Dinky.

'First the worst. Second the same.

Last the best, of all the game.'

Harry walked away leaving a very puzzled Dinky standing by the loudly ticking clock.

They all sat down to the evening meal. Tracy led off with, 'Now Harry, you can tell us every little smidgen. My ears are all agog.'

'So that's what's the matter with them. You had me worried,' laughed Strath.

Harry also laughed. 'I actually don't know whether my first day on the job was a success or not. I'd be inclined to call it a draw.'

Puzzled, Strath leaned forward. 'And what's that supposed to tell us?'

'Well, I made two friends and two enemies today.' He went on to explain what had happened and at the conclusion Tracy appeared rather concerned. Strath, however, dismissed the incident.

'That sort of thing goes on all the time, Trace. People will try anything at the expense of their fellows. Just keep your eyes and ears open, Harry. When I started my apprenticeship in the Acme Foundry the boys got up to all sorts of mischief and tried to put things over the tradesmen. I remember doing my time in the boiler shop. We had a large railway engine from one of the sawmills in at the time. One of the lads was put into the front of the firebox of the boiler that was being reconditioned and given a toothbrush to clean the soot out of the flues. He climbed in, and some bloody idiot closed the fire door behind him to give him a fright. That would have been bad enough but someone, they never discovered who, threw a smouldering piece of oily rag down the smokestack and when they finally found the guy he was completely round the bend. He spent years in an asylum for extreme mental cases and could be there to this day for all I know. Apprentices can do some bloody stupid and cruel things.'

After the dishes had been cleared away Harry brought out the papers for Strath to have a look at. They looked very official and were headed Department of Labour,Office of District Commissioner of Apprenticeships. Strath read them carefully and finally said, 'Well, it looks straightforward enough to me. You do ten thousand hours and at the end of that time I'll be able to ask you to fix my car.' He paused. 'For free of course.'

He peered back at the paper. 'I must say I really do like their language. Listen to this bit. It states "In witness whereof these presents have been executed by the parties hereto the day and year first before written."' He shook his head. 'Does this mean we have to pay people to write things this stupid? My poor old English teacher would have skinned me for writing like that in an exam paper!'

They all laughed, including the girls, who didn't know what it was all about.

To save a lot of trouble Strath signed as Harry's guardian and Tracy witnessed their signatures.

Harry had a shower and was in bed fairly smartly that night. First day on the job. Rather exciting really. His first letter would be to Maggot to tell him about a day in the life of a working man. He missed Maggot and wondered how well he was looking after his dog, Roy. He had given him to his old friend when he left. Funny. He sort of missed the dog a bit too. Just before he fell asleep he wondered what Lee was doing.

Quite a nice girl, that.

Next morning he arrived at work just as the garage was being opened up. He clocked on, slipped into his overalls and was hard at it in the smoko room by the time the bell went. He heard two journeymen say as they were changing, 'New boy a bit keen, ain't he? He'll wise up eventually.'

Nana had a name for those types. Small thinkers. He carried on and was finished by half past eight.

Dinky walked in and said 'Right, I'll show you how to get all the boy's smoko orders.' He handed Harry the little notebook. It had a list of names and the various prices of pies and cakes and all the sort of junk that the staff were in the habit of eating. 'Make sure that you don't muck the orders up. The boys get a bit snaky when you don't get what they want and you can get out of pocket pretty smartly. You make a stuff-up and it's out of your own pocket.'

It was a good opportunity to meet the staff and learn their names. There were twenty-seven all together, including the office staff. Harry looked at the notebook. Parts of it were indecipherable. It would need to be rewritten before it made much sense to anybody. Dinky saw him reading the notes intently and sniffed. 'Hope you can understand it,' he said with a smirk.

Harry was not to be drawn out. 'Swahili is only a little more difficult,' he said, smiling expansively. 'Then again, it could be a doctor's prescription. Don't worry, I'll get there.'

Dinky didn't have a clue what Harry was talking about and shrugged his shoulders. Maybe it was the name of a new milkshake?

A sudden thought struck him and his eyes gleamed momentarily. 'Look, Harry, I've just remembered I have to go down the block and pick up old Mrs Halthorpe's car for a grease and oil change. I'll just have to let you figure it out and get on with it.' Without waiting for a reply from Harry he turned on his heel and walked off.

Cunning so and so, thought Harry. He's going to try and drop me right in it. Well, Dinky boy, we'll just see about that. He quickly walked into the smoko room and retrieved the list that had been made out for the previous day. The cost of each person's order was written beside their name, as well as the change given them.

He had to be quick. There were a total of twenty names on the list and he only recognised four of them. Time was of the essence.

Frank's name featured halfway down the paper. Harry started with him.

'Smoko, Frank. Want the same as yesterday?'

'Why, er, yes. I guess so.'

'Righto. One mince pie, ninepence. Got the right change? No? Doesn't matter. Thruppence change coming up. Now, just point out Charlie to me, will you? Over in the lube bay? Great, thanks Frank.'

Harry made his way over to the lube bay, extracted the order from Charlie (also the same as yesterday's) and requested the whereabouts of the next client on his list. Following this procedure of using each person to point him in the direction of the next on the list, he soon had the orders sorted out, including the prices and change. Funny, this also followed a pattern of sorts. Nana always reckoned humans were creatures of habit. Looked as though she might have had something there.

He completed his task in double-quick time, raced over to the shop and placed the order. Tom Brekon gave him the same sort of ingratiating smile as he had on their first meeting, and for a moment Harry thought he was going to start rubbing his hands together like Shylock the Jew. Business can't be *that* bad, he thought.

Placing the orders in the box, he thanked Tom and sped back to the workshop and into the smoko room to do a quick check on the water heater. He had decided that until he was there a bit longer he just wouldn't take chances, especially with chaps like Pug around. It would be just like him to switch the heater off or something like that.

Walk softly and carry a big stick. Nana was sitting on his shoulder once more.

Fifteen minutes later as the staff filed in Harry had the bags of pies and cakes and various other items with their names printed on the side of them and handed them out to the men. It was all for show of course and went down quite well.

'Hey. Where's me bloody change?' asked Pug. 'I'm short of a shilling. You still owe me a bloody shilling. New boy's cocked it up, eh? I gave you a quid. How about it?'

Harry was ready for this. He appeared to be hesitant.

'Why, how much should be there, Pug?' Innocence itself was written all over his face.

This was Pug's big chance to show the new boy up in front of everyone.

'Eighteen shillings and ninepence.'

'Sorry 'bout that. I'm sure it was all right. Just to be on the safe side I'll put it down on the table and let Frank count it then,' replied Harry.

He pushed the coins over to Frank who was sitting opposite. 'Okay Frank, start counting,' he said with a smile. It was something like a poker game in the Wild West. He sat back and watched Frank carefully count out the change.

'Ten, fifteen, eighteen and six, seven, eight, ninepence perzackly,' said Frank. 'Yep, she's all there, Pug.'

The rest of the mechanics joined in the laughter. Pug went over to his table and glowered.

Later, Frank said to Harry, 'Well, I guess that will teach Pug to count his money properly next time, eh Harry?'

'Well, I really shouldn't tell you Frank, but he was quite right. He *was* a shilling on the light side till you started to count the change. I knew he'd kick up like stink and try and make a big thing of it. Thanks for your help, Frank.'

Frank gave a gleeful chuckle. 'Do you mean to say you palmed it?'

Harry grinned. 'Must tell you about my nana someday. I used to live with her and every night she would come in and sit on the bed and we would play euchre. I used to hide the cards under the blankets and cheat like anything. She would catch me and say that if I went through life like that I would end up in hell. I asked her if it was a sin to play cards and gamble and she said that euchre wasn't gambling. It was really my Uncle Jack who taught me to palm coins. He said it was a form of magic. So let's say I cast a spell on old Pug today.'

'Better watch your step, Harry. He's bad news.'

'Thanks, Frank. I'll try to remember that.'

The horn went for work and the room emptied. Harry cleaned up, couldn't find Dinky so knocked on the boss's door and asked what other jobs required doing.

'Just clean up the smoko room and then come and see me,' replied Jim.

'Finished that, Mr Schultz. That's why I'm here. Can't find Dinky.'

Jim led the way back into the now tidy lunchroom and looked around. 'You don't waste much time, do you Harry?' he said with a grin.

'My Nana always said if there's a job you don't like then get rid of it as quick as you can. I could always clean up the pigsty on the farm double-quick, Mr Schultz. Not much different to this.'

Jim looked sharply at Harry to see if there was any malice or cheekiness in his manner but he could see that the boy was just being very matter of fact. Jim hated smart alecs. Harry didn't seem to fit in that category. He relaxed. This was a change indeed from the usual run-of-the-mill apprentice. Time will tell, he thought.

'Have you got a driver's licence yet, Harry?' he asked.

'No, Mr Schultz, but I'd like to learn as soon as possible.'

'Right, we'll get on to that as soon as we can, Harry. Ah, here's Dinky. Now go and see what jobs he's got for you.'

Dinky showed Harry where the rubbish bins were and explained how often they had to be emptied. Together they loaded the drums on a trailer and then after securing them with a tarpaulin over the top Dinky hitched up the firm's Vauxhall van and both of them went to the tip and emptied the heavy containers.

'This is a bit of all right having two people to do this,' said Dinky. 'As soon as you get your driver's licence you'll be doing this off your own bat.'

Harry thought to himself I just can't wait.

Arriving back at the workshop Dinky went to great lengths to show Harry quite a few jobs which required doing. It was obvious to Harry that several of them had not been carried out for some considerable time. He wondered what Dinky actually *did* do with his time. Still, it was none of his business. The idea was to get promoted as soon as possible, but that didn't look as though it was going to happen tomorrow. He would just have to be patient and keep his nose to the grindstone.

And watch his back.

# CHAPTER THREE

Dinnertime at the Baines' house was nearly always quite an hilarious affair. With Strath at the head of the table one was never quite sure what was going to happen next. His two little daughters adored him and to see him playing up at dinnertime it was not difficult to understand why. While Tracy would put up a great show of being offended by his behaviour, she would sit and watch while Strath, with the aid of two soup-spoons, played a tune on himself. At times he would stand up and slap them together all over his body, while singing at the top of his Irish-tinted voice.

Often it was quite an effort settling the girls down to bed after that type of carry on. Strath would pretend to be in the dog-box and hide under their bed. Meanwhile Tracy would make a great show of searching for him, finally hunting for him in their bedroom. Strath, having sworn the kids to secrecy, would jump out and Tracy would pretend to be scared out of her wits, much to the delight of the girls. Another hour would have to be spent getting the girls to wind down. Highly exciting stuff and Harry, also joining in their games, was treated as one of the family.

They lived in a flat behind the dairy and one of the problems of course was that Tracy would also have to tend the shop during meal breaks. It was only on the weekends that both parents managed to have a little quality time off. Myrtle Brooks would do about six hour's work on a Sunday, which meant that the family could go to church. Strath, having been brought up in the Catholic faith, was a regular churchgoer and Tracy was intent on bringing the children up to 'follow the faith'. Two of her aunties were nuns and every time she visited them it was almost as if they were running a recruiting campaign for the Church. There were not very well disguised inferences that the two girls would make marvellous nuns, the attitude being, it seemed, that anyone who wasn't a priest or a nun would inevitably finish down in the fiery pit.

Harry, having spent some time being taught by nuns, had decided that the religious life was definitely not for him regardless of the hellfire and brimstone threat. He managed to get out of going to church and as Tracy was not the bossy type she resisted any attempt to order him to attend against his will. They were friends and what he did with his life was his business. She was, of course, inclined to be rather protective but there again that was only her nature.

She was slightly worried about the attitude of those men that he was working with and tried in vain to tell him to be aware of the dangers inherent with fellows like them. Harry was only too aware of what was going on but the last thing he wanted was for her to be worried so tried to make light of things, which only disturbed her all the more.

It had been rather a steep learning curve for Harry. Frank had begun giving him what could only be described as an intensively compressed driving course. He had also been given a few elementary lessons by Strath in his aging Chev Wentworth. To Harry it seemed like a massive vehicle but after a few short sessions driving around the back streets of the suburb in which they lived he was getting to feel more comfortable. It was only a matter of practice, Strath reckoned. Harry was not so sure about that but he was a very quick learner and before he knew it Jim had asked him into the office and said, 'You reckon you're ready to sit this licence yet, Harry?'

Harry stuttered his profuse thanks and was dismissed after being told to keep his eyes open for the traffic officer who, if all went well, would arrive to test him the following day. Jim wasn't one to muck about.

Strath was in high spirits at the tea table that evening. Anyone would have been forgiven for thinking that *he* was going for the test. He tried his damnedest to fill Harry's already bulging head with all sorts of belated advice.

Harry had a hard time falling off to sleep that night. His mind was too busy dreaming up all sorts of impossible situations he might get into during the test. Fantasising. Little was he to know that it would be rather different to that which he had in mind. The last thought in his head before sleep claimed him was that he had run down Mr Brooks while the testing officer was seated beside him.

He skipped breakfast next morning. Tracy was very understanding although rather mystified that a usually confident Harry could get himself so wound up over a simple thing like a driver's test. What she didn't know was that Dinky had told him in confidence that all of the last five apprentices from the garage had failed just because the testing officer had a snitcher on the boss.

Apparently it all had something to do with a dance the two of them had been at years ago. The way Dinky told the story it didn't seem possible for even a well-known racing driver to get through the driving test. Unfortunately, Harry didn't bother to check the veracity of Dinky's statements with Frank and, unusually for him, swallowed it hook, line and sinker.

The morning sped by and word of the impending test (thanks to Dinky) had spread around the staff. Frank took Harry for a last desperate drive along the route that he insisted everybody knew by heart. It was a standard test and he told Harry not to worry, it would be a breeze. Harry took heart that at least he would have the chance to drive over a familiar route. He was quite happy to be driving the firm's Vauxhall van. It had once been a sedan and had been converted into a van and was very comfortable to drive.

His confidence was restored after the drive with Frank, who informed him he had done everything just right. He tried not to think any more about the forthcoming duel with the law.

He was brought rudely from his reverie by a voice shouting his name. It belonged to Dinky. 'Hey, Harry, he's here waiting for you at the door.'

Harry saw the outline of the officer standing by the entrance to the garage. He went up to the imposing fellow.

'You wouldn't be Harry Evans by any chance now, would you?' enquired the tall figure with a big open smile.

Harry managed a smile in return and accompanied this gesture with a nonchalant thumbs up. 'I'm all yours.'

'And now, Harry, what marvellous machine are we going to drive out of here?' asked the officer with a very marked Irish accent.

'The Vauxhall's parked out on the street,' replied Harry.

Dinky, who was within earshot, piped up with a smirk, 'You'll have to take the Bedford van, Harry. Pug had to take the Vauxhall out on a job.'

Harry's heart skipped a beat. Was this another setup? he wondered.

The cop said, 'I'll be out in a minute – I just want a quick word with my friend, Jim.' Harry found out later that it had been Jim who had arranged Harry's test the previous evening. They were close neighbours and home brewers as well. Needless to say more!

Harry walked to the van waiting outside. Dinky was right behind him. 'He's not the usual testing cop,' said Dinky in a conspiratorial tone. 'I've never seen him before. You'd better watch him.' This was accompanied by a rather nasty-sounding laugh.

Harry waited beside the vehicle. The cop came out of Jim's office after a couple of minutes. He walked up to Harry and said with a grin big enough to match his frame, 'Well, Harry, are we going to get in?'

Harry climbed into the unfamiliar vehicle and deeply regretted that he hadn't had the chance to practise in this particular van. He adjusted the rear vision mirror with a great deal of show and waited for the cop's approval. The jovial Irishman didn't seem to take any notice.

'Shall I start now?' Harry asked.

The traffic officer laughed. 'Well lad, we're not going to get very far if you don't now, are we?'

Harry bit his lip to avoid blurting out a smart answer, started the van and, not being used to the vehicle's clutch, jumped clear of the park space.

'Bit of the old kangaroo petrol in the tank, Harry? Just try to relax a bit. Now, drive along the main street here. Good, now straight ahead. No, don't turn here, just carry along a bit. It's a lovely day for a drive now, don't you think, Harry?' He was obviously trying to get Harry to settle down.

And Harry did just that.

After driving a totally different route to that which Frank and he had practised on they stopped a few times and started off without too much trouble. Things took a different turn, however, when the cop directed Harry to climb up quite a steep street. Harry thought to himself that he had never in all his life been up such a precipitous incline.

'Stop,' cried the cop. 'That was dead easy now, wasn't it Harry? Now we'll try taking off and see how you go.'

It was then that all of Harry's chickens started to come home to roost. To his dismay he discovered that the van's handbrake didn't work at all. He just didn't have the experience to start off by using the footbrake and the clutch. After he'd stalled the van about four times the cop laughed and said, 'Harry boy, I think we've got a problem. This calls for a combined team effort.' He went on to explain that if Harry could work the accelerator and the footbrake, then he could let out the clutch.

After three attempts they pig-jumped up to the top of the incline. The Irishman called for a halt and indicated that they should stop at the top. 'Leave it in low gear, Harry. Leave what's left of the handbrake on and turn the motor off.' They both got out and the cop rolled a cigarette. He lit it and drew back deeply.

'Harry, me lad. Now just how long have you been driving?'

'About three weeks, sir,' said a very solemn Harry, steeling himself for a verbal dressing down.

'Well, I'm going to have a word with Jim when I get back and suggest he makes sure you get plenty of practice. Now, normally I'd fail you but the job you do is under constant supervision and you'll soon pick it up. Shall we say a small matter of fine tuning?' He stubbed his cigarette out. 'Now Harry lad, home James, and go easy on the horsepower.'

When they arrived back at the parking spot the traffic officer wrote out Harry's licence and gave it to him. 'Now don't go breaking your young neck just because I'm a bit soft in the head, Harry. I was supposed to give you a tractor licence test today as well, but my colleague will come up and give you a check before knock off. So keep an eye out for him.'

Harry thanked him and stood by the pavement while the Irishman climbed into his shiny black Ministry of Transport Clubman and drove off.

Nobody had said anything to him about a bloody tractor licence!

It was well after afternoon smoko and Harry, feeling very pleased with himself, went into the smoko room. As he did so Jim came out of his office and said, 'And how did it go Harry? Pass okay?'

Harry flashed his shiny new licence and grinned. 'Bit of a bother trying to start on Shepherd's Hill, Mr Schultz. The Bedford's a bit tricky on the brakes.'

'What do you mean, the Bedford? You were told to use the Vauxhall.'

'I know, but Pug needed it for a job and I was told to use the Bedford.'

'By whom?' Jim sounded rather terse.

'Dinky.'

'I'll bloody Dinky him. Tell him to report to me at once.' Jim swung into his office, leaving Harry to wonder what it was all about. He went and found Dinky, passed the message on, and moments later heard Jim's voice thundering, 'Come in here and shut the bloody door behind you.'

The stores cupboard was next to the boss's office. On impulse Harry quickly slipped in and though it was fairly cramped he could hear Jim's raised voice through the thin panelling.

'Righto Dinky, you little smart arse. Just what do you think you were up to this afternoon, telling Harry Evans to use the Bedford? You trying to be a bit clever, eh?'

Dinky's reply was unintelligible and Harry strained his ears even further. He spied an empty jam jar on the shelf and pressed it against the wall, putting his ear to it. He could now clearly hear Jim carry on.

'I told Harry to use the Vauxhall. Now just why did you have to change vehicles? You knew bloody well the Bedford's handbrake was supposed to be fixed this afternoon and wasn't to be used.'

'I'm sorry. I guess I forgot,' mumbled Dinky, clearly scared by the sound of things.

'There's more to this than meets the eye, Dinky, and from now on I'll be watching you like a hawk. Somebody could have had a bad accident. Now get out of here.'

Harry quickly stepped out of the cupboard and was back wiping down the bench in the smoko room by the time a now very red-faced Dinky came in.

'What was all that about?' asked Harry blandly.

'Nothing,' snapped Dinky. 'None of your bloody business.' Turning on his heel he stumbled out of the room and collided with Frank.

'Hey! What's the rush?' exclaimed Frank, but Dinky just pushed past.

'Pay no attention,' said Harry. 'He's just been bawled out by Jim.' He laughed, unable to contain his glee.

'Good one. I just came to see how you made out.'

'Got it!' cried Harry. 'And what's more, I have to drive the tractor this afternoon. Great, eh?'

'Good work,' said Frank. 'But have you driven the tractor yet?'

'No.'

'Well, we'd better give you a quick lesson on a Fergy then. Come on. I'll go and see Jim.'

Harry waited outside while Frank obtained Jim's okay and the pair went down to the tractor section where Frank went through the rigmarole of obtaining a tractor for Harry.

Reg, the head tractor mechanic, was only too pleased to sort one out and Harry gingerly climbed up on the machine. He had never driven a tractor before and it took a couple of minutes to sort things out to his satisfaction. He had just started to move forward and drive out to the entrance when out of the corner of his eye he caught sight of a blue uniform approaching down the main vehicle aisle.

He brought the machine to a halt as the cop approached. This one was definitely *not* Irish and looked mean into the bargain.

'They tell me you're Harry Evans and you're going to take a road machine test. Right?'

Once more Harry was going to take it, like it or not. He desperately wished he could have had a few minutes to drive the damn thing. The die was cast. Now or never. Do or die and all that sort of brave stuff.

'What would you like me to do? he asked.

'Oh, just reverse back down through the rear entrance and we'll see what you can do to impress me.'

Harry gingerly engaged the gears – fortunately these were clearly marked on the gearbox – and let out the clutch. It moved! It wasn't a very large tractor: Ferguson tractors weren't built in large sizes. The idea was that its newfangled hydraulic system was supposed to take all the hard work out of farming.

He reversed the machine out of the rear entrance and into the blind alley alongside the garage. The cop signalled him to back down along the alley.

Harry was slightly nonplussed. Which side of a blind alley was he supposed to drive backwards on? He backed along about twenty yards when the officer waved him forward. He managed to stop, change gear, and creep forward again. As he came abreast of the officer he heard him say, 'Now just drive around to the entrance and in through the main door.'

There was no traffic on the main thoroughfare, which was a relief, and Harry plucked up a bit more confidence. As he approached the main door, however, he saw to his horror all the staff standing there prepared to finish work for the day. He hadn't realised it was that late in the afternoon. The tractor was in a low gear which, combined with the low revs of the engine, meant that he was hardly moving. Harry could see the silly almost smirking, smiles on all their faces.

I'll show them, he thought to himself. I'll bloody show them.

He pulled the hand throttle wide open.

The engine coughed, almost stopped, then picked up and with a roar the machine sped forward and shot through the large front entrance. Smugly Harry saw the looks of alarm cross the faces of the assembled audience.

'This is really going to impress them,' he thought to himself.

At the same time he heard a shout behind him. He swung round in the seat and to his horror saw that the cop was being dragged by his leg along the oily garage floor. For a split second his mind went blank. He turned to face the front again and by the time he had applied the brakes and brought the tractor to a halt he had travelled almost the entire length of the garage. He switched off the machine and climbed down. By this time Jim and half the staff had reached the inert figure lying on the floor. They disentangled the officer's leg and helped him to his feet. The cop scowled at Harry and before Harry could proffer an apology said, 'Where's your licence, lad?'

Taking a pen out of his pocket he scrawled in the amended details and handed it back to Harry. Resisting any further offers of help he limped to the front of the building. The side seams of his jacket were torn and through the large rip one could see his white shirt dirty with oil. He was one bloody oily mess. Without slowing down he stooped and gathered his cap off the floor. He walked stiffly out into the sunlight and the mechanics could see him climb rather painfully into his car and speed off. To their delight he actually graunched the gears.

Jim came across and slapped Harry on the back. 'Harry, I've got to hand it to you. That's the best bloody entertainment we've seen here in a long time. For your benefit that fellow's name is Sligo and he would be about the meanest cop around. But he couldn't say a thing to you.'

Harry was totally mystified by all this.

'Why did he pass me when I thought I should have failed?'

'Because Harry, me lad, he was walking along behind you and went to hop on the drawbar when you opened the throttle. The tractor stalled for a moment then picked up. When that happened he managed to put his leg in the drawbar space as he was going to get on. Then you pulled away and trapped him. He shouldn't have tried to hop on the drawbar so he was at fault. He just couldn't do anything else but give you a pass with all of us looking on. Serve the beggar right.'

Harry looked at the driver's licence he was holding. For one fleeting moment he wondered whether it had all been worthwhile. It had been a pretty event-filled day. Just as well they're all not like this.

Yes. In the long run he decided it had been well worth the effort.

# CHAPTER FOUR

The next day found Harry at work bright and early, still a bit bubbly from the high he had experienced the previous day. He recalled Strath laughing so much at the tea table he had an awful feeling he was going to have a stroke. At one stage the tears were running down his cheeks.

No sooner had he entered the building than he heard Jim calling his name. 'Front and centre, Harry Evans.' It was a term he had picked up from the Americans during the war and it basically meant to whoever it was directed at: 'You are to come into my office and stand in front of my desk while I proceed to bawl you out.'

Harry's heart sank. He had known it was too good to be true and now he most probably would lose his licence, which had become something precious to him. Putting on as brave a front as possible he stood in front of Jim's untidy desk and waited with bated breath.

'Sit down, Harry,' were Jim's first words. Harry gingerly lowered himself into the seat from which there happened to be a spring protruding.

'Right, Harry,' Jim began poking tobacco into his evil-smelling pipe, which was usually a good sign that he was about to be expansive. Harry at this stage was about to break into a sweat. What's Schultzy taking so long about? he thought.

After prodding and tamping away at his pipe for what seemed ages, Jim finally looked at Harry and said, 'Harry, I've got good news for you.'

Harry waited expectantly.

'You've been here about a month now and you seem to be going okay. Ted Morgan, our heavy equipment manager, wants an apprentice to start in the tractor department. Now how would you like to do that?'

'Sounds rather good,' replied Harry. 'Would that mean that I wouldn't get to work on cars?'

'Hell no,' said Jim. 'There isn't always that much work in the tractor department. It varies and from time to time you would be required to work in the main shop. It would broaden your knowledge which is a good thing really.'

Harry decided to be slightly more bold. 'How come I get the chance and not the other apprentices, Mr Schultz? There are others senior to me.'

'Well, to be quite frank, I've been keeping a beady eye on you and you're doing all right. Don't let what I've just said go to your head but keep on the way you're going and you'll be okay. To be honest, I did have another in mind till you came along but he's blotted his copybook. It can happen, but them's the breaks.'

Harry screwed his toes tightly in his shoes to contain his excitement. He had a fair idea who Jim was referring to!

Jim continued. 'The heavy section does quite a lot of work out in the field so I guess you've done your dash as far as the smoko stuff is concerned. We're starting a new apprentice tomorrow so I'll get Dinky to show the fresh boy the ropes and you can start your new job straight away. Any questions?'

Harry sat thunderstruck. Things were just happening too fast.

'Not at this stage, Mr Schultz. Can I come back if I think of some?'

'Sure thing, Harry, and keep up the good work. You can now go and report to Ted. I've jumped the gun and taken the liberty of telling him you will be working in the tractor department.' He smiled. 'I knew you would take it.'

Harry rose to his feet and left the office in a daze.

"Send Dinky in as you go,' came a voice from behind him.

Harry knocked on the door of the heavy equipment section and a voice asked him to come in. Ted Morgan was a Canadian by birth and although his accent was not very pronounced one could be forgiven for thinking he was an American. Ted, however, would not forgive anyone who took him for an American. The biggest insult was to be called a Yank. Ted had made this abundantly clear to those who were foolish enough to make this mistake. He loved the outdoors and after having served his time as a diesel engineer he had then spent a great deal of time in the Canadian outback working on timber projects. He knew his bulldozers backwards.

Some said he was obsessed with anything that made a diesel engine noise and anything that had a bloody big blade on the front. The bigger the better.

Because of his forestry and engineering experience, Ted spent his years during the war building airfields and bridges. He had somehow found his way down to New Zealand to visit his mate Rex who he had hunted with in Canada before the war, and finished up by marrying Rex's sister. He didn't really take kindly to being tied to an office desk and used every opportunity to get out to field jobs where he could tangle with problems associated with heavy bulldozers and the like. The hunting in the backblocks was right up his alley or, as he put it, right up his valley. He maintained he was a New Zealander with a bloody awful accent.

He was an excellent shot and as he and Rex retained a brotherly love for each other and the companionship of hunting and the outdoor life, it was no wonder that Rex's sister was wont to say that she sometimes wondered whether Ted had married her or Rex. She was a wonderful person, however, and jealousy was not in her make-up. Ted considered himself to be very lucky to have the best of both worlds.

He was busy checking time sheets, a chore which did not bring much joy to his soul, so when Harry knocked on his door he had no trouble putting the unsavoury task to one side.

'Sit down, Harry. Make yourself comfortable. So you want to be a diesel man, do you?'

'Well,' said Harry rather diffidently, 'I only learned about this new job about fifteen minutes ago and it's all come as a bit of a shock. To be quite frank my mind's still in a whirl.'

'Well, we'll just have to try and sort you out. The firm's franchise deals in Caterpillar on the heavy side and Ferguson on the light side. Quite a few returned soldiers are getting back to life on the farms and there's a hell of a lot of work to be done clearing up things that were neglected during the war. I deal not only with sales but also servicing and it's quite an interesting job. You'll get out of the shop a fair bit, especially with the heavier stuff that can't easily be transported back here. I do a fair amount of demonstrating, particularly with the Fergys, and I'll need back up to do this.'

He smiled as a thought occurred to him. 'I saw how you managed to obtain your tractor licence yesterday and tomorrow you're going to take a drive on a Fergy to Outram where I'll demonstrate it. Normally we'd transport it by truck but the new vehicle we've just obtained hasn't quite finished getting the new deck on so just this once we'll do without it. It will be a good chance not only to get a bit of driving experience but also to see what demonstrating involves.'

They went out to the showroom and Ted gave Harry the dealer registration plates to fix to the machine so that everything was legal and roadworthy. Together they spent the rest of that afternoon preparing the implements and spares and sales pamphlets. To Harry this was quite an experience, and Ted proved to be a good teacher to a very eager pupil.

Harry was to drive the machine from work first thing in the morning and by the time he reached the farm where the demo was to be held Ted would have everything set up. That was the general idea anyway.

Tracy and Strath were just about as excited by Harry's good fortune as he was and sleep that night didn't come too easily to him.

The following day dawned bright and clear and matched Harry's disposition. Owing to Tracy's insistence, he had dressed warmly and had a raincoat with him, just in case.

He felt quite important driving a machine that no one else seemed to be on the road with and, what was more, it was shiny and new. It took roughly an hour and a half to reach the farm and he pulled up alongside Ted wearing a smile of satisfied accomplishment.

Ted introduced Harry to the owner of the farm, which made him once more feel quite important. Ted was a person who didn't talk down to him as an apprentice, which made all the difference. Indeed this was onc of the reasons why his staff liked and respected him.

The Ferguson, being an English tractor, possessed some fancy new innovative ideas. One of its great selling points was that it incorporated a newfangled hydraulic system. If, for instance, the plough it was pulling struck a submerged object such as a stump, then, by means of the machine's linkage, the pressure could be taken off one driving wheel allowing it to spin and thus reducing the liability of the tractor being damaged. Often its drawbar would be able to lift not only the plough but also the stump which would sometimes be jammed on its point.

This invention was a great boon for the farmer who now had an easy means of lifting heavy weights – something that could not be accomplished so readily beforehand. One only had to back the machine up to a fence, put a chain around the post and move a small lever and hey presto! – the post was extracted smoothly and with minimum effort. This proved to be tremendously popular, one farmer unfortunately becoming so enthusiastic that he went around extracting such a large number of his old posts that he finally reached the stage of not having enough new ones to replace them.

Ted was not only an expert but a showman as well and under his capable hands he practically had the tractor talking. The farmers lapped it up. They recognised and appreciated a skilled ploughman in their midst.

There were a considerable number of landowners attending the demonstration and they all seemed very interested in the machine. Lunch over, Ted beckoned to Harry and said, 'There are a few fellows here who have said that would they like to see the new type of swamp plough in action. Hop into the van and go back to the shop and get it. You'll have to get a few of the lads to give you a hand on with it.'

Harry climbed into the van and drove back thinking this was a job of a lifetime. He wasn't learning much in the way of mechanical things but it sure was a lot of fun. What's more he was also getting paid for it!

He drove into the heavy machine section and went for help to lift the heavy swamp plough onto the vehicle. It took three of them heaving heartily to slide the implement on.

On the return journey Harry started to feel more confident handling the vehicle and increased his speed. It was a lovely day and this was the life. Yes siree, this was the life! He even started to whistle. Things were really looking up.

By this time he was hitting about sixty miles an hour. Boy! Am I good, he thought to himself as he went to turn a gently sloping corner. He could hear the tyres starting to protest slightly. Absolutely nothing to it, he thought. Good old Sterling Moss couldn't do much better. He was halfway around the corner and thought he had it made when without warning the heavy swamp plough toppled over. It had not been secured. It was also top heavy and the weight change, coupled with the loud crash from the rear of the vehicle, startled Harry. He involuntarily flinched at the wheel and tightened the turn even further. The van started to lean over at an alarming rate. Harry reversed the direction of the steering wheel whereupon the van went over on the other two wheels. Narrowly missing a concrete pole he again swung the wheel the other way with a vicious oversteer. Once more the tyres protested and he was heading for a stone wall. More in desperation than following the standard procedure for a skid, he straightened the wheel and luckily for him the van was once again heading in a more or less straight line down the road. Harry gently applied the brakes and drew to a halt at the side of the road. He lifted his hands from the steering wheel and looked at them. They were shaking like fury. He felt sick in the stomach. He glanced behind him at the the source of the trouble. The plough was lying on its side. Perhaps he would have been better off to put it in that position in the first place. He was lucky there was no other vehicle on the road. He sat there for what seemed an interminable period before screwing up enough courage to start the motor and drive off, somewhat chastened, at a considerably reduced speed. He realised he had been extremely lucky and would probably remember that driving lesson for the rest of his life.

On his arrival back at the farm and with the help of several of the farmers, he unloaded the plough and hooked it onto the tractor. It was found that the temporary dealer number-plates were interfering with parts of the attached implement so Harry removed them and placed them both in the van. For the rest of the demo the farmers took turns driving over the ploughed field where Harry had driven hidden spikes into the ground and where Ted would proudly point out to the assemblage that the machine wheels would slip and save further damage when the plough struck the hidden object. The farmers were suitably impressed. At the conclusion of the display they all adjourned to the farmer's woolshed where the firm had put a keg on and provided other more solid refreshments. Everyone, including Ted, was in jovial mood. The day had gone off extra well.

They were all talking ten to the dozen, tongues loosened by a few beers, when Ted told Harry to get on his way back before it got dark, as the tractor wasn't fitted with headlights – he'd better get his A into G. With a final wave Harry took off through the farm gate and was on his way. He was barrelling along in fine style when he happened to glance behind and spotted a traffic patrol car on his tail. He giggled to himself and thought, Well, I don't think I'm capable of outrunning him with this machine. It's not really designed for racing. The patrol car drew abreast and Harry was surprised to see it was driven by Officer Sligo whose clothes he had successfully ruined the day before. They recognised each other at about the same instant.

To his surprise the officer signalled Harry to pull over. Ah! thought Harry. He can't get me for anything on this machine – I wasn't doing anywhere the speed limit. Ted had told him the top speed was roughly eighteen miles an hour and he hadn't had the throttle wide open so it was with more curiosity than concern that he viewed the cop walking purposefully towards him.

He looks mean enough, thought Harry. Wonder what's up?

'Afternoon,' Harry said with a smile. No use pushing your luck. Especially not with this fellow.

'Ah, Mr Evans. We meet again.' The cop smirked. 'Didn't take you long to start breaking the law now, did it?'

Harry was completely nonplussed. 'Breaking the law?' he asked incredulously.

The cop with a bland smile said 'Now, Mr Evans, you know very well you can't drive along the Kings Highway without number-plates, don't you?'

'Aw, heck. That?' said Harry. 'My boss has just been demonstrating this tractor and we took the number-plates off. They were in the way and I guess I forgot to fit them back on.'

'Well, I guess that's not good enough, is it now? I guess also that until you put some plates on that machine you'll just have to drive it into that paddock and leave it there. Now how does that idea strike you, Mr Evans?'

Harry groaned inwardly. He wasn't too sure about leaving the company's machine in a stranger's paddock where it could possibly have parts flogged or damaged. He didn't have any money on him to ring the garage and he certainly didn't know how to get hold of Ted.

'I'll also have to write you out a ticket for not displaying a number-plate in accordance with the Transport Department requirement. I won't ask you to produce your licence as I am quite aware that you possess one and that it is fully up to date.'

Now isn't that just bloody lovely of you, thought Harry, inwardly seething by now and trying desperately not to show it. He managed. Just.

With greatly exaggerated effort the cop wrote the details into his little book and then with a flourish ripped out a copy and handed it to Harry.

'Now Mr Evans, I suggest you get that machine into the paddock smartly.'

Harry once more climbed onto the tractor. As he was about to start the machine he glanced up and was thrilled to see Ted hurtling around the corner. He obviously had been really motoring, and brought the van to a rough halt beside the traffic officer's vehicle.

Harry breathed a sigh of relief. Good, he thought. Here comes me boss, he'll fix things up.

Ted stepped out and walked up to the officer with a puzzled look on his face. 'What seems to be the problem, Officer?'

'Are you his employer?' asked the cop.

'I am the divisional manager of the section in which he works. Yes, I am his boss. Why? What's up?'

'I have just given him a ticket for not displaying a registration plate.'

'But I have them in the van,' Ted replied testily.

'They were not on the machine when I gave him the ticket.'

'Well, we'll put them on straight away,' protested Ted.

'Sorry, sir, deed's been done. The law's the law, you know.' The cop continued smugly. 'Your firm may register your disapproval through the approved channels in writing.'

'My bloody oath I'll be registering my disapproval.'

Ted was starting to lose his cool. The cop, noticing this, began walking to his car. He drove off leaving Ted in high dudgeon.

'Okay Harry, get these bloody plates on and let's get you home before it gets too dark. We can make better speed if I tow you.'

In no time at all they had re-attached the offending plates and the towrope was laid out. Ted tied the rope on, expertly. Harry wouldn't have had a clue; knots were definitely not his specialty. The granny was just about his limit.

'Let's go, Harry,' Ted shouted, and dived into the van. Harry let the brake off and they were away with a hiss and a roar. It was surprising just how fast the van could tow the tractor. Harry had the wind up several times as the large tyres were inclined to bounce at the slightest imperfection in the road. The bumps seemed to be magnified and more than once he was sure he was going to be hurled from the seat as if it were a sling shot. He had a distinct feeling he should have been elsewhere.

It was just on dusk as they pulled into the workshop entrance. Ted unlocked the doors and Harry started the tractor and slowly drove in. He was stiff with cold. He clambered down unsteadily and said, 'Well, I certainly don't want another trip like that in a hurry.'

'Never mind, Harry,' said Ted. 'You did well. The first thing I've got to do in the morning is write a letter to the Transport Department and get your licence sorted out. I'd certainly like to sort out that bloody idiot of a jumped-up cop while I'm about it.'

He looked at Harry and said, 'Just clock out and get on home. I've got a bit of paperwork to complete. Do you know that we sold three tractors today and I've got four more farmers interested? A bloody good day's work. Tomorrow it's all on to complete the delivery truck. The sooner we get the new deck on the better. I'll see you tomorrow. Good night, Harry.' He paused and added, 'Thanks for a good day's effort and don't worry about the cop – I'll fix that.'

Harry walked outside to the tram stop. '*We* sold three tractors, he repeated to himself. 'Not I but *we*!' It made Harry feel as though he was part of the team and gave him a warm, fuzzy glow. It was quite dark now and he could feel the wind on his cheek and smell rain coming. Two minutes later he boarded his tram and paid his twopence fare. It was way past knock-off time and most workers were at home. The picture-goers would crowd the trams in about an hour's time.

Life in the city was much different to his hometown. Busy, bustling and not altogether to his liking. Still, in a way it could be considered exciting. Perhaps he would feel better once he had become accustomed to it. It was a case of wait and see. He wondered what his friend Maggot was doing.

'My, Harry, you're late tonight,' said Tracy with a smile when Harry finally arrived home that night. 'Time for a quick wash and tea's on the table.' Strath and the girls were already halfway through their meal.

'How did it go today, Harry?' enquired Strath.

It took the remainder of the tea session to tell them all about the adventures he had been in that day. He did not, however, mention the fright that he had been given by the van. Too embarrassing.

It wasn't until the dishes and the children had been put away that Strath put his newspaper down and said rather seriously: 'Harry, I think I've got a place where you can go to board. I was having a beer with a fellow who works with me at the gasworks. He's got a spare room and he's not very keen on gardening. He lives in quite a big house with grounds. It used to belong to his mother. It's a bit big for his wife to handle the grounds and gardens. Maybe you could come to some sort of agreement with her to do some work and possibly offset your board. He couldn't care much about the house. I've known him for a while and he likes his drop of whisky. He's a bit on the lazy side but it might be to your benefit. I said I'd speak to you about it. How do you feel?'

'Just where abouts is the place Strath?'

'In Maitland Street. About a mile from where you work.'

'What do you think, Tracy? Good idea?'

'Well, as I said when you arrived here, it was only temporary and please don't think we're trying to get rid of you… '

Harry interrupted her. 'Oh, don't be silly, Tracy. I was only asking what you thought of it.'

'I think you'd be best to go and see the place. Would you like me to go with you?'

'Heck no. When do you think would be the best time to pop along, Strath?'

'Well, I tell you what, Harry, I know that Tas will be at the pub at eight o'clock tonight – he goes there every evening. I'll take you along and you can have a chat with him. Okay?'

'Will I be allowed in to the pub, Strath? Don't forget I'm underage.'

'As long as you're with me you'll be okay.'

They had a game of crib until it was time to go. Tracy made

them both put on their coats and scarves. The night was getting cold and it had started to rain.

'I think I could do with a rum and raspberry tonight,' chuckled Strath.

The hotel was a good ten minutes' walk from the house and Strath had a careful look around before ringing the doorbell twice. It was the first time Harry had been in a pub and he found all the secrecy surrounding the entrance to a hotel rather exciting. It was something like a bad film.

As all hotels were closed at six o'clock anyone who was not a bona fide traveller or a guest of the establishment was liable to a hefty fine if they were caught drinking after hours. Depending on the area, some hotels were busier than others with this illicit trade of supplying liquor. It was well worth the risk and the practice was to slide up to the front door and ring twice. At times trade would be so brisk that a person would be placed outside to vet the callers as they arrived. If the law was spotted coming down the street then the doorbell would be rung once, or whatever the signal happened to be, and there would be a general exodus from the rear of the hotel. To overcome this, on entry to the establishment a guest book would sometimes be produced and the drinker would sign this as being a bona fide traveller who was staying the night. It was quicker to produce this item of evidence to the police than to have half-pickled drinkers wandering around the back of the pub asking, 'Have they gone yet?'

The door opened slightly and a voice said, 'Oh, it's you, Strath. Come in. Bloody cold night, eh?' A moment's hesitation. 'Who's with you?'

'My young cousin, come to see Tas. He in yet?'

The publican chuckled. 'And just when isn't Tas ever in? You'll find him down in the Snug Bar.'

The publican was behind the bar. 'What's your poison, lad?'

Before Harry could order a beer Strath intervened. 'A stout and raspberry for Harry here and make mine a rum and cloves.'

He duly paid the money, picked up the two glasses and went

over to a solitary drinker sitting at the table watching two men playing darts. The room had a fire burning brightly and it was a cosy sort of setting.

'Hello Tas,' said Strath, motioning Harry to be seated. 'Like you to meet Tas Mann, Harry. This is the young fellow I was telling you about, Tas.'

Harry held out his hand. Tas shook it a little too vigorously. His eyes were bleary and he obviously had been there for a while. He was about fifty and looked about sixty.

'So this is the new helper.' He laughed. 'Looks strong enough, Strath, eh?'

'I brought him along to see whether he would fit the bill. Maybe discuss the board and all that.'

'Oh, shit on that.' Tas hiccupped. 'Got nothing to do with me. Missus handles all that sort of stuff. She needs a hand in the garden and a few other things need doing round the place. None of my business. He better go and see her. Yes, he better see the liddle lady himself.'

He squinted owlishly into his glass. 'Know where I live, boy?'

'No,' said Harry, 'but I can find it okay I'm sure.'

'No time like the present, lad. We'll go now. I've had me quota tonight.' His glass was empty and he rose unsteadily to his feet.

Harry glanced over at Strath. He hadn't even tasted his drink yet. It seemed to be rather rude of Tas but he was obviously past noticing any social discrepancy on his part.

'I'll go with him, Strath,' Harry said.

It was Strath's turn to look embarrassed. 'What about your drink, Harry? We've just got here.'

Harry downed the glass in one go. It was only a little lady's waist anyway. He stood up and winked at his cousin. 'Gotta look after my new landlord now,. haven't I?'

Tas went to take a step and leaned on Harry rather heavily.

'Whoops-a-daisy,' he said. 'Night, Strath.'

The publican saw they were leaving and managed to get to the door before them. 'Wait one minute,' he said. He opened the door and looked up and down the street. 'Okay.' He let them out into the inhospitable night.

'Night, Ces.'

'Night, Tas.'

They started to walk down the street, Tas humming softly to himself and their heads down in the wind which seemed to be increasing in strength. Fifteen minutes of walking brought them to a rather forbidding stone wall. It reared about eight feet into the air. An ancient wrought iron gate barred their entrance. A street lamp accentuated the bleakness. By its light two hideous gargoyles frowned down on them. Harry wondered where the drive to the house was. It took a while for it to sink in that they were at the back gate. One of the hinges was broken and Harry had to lift the gate to get it to swing sufficiently for them to get in.

The path was overgrown with branches and littered with debris. Harry thought to himself that his nana would have had a fit to see such a neglected pathway. He couldn't make out where the rest of the garden, if you could call it a garden, was. It was pitch black looking up to the house and Harry could make his way along the path only because the street lamp cast just enough illumination to see by.

Tas stumbled his way up the path talking to himself. 'Almost there, Harry,' he chuckled.

They reached the back door and Tas opened it and almost fell. 'Oops, somebody keeps pushing me.'

Harry was not impressed. Just what sort of person and situation had Strath introduced him to? He was starting to have serious doubts as to what his future lodging was going to be like. He could just imagine living with a person like Tas and most probably his wife would be an ogre (or was it ogress?) too.

Tas took off his coat and hung it in the porch. He called out, rather loudly, Harry thought, 'I'm home.'

Then, 'Where the hell is that girl?'

The door to the porch opened and a flood of light filled the area.

'I'm here, Tas,' Harry heard a woman's voice say.

'Good, come and get my boots off. Me gout's giving me hell. D'ya hear?'

He sat down heavily on the solitary chair in the porch.

A slight figure stood awkwardly in the doorway. Harry could see a that pair of crutches caused the awkwardness. With a quick movement a woman moved forward and sat down on the floor on the mat in front of Tas. Harry could see she had long hair down to her waist. She swiftly undid the bootlaces, removed the boots and slid back on her bottom.

'That's better,' Tas said, and stood up.

He walked to the door, making no attempt to help the woman. 'Follow me, Harry,' he hiccupped.

Harry followed him into the house. The woman scrabbled to her feet and brought up the rear, boots in her hand. They walked into the kitchen and Harry could see that it was massive. The woman clumped over to the coal range and placed the wet boots on the rack above. She turned and faced Harry. She didn't smile.

Tas belched and said, 'Shake hands with Harry, m'dear. He might be going to live here. Eh, Harry?'

Harry held out his hand. She took it. Hers was warm and gripped firmly, as if she meant it to be a welcome. Her eyes were flickering nervously. Harry wasn't quite sure how to read the situation.

'She'll tell you all about it. I'm off to bed.'

With that remark Tas walked out of the room. Harry heard his stockinged feet thudding up the hallway. His gout must having been giving him heaps.

The two were left in the room facing each other. She leaned on her crutches and stood watching him. Her face was expressionless.

Under the light cast by the large old-fashioned type of chandelier, Harry could see her more clearly. He tried to look at her face but his eyes were drawn to the reason she was leaning on crutches: she had only one leg.

She saw him staring and with a resigned sort of look said in a low voice, 'Would you like to sit down?'

He almost dived into the chair to hide his embarrassment and looked across at her once more.

Harry was surprised by her youthfulness. He had imagined Tas to have a wife about fifty-odd but this woman would be no older than twenty-five, maybe less. She had waist-length auburn hair. He noticed there were marks on her dress under her armpits where the crutches had worn the fabric thin.

She returned his gaze with an innocence that was hard to describe. He actually felt quite uneasy under her intense look.

Finally she spoke, rather tersely, he thought: 'Tas brought you home or did you bring Tas home?'

'I beg your pardon?'

'I mean did he bring you home as an excuse for being late? He's never bothered himself before this.'

'I came home with him because I thought that you had a room to rent and he said it would be up to you.'

'Oh,' she replied, sounding rather mollified. 'I guess I got it wrong. I thought he said something totally different.' Her voice dropped even further. 'I'm very sorry.'

Harry felt the conversation was getting nowhere and it had been a long day.

'Well, have you got a room to rent? And what would be the weekly rates?'

'Bed and breakfast, cut lunch, evening meal, washing and ironing would be thirty-eight shillings.' she sounded as though she had rehearsed this announcement. She had too.

'Boy!' said Harry. 'That's pretty steep, isn't it? I only get two pounds sixteen a week as an apprentice.'

She frowned. 'To be quite honest I haven't taken in boarders before and I thought it would be a good idea to do this so I could get some work done on the garden. I suppose I was expecting the person to be on a man's wages... ' She realised this didn't sound at all tactful and sensed Harry's hackles rising. 'Tas doesn't do anything in the grounds so I was hoping to get some help out there... ' Her voice trailed off and she looked so downcast all of a sudden that

Harry began to feel sorry for her.

'What do you suggest then?'

'Do you know anything about gardening? I can only manage a small area outside and it then gets a bit beyond me. Maybe I could reduce your board to suit. Say twenty-five shillings? Would that be a bit better?' she added rather tremulously. She was getting worried now.

Caught short for words Harry looked at the ceiling.

'Could I have a look at the room please?' He was a stranger to this sort of goings-on and dearly wished Tracy was beside him to help with the right questions.

She nodded, then adroitly lifted herself out of her chair and with a smooth movement of one crutch walked over to the door leading from the kitchen. Switching on the light she waved her hand at the large area and said, 'It's the warmest room in the house and you've got plenty of space.'

Harry saw it contained a double bed with great big brass balls on the top of each post and a huge chest of drawers. An old-fashioned washstand complete with basin and ewer stood by the window and completed the rather sparse interior.

Not quite sure what to do next he went over and sat on the bed. He tried to give the impression he rented rooms like this every day. The bed felt quite firm, not like the kapok one he was used to back home. There was a massive tallboy in the corner he hadn't noticed before.

The room looked rather comfortable. It would be *his* room. He would be paying for it. This thought made him feel quite good.

He sat there for a minute. Tas's wife eyed him anxiously. She had taken to him instinctively when he first mentioned the room. He didn't know how desperately she was hoping he would rent it. Her heart was starting to thump. She didn't understand why. It was only a room, she thought to herself. It's only a room. Most importantly though, it meant company. Would he take it? *Oh, please take it.*

After what seemed an eternity he looked up at her and said,

'How big's the garden then?'

She let out an audible sigh of relief. He was going to take it. She knew.

She smiled for the first time. 'Oh, it's big, but I'm sure you can handle it all right.'

He hoped there wasn't a garden the size of a rugby field outside but he couldn't check that tonight. He made his decision swiftly. Devil take the hindmost when it comes to making your mind up, Nana always said.

'I'll take it, Mrs... ' Harry paused a moment. 'Mrs Mann.'

He shook her hand to seal the deal. Her handshake somehow felt different this time.

'Helen. Call me Helen. Would you like a cup of tea... Harry, wasn't it? Sorry, you didn't tell me your last name.'

'Evans. Harry Evans. Thanks for the offer but I better get back. When would you like me to shift in Mrs... er... Helen?'

'I think you better decide that Harry. Any time is suitable as far as I'm concerned.'

'Saturday?'

'Fine. I'll expect you. Now I'll show you out the front door.'

'Sorry, Helen, but I had a nana who was a bit superstitious. First visit – must leave by the door you came in otherwise you don't come again. Silly, isn't it?'

She laughed, slightly more freely. 'We have something in common, Harry. My mother was superstitious about that. I'm a bit that way myself too.'

Harry went out and found his way back down the garden path in the dark. He'd have to buy a torch.

It was a good forty minutes' walk back to Strath's by the time he had taken two wrong turnings. Tracy was still up and eager to hear the news.

'Tell me about her, Harry,' she said.

With some difficulty he tried to describe Helen, managing a fairly accurate one except for her eyes. He didn't attempt those. To him there was something indefinable about them. So intense. Pain-filled? No, he was at a loss.

His description of Tas was not the most complimentary. Tracy, however, hurriedly stepped into Tas's defence.

'I believe he's an old friend of Strath's who's had a hard time and if Strath put you onto him I wouldn't worry too much. She sounds rather young to me. How old do you really think she is?'

'Dunno. She looks about twenty-five to me, maybe younger. I reckon Tas won't see fifty again.'

'Strange.'

'I can shift in next Saturday she said.'

'I'll miss you, Harry. It's been good having you here. The kids have really enjoyed it.'

'So have I.'

'You having a bath?'

'I'd better.'

'Well, I'm off to bed.'

'G'night Trace.' Harry paused and looked at her. 'And thanks for putting me up like this.'

'Silly.' She gave him a big peck on the cheek. Tracy was a big softie really, Harry thought to himself.

# CHAPTER FIVE

Ted called Harry into the office next morning.

'I'm going to put you under a journeyman from Monday, Harry. Reg is his name. He's been on an extended holiday and just got back this week. He's one of the best in the business and while you're going to be carefully absorbing all that he says and sucking his brains, I'm going to be right behind you finding out if you're listening to him or not. Got that? I like your manner and your openness. You've got a lot to learn and by God you're going to top the apprentice exams this year. Don't try and tell me it can't be done. I've just decided that this is what the tractor section needs. Reckon you can do it?'

Harry stuttered. 'I'll certainly do my best, but I don't know whether or not I can do it. I haven't even picked up a spanner yet.'

Ted gave a great big grin and reached into his drawer, pulled out a tiny four-inch adjustable spanner, and placed it on his desktop.

'There,' he said, 'try that for size.'

Harry leaned forward and picked it up.

'Well, that's your first hurdle over,' grinned Ted and they both sat there and laughed. 'Keep it,' he added.

'Don't think I'm doing this just for you alone. I want this franchise to be a winner this year and we're going to pull all stops out to get there. Get my pitch?'

Harry nodded, too overcome for words. Ted's enthusiasm was infectious.

'Right, Harry, down to earth once more. Get out there and I want the tractor section cleaned up. I want to see my face in the floor even if it is concrete.' He pretended to scowl. 'Now, out!'

It was the hardest day's work Harry had put in since he had started with the firm. Ted certainly knew how to get the best out of anyone.

Saturday. The big day. Harry only had two suitcases to shift. Strath ran him around to Maitland Street in the Wentworth, and the two girls came for the ride, chattering away like crazy.

Harry stepped out and Strath, shaking his hand, wished him, 'All the breast mate.' He drove off, the two little faces waving out of the rear window. Harry returned their salute, hefted his luggage up, and manoeuvered through the big wrought-iron gate and up the drive. Somehow the grounds looked totally different in the daylight and he had to keep telling himself it was only the rear of the property that he had seen. He dropped the suitcases and looked around. There was quite a bit of work to be done. The place looked rather neglected to say the least.

He puffed his way up to the front entrance and pulled the bell rope. Seconds later he heard a jangle coming from the depths of the big old house. It looked like one of the originals in the street.

He recognised the clump of Helen's crutches on the passage floor. The door opened and there she stood.

'Oh, good, you did come after all. I had a funny feeling you might have changed your mind.' A big smile spread over her face. She looked relieved and happy. Harry thought to himself that she looked even younger than when he first saw her. She wore a summery sort of dress and had a silk scarf in her hair. Nice.

'Come in. Come in,' she said almost insistently.

She led the way to his bedroom and immediately Harry spied that something had changed. There was a small bedside table with a lamp sitting on top.

'I thought you might like to read in bed, Harry,' she said.

'You must be a mind reader. I read anything I can lay my hands on actually. That was a nice thought. Thank you.'

She blushed with pleasure. 'I read an awful lot myself. Anyway, come out to the kitchen and have a cup of tea. Then I'll show you around the house.'

She once more led the way and Harry could not but admire the dexterity with which she manoeuvred on her single crutch. He noticed there were no floor coverings. He would learn later that loose floor coverings and crutches did not go well together.

The tea made and hot scones placed on the table, Helen edged herself onto a chair and let out a sigh of relief. 'Well, here you are at last. Now tell me something of yourself. You're an apprentice, right?'

Harry told her a little of himself – enough to get started – then enquired where Tas was.

'Oh, he's at work. He starts at the gasworks at five o'clock each morning and finishes at about four in the afternoon. He generally goes straight to the pub after work and comes home about eight thirty or nine o'clock in the evening.' She seemed slightly embarrassed. Funny, thought Harry. A hell of a long time to be away. Not much of a home life.

'He's an alcoholic,' she added.

'Oh, I am sorry.' This was embarrassing.

'No need to be. There's nothing we can do about it,' she replied simply.

There was a moment's awkward silence.

'Sugar?'

'One lump, please.' It was an old silver tea service. Most probably brought out to impress him.

'How old are you, Harry?' The question was rather direct and found him with a large lump of scone in his mouth. He hastened to clear it away before he blew a handful of crumbs at his hostess.

'I'm sixteen.'

'That's how old I was when I came to work for Mrs Mann. Seems years ago now,' she said rather wistfully. For a moment she seemed lost in a reverie. Harry finished his mouthful and sat ready to fend off another question.

'Do you like gardening?'

'As a matter of fact I do. My Nana always had a big garden and I was forever helping her in it. I can tell a weed from a wisteria and a pumpkin from a pea.'

She relaxed and laughed. 'Well, that's a relief anyway.'

They finished their tea and Harry carried the dishes to the sink despite protestations from Helen.

'Would you like to have look around the property now?' She seemed in a hurry to get him on the job. The sun had come out and it looked as though it was possibly going to turn into quite a nice day.

They inspected the front of the grounds first. It was all badly overgrown and would need a vigorous pruning, as Nana would say. That was her idea of giving something a bloody good going over. The same could be said of the garden at the rear.

Helen explained the grounds had been part of an old estate that had been subdivided. The original house had been two stories. When it burned down at the turn of the century a single-story house had been built to replace it. Six bedrooms in all. It had belonged to Tas's grandfather and must have been a fine place in days gone by. Though it retained some of its former glory the grand effect was unfortunately somewhat undermined by the state of the grounds. If Tas had ever had any interest in its welfare this was obviously discontinued a long time ago.

'Any reason for that?' enquired Harry.

'It's a long story and a sad one at that.'

Harry decided not to push that line any further.

They both struggled along an overgrown path to a building at the back. Harry was amazed at the amount of undergrowth.

'Doesn't anyone come here, Helen?' he asked.

'I came up here before I lost my leg.' It was the first time she had mentioned this. 'That was about two years ago,' she added.

Harry tried the door of the garage. 'Locked.'

'The key's under that brick.'

It was still there, guarded by an army of earwigs who scurried off in a huff. Harry turned it with some difficulty and went in. She followed.

Gloom and dust and cobwebs. The interior was composed of a double garage and a remarkably well-equipped workshop. A sheet-covered car stood forlornly on the left-hand side.

'Will Tas mind me looking through here?'

'No,' she answered simply. Just like that. Harry still hadn't figured this young woman out.

She looked around. 'Looks just like it was that morning.' She gave a little shiver. 'Let's go back, Harry.'

'I was looking for some gardening tools. Must be some somewhere in here, Helen.'

As he spoke he spied what he was seeking standing in the corner amongst a whole lot of other gardening equipment. A slasher.

'That'll do the trick just fine.'

After securing the door they made their way back to the house and went inside. Helen sat down. She was a little white-faced. 'My foot's hurting again.'

She saw Harry look down. 'No, not that one – it's all right. It's the one that's missing that hurts.'

Noticing his puzzled look she explained patiently 'I get ghost pains in my missing leg. Quite funny and quite sore at times. Strange, isn't it?'

'Can I do anything to help?'

'There are a few little things that I find rather difficult to manage. Like filling the coal bucket – that's about the top thing on the list. Takes a bit of heaving.'

Harry filled the surprisingly heavy coal-scuttle and brought some more firewood in. He wondered how she managed it. Gratefully she said,' I think we'll light the front room fire tonight. I don't usually, but seeing we'll be using it more from now on we might as well, eh?'

As Harry walked up the hallway he passed two doors opening onto bedrooms, and could see quite plainly that one showed a feminine touch and had a single bed, while the other had a double bed and no trimmings.

'The end room on the right, Harry,' Helen called. He opened the door and found himself in the drawing room. He set the fire and gazed around. It was neat, clean and tidy, showing signs of bygone elegance though rather straight-laced in design. The furniture had antimacassars on them and there were a few frowning faces looking down from the walls. A comfortable sofa looked out of place.

He heard Helen behind him. 'The oldies,' she said, in a sepulchral voice. 'Takes a lot of cleaning.' And giggled almost like a little girl.

That afternoon Harry spent some time sorting out what little clothes he had into the drawers and then walked down to Strath's place to pick up some washing he had forgotten.

'What's the place like?' Tracy asked eagerly.

Harry tried to tell her as much as he could but when it came down to tin tacks it wasn't very interesting. He was back at the house by four o'clock and as he walked in he heard Tas's voice, raised and angry.

Tas swung around on Harry's entry into the kitchen and dropping his tone said, 'Oh, there you are. All settled in?'

Harry said he was quite happy and added that he had been up to the shed to see if there were any garden tools.

'Help yourself, lad. Help yourself,' was the answer which somewhat surprised Harry.

'I won't be home for tea,' Tas stated to Helen in a colder voice, and walked out. Bloody rude, thought Harry.

Helen didn't seem to take any notice. 'What would you like for tea, Harry? Any favourite meals?'

'I take it as it comes, thanks. Though I must say I don't particularly care for tripe.'

'Right then. I've had a roast on and I'll use the cold meat for lunches next week. I don't like tripe either.'

That having been decided, Harry went into the washhouse and asked where the spuds were.

'What for?'

'To peel of course. You want a hand don't you?'

She seemed rather puzzled and a bit reluctant. 'Yes but… '

He smiled. Obviously his offer of help surprised her. 'Then where have you hidden the spuds?'

Harry was sure she had never been used to having a male doing a bit of fetching and carrying. She was so appreciative, it was a pleasure just to listen to her.

It didn't take too long for her to accept the little aid he was giving her and soon they were chatting away at the bench about all sorts of things.

Later, when they had finished dinner and put everything away, he lit the front room fire and both of them sat at the card table. He showed her some amateurish tricks and then taught her the rudiments of euchre. She knew how to play snap and happy families and had a smattering of the values on the card faces but that was about all. She was an eager student and her face was flushed with each little bit of praise Harry handed out. He tried to sound reluctant when he did it, which pleased her even more.

Harry was warming to her character more and more as he listened to her, though he was surprised by the different types of personalities she had displayed in the very short time he had knew her. One moment she would appear to be a very intense woman and the next minute almost childlike. It was all very perplexing.

It was close to ten in the evening when Tas stumbled in. He sat down in front of the fireplace and said, 'Getting a bit cold out there tonight – might be a frost tomorrow. Saw Strath down at the pub. He asked how you were getting on. I said you were settling in just fine, Harry.'

Harry couldn't quite see how Tas could figure that out as they had spent little more than five minutes in each other's company at the house. Still, he didn't say anything.

'Would you like something to eat, Tas?' enquired his wife. Harry suspected she knew the reply.

'No. Had a pie at the pub." He let out a rather stale, beery yawn. 'Well, I'm off. Work tomorrow.'

'But it's Sunday,' protested Harry.

'Nothing like a bit of overtime to keep the pay packet up, son,' was the reply, and with that he rose and went out of the room.

'I think I'll turn in myself,' said Harry. 'Thanks for the game. I really enjoyed it, and I won't let you beat me so easily next time.' He grinned. And off he went.

He undressed and got into bed. He decided he didn't want to read and switched out the light. The bed was cold but soft and funnily enough he was tired. He could hear Helen moving around in the kitchen, her crutches making a sound of their own. The grandfather clock in the hallway struck eleven. The last thing he heard was the toilet flushing next door. Noisy thing, he thought. He didn't even manage to run through the events of the day. Sleep claimed him.

It was the same sound of the toilet which roused him from a deep sleep some time next morning. He lay there in the darkness, trying to figure out exactly where he was. He heard someone at the coal range, the clang of the grate being cleaned, then a minute later the familiar sounds of a fire shovel in the coal-scuttle and the scrape of a kettle being slid over the top of the range. These sounds were readily identifiable to one who had grown up with a bedroom near a kitchen. They signalled the awakening of the house, and sometimes the reluctant listeners, who desperately sought shelter for one more moment between the now thoroughly warmed covers.

Harry switched on the lamp and lifted his trousers off the back of the chair. Pulling them on he picked up his towel off the rail behind the door and went into the kitchen.

Helen was standing with her back to him. She wore a candlewick dressing gown and her hair was in two long braided plaits. He could hear Tas in the bathroom.

'What's the time?' asked Harry. Helen spun round awkwardly and for a moment he thought she was going to lose her balance.

'My!' she exclaimed, 'You gave me an awful fright. What are you doing up, Harry?'

He glanced at the clock on the mantelpiece. 'Ten past four? Do you always get up this early?' No self-respecting person should be out of bed at this ungodly hour, he thought to himself.

At that moment Tas came out of the bathroom, his red woollen singlet not quite tucked into his trousers and his braces hanging at his sides. 'Hello, Harry. You going somewhere?'

'I thought it was time to get up. I've just remembered it's Sunday. Bit early, isn't it?'

'Well, young feller, I start work at five o'clock so I've got get going sometime, haven't I?' Tas said, with the hint of a grin. It was the first time Harry had seen him show any sign of humour at all. 'Helen gets me breakfast and makes me lunch. Just gives me time to get there. You might as well go back to bed. As you say, it's Sunday. Lie-in day. Lucky bugger.'

'Would you like a cup of tea, Harry?' Helen asked.

'Thanks. I think I'll just go back to bed like Tas said. It *is* a bit early, isn't it? Sorry to have bothered you.' He closed the door behind him and climbed back into the warmth.

He lay there for a while then got up and retrieved a book from his suitcase. A cowboy one. He didn't actually care for Westerns, but Tracy who did, had thrust it upon him. He thought it might help him get back to sleep. Twenty minutes later he heard the front door slam. He could still hear Helen moving about in the kitchen. Strange woman. Interesting in a way. He heard the kitchen light switch click then click again. Then came a tentative knock on his door.

'You awake, Harry?'

'Come in.'

The door opened and she clumped in. 'I was just going to go back to bed and I saw your light was still on. Sorry for waking you up, but I guess it's just one of those things in the morning. It's pretty hard to get around quietly on these things. The cold weather. It makes my leg ache in the morning too.'

'Which one – real or the ghost? Sorry. Didn't mean to be funny.'

She let out a girlish giggle. 'A ghost. I rather like that. I never thought of it that way. "Helen with the haunted heel".'

'No, truly, I'm sorry, it wasn't meant that way at all.'

'But Harry, I think that's priceless. Honest I do. You know something? I haven't felt so good about my leg for ages. Do you mind if I sit down?'

Without waiting for a reply she half twisted round and slid her backside up onto the bed. She laughed again – it had a kind of a throaty, exultant ring to it this time. 'Harry Evans, you've got a ghost on your bed.'

In a way it was rather intimate, two people laughing about a missing leg in a cold room at five o'clock in the morning. Somehow it made sense.

Harry recovered first. 'Tell me, Helen, do you get up every morning to cook Tas his breakfast?'

'Why not? I'm his wife and servant and there is no one else to do it. I don't mind really because soon as he's gone I either go back to bed or sit in front of the range where it's warm and read a book. I don't go out anywhere and I can't do anything much in the garden – that's why I'm so glad that you have arrived. I don't think I have talked so much since Tas's mum died.'

'How long ago was that?'

'Let's see. It would be exactly two years and one month ago. I remember because I unfortunately reminded Tas of it four weeks ago and he went out and got really blotto, it upset him so much. It all came back to him and he doesn't like to be reminded of it.'

'What did she die of?'

'He killed her,' Helen said simply. 'I think I'll go back to my room now.' With that remark she slid off the bed and walked out, closing the door behind her.

Harry switched off the lamp and lay there in the darkness. His mind was a jumble of emotions. What a mystery. So many unanswered questions. It really was quite mind-boggling.

Nothing was said about the conversation later that morning and Harry went out to the stables and retrieved the slasher. He carefully sharpened it and got to work. He had decided that whatever the mystery it had nothing to do with him and if Helen didn't want to tell him then that was her business. He had just completed two good solid hours of sweat-producing labour when Helen made her way cautiously along the tangled path. She had a thermos of tea and some scones in a basket which swung dangerously as she walked.

'Let's have a morning picnic.'

They sat in the sunlight on a couple of old kerosene boxes Harry brought out of the stables and sipped their tea.

Helen was the first to speak. 'You've certainly made a clearance here already, Harry.'

'I haven't even scratched the surface yet,' he stated rather apologetically. He was justifiably proud of his efforts but didn't want to skite about it. 'Just wait till I burn a bit of this old rubbish and then we'll see what's what. Hope the neighbours don't mind too much.'

It was getting late and the shadows were beginning to lengthen by the time he decided to cease work. He stood back and contemplated the result of his efforts. Nana would have been satisfied with that, he thought. Quite a few of his labours he mentally based on obtaining Nana's approval. It kind of kept him up to scratch.

Tas was home sitting in front of the stove.

'Been busy, lad?' he enquired.

'Yes. Funnily enough, it's quite enjoyable up there. I've had a good day all told. How much do you want done up there, Tas?'

'Ask the missus. Nothing to do with me,' replied Tas abruptly. He was getting rather hard to tie down to a straight answer.

Harry went and washed up for tea.

Monday. Same noise. Same routine. Harry rolled over, pulled the covers over his head and tried to go back to sleep. He heard Tas go and knew that Helen was still up in the kitchen. One of her stay-up-in-front-of-the-range-and-read mornings. He desperately wanted to go and have a pee but knew that would be the end of any chance of getting back to sleep. He endured it until he heard the chimes for six thirty then capitulated to the needs of his bladder.

The coal range was going full tilt and the kitchen was cosy. He finished his toilette and, fully dressed, went and sat at the kitchen table. Helen soon had a breakfast of bacon and eggs for him. His lunch tin sat next to the plate.

'Your lunch,' she said unnecessarily. 'Hope you like cold meat. I've put tons of pickles on.'

'Sounds fine thanks,' said Harry. 'And what are you going to do today?'

'Just the same as I do every day. Clean the house, polish the floors, and read a book.'

'Which library do you go to?'

'Oh, I never go to the library. Mrs Jenks next door calls in every Thursday and changes my books. She knows what I read and gets them for me. She's been doing that ever since I lost my leg. The butcher and the grocer are very helpful too. They take my order on a Tuesday and deliver on a Friday. I make my own clothes.'

That's the second time she's mentioned her leg, Harry thought to himself, but still nothing about how she came to lose it. And how the hell did Tas kill his Mum? It was all a big mystery that would clearly take time to solve.

He deliberately left early for work that morning so he could time himself. It was just as well, as he made it to the clocking-in point only moments before the horn sounded. Ran that a bit fine, he thought.

'Hot to trot, Harry?' Ted's voice broke in on his thoughts. 'This is Reg, who's going to teach you everything. Right, Reg?'

Harry took to Reg straight away. As he would find out later, Reg was an inveterate leg puller and Harry likened him to Harpic, one of the friends he had left behind in Thexton. He had a continuous twinkle in his eye and a boundless sense of humour.

'Ted, just what on earth have I done to deserve this?' Reg asked in mock dismay, his eyes rolling upwards.

'I apologise, Reg. It was all I could get you at such short notice,' replied Ted in like vein. Harry caught him winking at his new mentor. They shook hands.

'I'll leave you to it,' said Ted. 'I just can't stand the sight of blood.' With that he walked away leaving them eyeing each other.

'Well, I guess we better get started,' said Reg. 'I'll have to find me way around again. Been over in Aussie for two months and it looks like the work has piled up a bit. But not to worry, nothing's impossible. Ted tells me you've just started. Well, you'll be working under me and if there's anything you want to know then ask. Simple as that. Don't take anything for granted and remember somebody's life may depend on the work you do so double-check everything. Got it? Get it? Good.

Ever done any arc welding? No? Well, you're going to be sick and tired of it by the time you've finished because my idea of teaching welding is practice, practice, practice. I'll set up the machine with the correct settings and if at any time you've got nothing to do then sit down and start on this.' He walked along to where two great big sets of tractor tracks were set out on the floor. 'These thingummies are called grousers and they have to be built up with hardened rods. Now take a hold of that gismo and watch me.'

He went on to warn Harry of the dangers of looking at a welding arc with unprotected eyes. Harry had been burned when he was a child and didn't need any persuading. His father had been an engineer. He picked up a welding shield and after a bit of fumbling fitted it onto his head.

Reg struck an arc and started to weld up the track. He was a good instructor and soon Harry had grasped the basic essentials. As the work was not of structural importance the finish didn't matter. Reg explained that he was just adding some meat to the tread.

'You might as well be practising on that as on any old piece of iron. Now from now on I want you to work on that if you've got nothing else to do. Okay? Can't stand apprentices hanging around with their fingers up their bums. Don't forget to clock on and off all the same. It's still got to be charged out.'

This went down well with Harry as he was not one to be idle and it was hard trying to invent jobs at times. He toiled away happily.

Helen and Harry sat at the big kitchen table having their tea. Tas had not yet come home.

'Does he do this often?' enquired Harry.

'Do what?'

'Not come home for tea.'

Helen paused, wiped her lips on the serviette and thought for a moment.

'I used to worry about Tas a lot, but I guess I've become quite used to his habits now. It was quite different when his mother was alive. He seemed to have some sort of purpose in life. As you can see he drinks a lot. Too much. He seems to be getting even worse. He's not so even tempered as he used to be.'

'Does he hit you or beat you?'

She laughed. 'Oh, heavens no. What made you think that?'

'The drunks I've usually come into contact with seem to always take it out on their wives or their girlfriends.'

'No, Harry, Tas is a very kind person. Maybe a little short at times, but kind.'

Tas still had not come home when Harry crawled into his bed but the next morning there he was, large as life, sitting at the table having breakfast. Even though it was early Harry decided to join them. He had to find out something about Tas eventually.

'Ran into Strath at work. He said to say hello,' Tas said, chewing on a large piece of toast.

'Good. I must go and visit them next weekend.'

'Must be off now. Bye.'

They both heard the front door shut.

Harry sat there at the table staring at his cup. 'Doesn't say much, does he?'

Helen looked at Harry speculatively from across the table. 'No. He never has been one to talk very much really. Are you going back to bed?'

'I might as well try and get an hour's sleep. It's a habit I'm going to have to develop. What are you going to do?'

'Seeing I've got no one to talk to I'll just sit here in front of the fire and read a book like I usually do.' She sounded just a little petulant.

Harry could have kicked himself. She was just dying for company and the chance to talk. Here he was saying Tas didn't say much. He was just as bad. He tried to make amends.

'No,' he said cheerfully, 'I've just changed my mind. I'm going to sit here where it's warm and talk about anything and everything with you. How does that sound now?'

She brightened perceptibly at that and he could see he'd hit the right spot.

'What would you like to talk about? Finance, cows, work, state of the nation, war, or what?'

'You, Harry,' she replied. 'Let's talk about you.'

'All right. Only on one condition.'

'What's that?'

'That we talk about you tomorrow morning.'

'Fair deal.'

They sat there at the table that morning and in the next brief hour Harry had told her everything about his life. Well, not quite everything, as there were a few items that he would carry to the grave. He was also very careful to leave out the more intimate details of his previous love life. That included his relationship with Angie; he did not think Helen would be impressed by the fact that he had had an affair with someone twelve years older than herself.

When he eventually left for work he was completely unaware that he left behind a sensitive young woman who was very much aware that the more she got to learn about him and his ways, the more she was attracted to him.

Her head bowed to the book but she didn't realise for quite some time that she was holding it upside down. She would have to conceal her innermost feelings very carefully in her further dealings with him. Could she do that successfully? She tried desperately to suppress a terrific surge of desire that coursed unbidden through her body. Never in her life had she felt anything like it. On impulse she stood up and without the aid of her crutch hopped in through the open door of Harry's bedroom. She stood hesitantly beside his bed then let her dressing-gown slide to the floor, lifted her nightdress over her head and climbed naked into his bed. She detected the remnants of his body warmth in the mattress. She lay there for a minute, then plunged her face into his pillow. She could smell him. She wallowed in the sensuality of the moment. God! What was happening to her?

This was totally different to the last time she had lain in this bed. Her mind wandered back to an afternoon over two years earlier.

*She had been ironing clothes in the kitchen and heard the car roll up the driveway and stop outside the garage. There was the sound of the double doors opening. They always seemed to make a grinding sound – maybe needed a touch of oil. Five minutes later he came in through the back door, his eyes agleam with excitement. He had only been home four months from the war, having been wounded in action and discharged because of the silver plate in his head. He said it stopped him from thinking straight at times. He had made several attempts at being more intimate with her and she was flattered by his attentions, though at the same time she felt frightened by his changeable manner. He was quite good-looking and gallant. Before he went away he tried many times to be persuasive with her. She had resisted in a laughing fashion and treated him more or less in a sisterly way. He had, however, never really forced his attentions on her. He had already asked her to marry him several times and she had thought to herself she could do worse.*

*He had been away for the weekend at his favourite hobby, rock hunting. She had been thinking about his proposal and had made up her mind to say yes. She still was not too sure whether she loved him but if an opportunity like this existed then she felt sure she should take advantage of it. She had no other relatives. What had she to lose? Times weren't that good and this seemed a secure proposition.*

*He came up behind her and buried his face in her neck. She squirmed and went to slip out of his grasp. He whispered into her ear, 'Well, have you made up your mind yet?'*

*'Yes.'*

*'And what's the answer?' He sounded rather confident.*

*'Yes, George. I'll marry you.'*

*He let out a whoop and grabbed her hand. 'Come with me.'*

*He led her into the room beside the kitchen. She went reluctantly. He spun her round and pushed her back onto the bed. Leaning over her he pulled her dress up. She lay there in disarrayed dismay, stunned into immobility by the sudden fierceness of his actions.*

*'George! Please! What are you doing?' she gasped, temporarily winded. 'No, please, not yet. Not until… '*

*'No time to waste, darling. I think I've been bloody patient. Don't have to wait till we're hitched and all that nonsense. Now's the time for some action. You've given me your answer.' He unbuckled his belt, slipped his braces off his shoulders and knelt over her.*

*Her recollections were hazy after that. She remembered him grunting as he thrust at her almost like an animal. She had hoped that it would be loving and gentle, but it wasn't anything like that. A woman's duty according to her mother was to do her duty towards her husband and no excuses. This was what she had to put up with, apparently. She just had to lie there and accept his rutting. He finished. Stood up, buttoned up his trousers and said in a throaty voice, 'Well, I guess we'll be having some more of that later.' With that remark he walked out the door and later she heard him working in the garage. He was even whistling! She went and washed herself then went back to her ironing. What had she let herself in for? A tear rolled down her cheek, it was followed by another. She hurt inside and not only physically. A minute later the torrent began. Her only consolation was that no one could see or hear her.*

# CHAPTER SIX

Harry changed into his overalls and began work on the welding. He had only used three rods when he felt a tap on his shoulder. It was Ted standing there with a grin. 'Harry boy, you're having fun, aren't you just? Well, sorry about this but I've got another job for you. We're going to have to finish this deck for the display vehicle. You can work with Seth and Joe – give them a hand. By the way, have you got your heavy trade licence yet?'

'No, not as yet. I haven't had a go at a truck. In fact I've only just got my light licence.'

'Right, Harry me lad, we'd better do something about that and smartly.'

Ted it seemed, didn't muck around about anything. Wham bam and there it was.

Harry had been at work for about three months when the boss sent for him. 'Looks like we might have a little bit of a problem. The Trade Certification Board wish to speak to you down in the council chambers, tonight at seven o'clock.'

'Who are they?' enquired Harry.

'Oh, just a pack of old farts who keep an eye open for bad practices by employers and the like. Their secretary just rang and asked that you attend their meeting – tonight. Wouldn't say anything else. Better come and talk to me tomorrow morning and see what it's all about. I guess it should be straightforward but you never know with these things.'

Harry hurried home and duly got changed into respectable clothes and caught a tram to the council building. It was after hours and it took a while but he finally found the chamber where the meeting was to be held. He was a little early, just in case. He walked into the room and was met by an elderly man who asked him his business. When Harry told him he shortsightedly perused a sheaf of papers and was told to wait in an adjoining room. An hour later the same gentleman came back and told him, 'The Board will see you now.'

Harry diffidently entered the room. There were twelve ancient gentlemen seated at a great big table all looking at Harry. There was a single chair facing them.

'Come in, Mr Evans, and please be seated,' said the grave-faced man in the middle. Harry had read books on the Spanish Inquisition and an image of them all wearing black cowls came to mind. He pictured himself as a heathen or a convict all set for the gallows or whatever they used in those days. He sat down.

'Now, Mr Evans, my colleagues and I compose the committee of the Trade and Manufacturing Board of Dunedin. It has come to our notice that you have applied to undertake an apprenticeship in the art of motor engineering at the firm of Blackwell Motors of South Dunedin. From looking through your records it has also come to our notice that you have only completed one year's secondary schooling and as your apprenticeship in the motor trade requires at least two years this does not comply with the statutory requirements of the trade. Now what have you to say about that, Mr Evans?'

This came as a complete shock to Harry as he thought everything had been in order.

He vainly tried to collect his thoughts before replying.

'I'm afraid I was unaware that I was supposed to have two years' secondary schooling. My grades have been fairly good though, and to be quite honest I've been told I was a year ahead in my studies. My mother couldn't afford to keep me at school – that's the only reason I left. I would have dearly liked to have stayed on. I'm afraid I can't do much about it, but I'll be very sorry to throw away the only chance I've had, and I wont without some sort of struggle. Is there anything I can do perhaps to make it up?'

Harry thought to himself, they've already got things cut and dried and they're only going through the formalities. I guess I'll just have to sit here and wait for the firing squad. He felt sick in his stomach.

The three middle men conferred for a minute then the chairman cleared his throat and raised his voice. 'Ahem, Mr. Evans, would you mind leaving the room while we discuss this further?'

Harry got up and went out. Sitting on the cold leather seat in the waiting room he thought perhaps he might have a chance of getting a job at the gasworks with Strath or Tas, though it certainly wasn't the kind of employment he had his heart set on. He waited somewhat impatiently. Let's get it over and bloody done with, then I can go home, he thought disconsolately.

After an interminable period the door opened and Harry was once more summoned in. He sat down without being bidden.

Again the chairman cleared his throat and in a pompous tone said, 'Mr Evans,. we have reviewed your case and discussed at length the considerations involved. Obviously you were unaware of the trade requirements and to some extent this was due to an oversight by your employers. We have had excellent reports of you from them and their support of you remaining on their payroll is rather surprising. This is very encouraging as far as you are concerned but it does not preclude the fact the trade requirements are not being fully satisfied. My colleagues and I, after due discussion, feel that an extra period of education in the trade must be added to your apprenticeship. We find that you also have not commenced night school as required. Why not?'

'As I understand, sir, the night school starts in two week's time. I did go along to enrol and was told that term starts in a fortnight.' He almost added 'Your Honour.'

A few of the old farts nodded their heads as if in agreement with Harry.

'Fair comment, Mr Evans. We have therefore decided that in addition to the night school syllabus as laid down for apprentice motor mechanics you will complete an extra night per week for the period of one year from commencement. This we consider to be the minimum requirement we can ask of you to bring you into line with others of your trade. If there is any reason why you do not fulfil these obligations we will request your presence once more in front of us. Is that not only satisfactory but is it also fully understood, Mr Evans? Or would you prefer to go away and think on it?'

Harry could see no reason for delay. To him it seemed to be a very generous deal. An extra night a week in lieu of one year's secondary! Yes siree! He found it difficult to contain his elation.

'Thank you for your kind offer, sir. I accept it gratefully.'

'Thank you, Mr Evans. That will be all.'

Harry almost pole-vaulted down the stairs and into the street.

He received the revised and amended apprenticeship agreement the following week. Part of it read '... by virtue of a resolution of the New Zealand Motor Trade Apprenticeship Committee the said apprentice is required to enrol in and attend evening classes during the first three years of his apprenticeship. Attendance at one extra evening class per week to be made during the first year to comply with the special conditions as agreed upon... '

Half an hour later he was home recounting his good fortune to Helen. She had never seen him so excited.

'What have you got to do now, Harry?' she asked.

'First thing is to get to the school and enrol.'

'But I thought you said you had already enrolled?'

'Er, yes. I must have given them that impression.'

'I only wish we could go out and celebrate,' said Helen rather wistfully.

'It's a bit late now but if you like you can try and beat me at a game of euchre,' he said with a laugh.

Later on she said, 'You know, Harry, I've been thinking about breakfast.'

'What's wrong?'

'Well, I get up each morning at four o'clock and wake you up most of the time.'

'I'm almost getting used to it now, Helen.'

'Yes, I know, but I still have to get up later to get you away to work and it's almost the start of two mornings. What say if I was to bring you breakfast in bed and then I wouldn't have to get up again?'

Harry pondered. 'What's best for you. That's the most important thing.'

'If you wouldn't mind I reckon it would save me that extra time. I can then kill two birds with the one stone.'

'Oh, your cooking's not *that* bad!' he said with a big grin.

She threatened to throw a cushion at him. 'Well, what do you think?'

'If it's okay with you, then let's try it.'

Helen didn't get to sleep straightaway that night. All sorts of little fantasies and plans were running through her head.

Next morning it wasn't till Tas closed the back door and Harry heard his footsteps passing his window that there was a knock on his door.

'You awake, Harry?'

'Come in if you're good-looking,' he replied and sat up in the bed. She managed the tray quite skilfully and came to his side of the bed. 'There,' she said rather proudly, as she laid the tray down in front of him. 'Now what do you think of that? As soon as you're finished you can go back to sleep.'

'That looks great. And I get two cups of tea too.'

'Oops, I must have put my cup on too. Never mind. You finish your breakfast and I'll go out into the kitchen and finish mine.'

'No need for that. Just grab a seat and join me.'

She slid up onto the bed and Harry held out the cup for her. Her hair wasn't in braids this morning and looked soft.

'Well, Harry, you've been here four weeks almost to the day. Are you happy here?'

Harry was halfway through a piece of toast. 'You certainly spoil me Helen. You really do.' He finished the slice and paused. 'There's only one thing puzzles me.'

'What's that?'

'Tas has really got me baffled.'

'Why?'

'Oh, never mind now. By the way, you promised to tell me all about yourself ages ago and you never did. Why don't you start now?'

She had been very careful to keep completely out of his bedroom while he was in there. She decided she just could not trust herself. But the meeting this early morning was on her terms and she had thought out her plan of action very deliberately. Harry couldn't have said anything more encouraging. She started to tell him of her early life.

She had been a happy only child who enjoyed school. She was so lucky to have had a wonderful dad and mum. They lived in a logging camp down South Westland, in a rude sort of collection of workers' huts near the sawmilling settlement, and only had to walk a short distance to the nearby school. There were twelve pupils altogether and the teacher was an Englishman who was not only interested in stars but was a wizard in mathematics. He had a tremendous way of putting things across and it was little wonder that she became so interested in numbers.

Helen sat on the bed absorbed in her tale, her eyes all lit up. Harry was under the impression that she was excited by her tale, but little did he know it was the mere fact of being on his bed talking to him in this manner that was causing her flushed condition.

'Did you know that nine is a magic number?' she asked suddenly.

'No.'

'Well, it is. That's what Mr Drake taught us.'

'Can't see that it's more magic than any other number,' said Harry.

'Well, it's not easy to explain but Mr Drake said that it would always turn back into itself whatever you did to it.'

'No,' said Harry, 'I still don't quite see what you're getting at.'

'Try multiplying nine by itself and the answer always adds up to nine.'

'Okay, said Harry. 'So nine times nine equals eighty-one. That's not nine is it?'

'Now, add the eight and one and you've got nine. Got it?'

'Yeah,' said Harry. 'Four times nine equals thirty-six. Three plus six equals nine. Wait. It can't always work out that way. Hold on,' he said, 'I'll try a hard one. How about nine times ninety-nine equals… er… eight hundred and ninety-one. That's not nine, is it now?'

'Just keep adding,' Helen said smugly.

'Okay. Eight plus nine equals eighteen. One plus eight equals nine. By crikey, you're right. I never knew that. Gee that's clever.'

'I thought so too and that's how Mr Drake used to teach. He made everything so simple. Try writing out the nine times table up to ten and you'll find the answers always add up to nine. Clever isn't it?'

'It certainly is all right. Did you like school?'

'It was easy. The trouble was when my father shifted from the West Coast to Christchurch with Mum and me. He was called up shortly after into the army and trained as a Bren gunner. They were out on night manoeuvres at Burnham military camp when the machine turned over and burned, with him trapped underneath. Mum never recovered from it and we shifted down here to Dunedin. I was going to school at Dunedin Girls High and the principal was Tas's mother. She was just about to retire when my mother died. She took me under her wing and offered me the job of companion-housekeeper. She was a wonderful person and taught me a lot though she never forgot she was a schoolteacher. She had two sons, George and Tas. Tas was the eldest and was very protective of both his mum and his young brother. George was the engineer and all the tools in the stables belong to him. He loved playing lead soldiers and he even made his own. He had a little furnace. It's still out there I think. He had a bit of a crush on me right from the moment we met. He was a lot of fun. We all used to drive out in the country a lot and it was a happy sort of existence. I was always treated as one of the family and felt protected.

*Crush had invaded him again. The attacks were increasing not only in frequency but in intensity too. His resistance was wearing down. He found he could not rally so easily from each attack. Not only that but his memory was also getting more confused. He realised his attitude towards Helen was becoming more aggressive. He had to be more firm with her. She wasn't fooling him one little bit. She was keeping secrets from him. He knew she was waiting to kill him. He was clever enough to recognise this. Both she and Tas were plotting something. It was the gold they were after. This was a pity because he was originally going to share it with them. But not now. Oh no, not now. He could see through their scheming. Even his mother was in on the plotting against him. He would have to be more careful. He sat back, forcing a smile, and joined in the chorus. He would play their little game. Crush had faded for the moment.*

'Well, we were driving out one day with Tas at the wheel. We were even singing. His mum was sitting in the front seat when one of the tyres blew out. I was thrown clear. So was Tas. We were sitting on the same side of the car. I was only bruised, and so was Tas, but his poor mum was trapped. I remember holding George's head in my arms but he died almost straight away. The car was right on top of a cliff and I remember Tas telling me to get clear. He disappeared for about twenty minutes and then I heard a tractor coming. He'd had managed to get help. I was so glad. I'd tried to shift Mrs Mann but she was stuck. She was unconscious and bleeding badly. The man on the tractor put a wire strop on to the car and went to pull the vehicle to safety. Tas made me move away from the car, but as the strop tightened and the car started to move it somehow caught on a big rock and dug in. I could see the strop looked really taut. Then it snapped. I can still remember a funny whistling sound as it flew through the air and I felt a burning sensation in my foot. I looked down and saw the wire strop had cut my foot almost right off. Clean through. It didn't even hurt much. The car rolled off the edge of the cliff and went bouncing down into the river and when it reached the water it sank very slowly. I can see it now, even after all this time, all in slow motion. Tumbling over and over. It was awful and we couldn't do a thing about it. Tas was screaming at me to climb up onto the road. He hadn't realised

I had been hit and just how badly I was bleeding. It was lucky that the farmer had been a medical orderly or a stretcher-bearer in the army and knew exactly what to do. He had seen a lot of legs blown off. I woke up in hospital and my foot had gone. The next thing I knew was that a clergyman was standing by my bed and I was married to Tas. Just like that. Later gangrene set in and they had to take it off above the knee. That was two years ago and at times I can still see and feel it all happening.'

She shuddered and Harry could see the tears filling her eyes.

'I didn't mean to tell you all that, Harry. It just sort of came out. I've never told anyone about it all since the police questioned me. Though he has never admitted it I know that Tas has always blamed the accident on himself.'

She sat there very quietly. 'My foot's got cold,' she added unexpectedly, and she lifted a corner of the quilt and slid her leg under the cover.

Harry lay there pondering her story. It was incredible what she had been through.

'Tas married you,' he repeated her words. 'Just like that?'

'I didn't know at that stage what it was all about. I guess I just went along with what he wanted to do. I don't know, Harry. I was so messed up. I wasn't thinking straight. Looking back it seemed to be the only thing to do.' She paused for a long period then continued on.

'The only family I had and they were all gone. Just like that. Tas was so kind. And I had lost my leg. Look at me, Harry, I'm so ugly. I'm not whole, I'm incomplete. Look at my ugliness, Harry. Look at it.' With that she quite violently wrenched her nightdress up to her hips and exposed her stump. It was pink and Harry could see the angry white lines of the stitch marks. That wasn't all that was exposed to his gaze. His reaction was that of any normal young man.

'It hurts, Harry. It hurts like hell. Not only physically but in my head too. Am I mad, Harry?'

He leaned forward and took her shoulders in his hands. 'Of course you're not mad.'

She could smell him again and leaned forward into his chest. Instinctively his arms wrapped around her. It was the most natural thing to do to a suffering person and he really felt for her in her pain.

She swivelled around in the bed so she was beside him and nuzzled into the hollow in his shoulder. He could feel the wet tears against his throat. 'Tell me I'm not mad, Harry. Please not mad. Ugly maybe, but not mad.'

'No, you're not, Helen. You're not ugly either.'

Without thinking he took hold of her dressing-gown, which had slipped off her shoulder, and pulled it back up on to her. As he did so it fell open. She was wearing only a loose, thin nightie and for a moment he caught a glimpse of an exposed nipple. She could feel his heat. He could suddenly sense hers.

'Here,' he said, 'you're getting cold. Get in beside me. I'll make you warm.'

As she slid down beside him her nightie rode up even further but she didn't do anything to adjust it. She put her arms around his neck and pushed her face once more into his neck as if to hide herself. She didn't dare look into his eyes – he might have read in them what she desperately wanted him to do. Do? She didn't even know what she wanted herself.

He lay with her cradled in his arms and he knew that his hardness was betraying the fact that he was not unaffected by her closeness. He ran his hand over her back and she shivered in anticipation of things she thought could happen only in her dreams.

They lay there together for quite some time, both of them completely immersed in their thoughts. Then very slowly she started to rub the stump of her leg against his hip. He slid his hand down and began stroking the maimed leg. He could feel the dimpled scar tissue on the end of it. He massaged it gently and she gave a murmur of satisfaction.

'Mm. Feels better already.' She nibbled his ear. To Harry it signalled her tacit consent.

'Foot cold?'

'Hadn't really noticed.'

'But that was why you got into the bed, wasn't it?'

'Come to think of it, yes, it *was* cold. Doesn't seem to be now. Can't understand why not.'

'Be serious. What about Tas?'

'What about Tas?' she said almost belligerently.

'He's your husband.'

'Do we have to talk about him?'

'Not if you don't want to.'

'I choose not to just now.'

Harry changed the subject abruptly. 'Your hearts beating awfully fast.'

His hand was cupping her breast. The last time he had done this was with Angie. He had a quick flashback. He sensed that Helen was an amateur by comparison.

'Let me take your nightie off.' He went to remove it for her. Suddenly her whole demeanour changed and she drew back. 'No, Harry. We'd better not.'

'Why not?'

'You'll be late for work. You'd better go. No, Harry.' She was more insistent.

'Kiss me, Helen.' He paused. 'Please, Helen.' He sounded just like a little boy asking for a lolly.

'All right.' She tried to make it sound reluctant and wondered whether it sounded convincing. She moved eagerly towards him.

He took her head in his hands and kissed her long, gently and insistently. She could feel things happening to her that she could not later describe even to herself. She could feel his eager hardness pressing against her. His hand once more slipped down and began fondling her more intimately – gently, and to her surprise, expertly. He knew exactly where to explore. It shocked her not a little to realise that this was no novice.

She shook loose from his grip. He relinquished his hold on her surprisingly readily.

'I'd better get up, Harry. No. Sorry, but I've just got to get up.'

At that moment the tray, which both had forgotten about, fell off the bed and with one hell of a crash landed on the floor. It was sufficient to break the spell. Helen slid out of the bed, picked up her crutch and left the room. Harry heard her bedroom door close behind her.

He lay there for several minutes wondering what action he should take next. Hearing the hall clock chime seven he leapt out of bed and performed his ablutions. Then he cleaned up the tray and brought it out to the kitchen sink, picked up his lunch from the bench and went out into the crisp morning. He was going to tap on her door and say good bye or something to that effect, but decided against it. He couldn't explain why – maybe it was embarrassment or something.

He walked down the street, his mind in a daze.

Helen lay in the darkness of her room. Questions ripped through her mind. Had she gone too far? Frightened him off? He seemed eager enough. She could still feel his hands on her. In her – even if it was only momentarily. Her face flushed. She re-ran those sensual moments through her memory. Never even in her wildest moments had she imagined those feelings that she had just experienced. She ran her hands over her body, re-enacting his explorations. More. She wanted more. And she was determined that was exactly what she would get. She lay back on her pillow wallowing in a haze of sensuality. Funny, the ghost wasn't hurting at all. She rose once more and went into his bedroom. He hadn't made his bed this morning like he usually did. Maybe he had something else on his mind. She allowed herself a congratulatory chuckle, shucked off her nightie and slid once again between his warm bedclothes.

Her thoughts wandered once again to that prior period after her virginity had been rudely wrested from her. No, it wasn't rape in the true sense though she bitterly regretted she had not been given the chance to give herself more freely. Rape? What was the difference? she thought. Not only was her womanhood transgressed but her soul too, which she supposed was one and the same thing. She lay there, her thoughts a mixture of past and present events.

*She had gone to the doctor immediately her period was late. The news couldn't have been worse: she had definitely fallen pregnant. She had been made love to several more violent times since the initial approach and she found she was too frightened of him in his moods to even contemplate resisting. She just lay there inert, submitting without question to his at times animal-like rutting, and thinking how uninteresting the whole business was. Her opinion of men had sunk to an all-time low. Mrs Mann had not been informed of their unofficial engagement and Helen wondered how she would take it when she was advised that her young companion/help was cohabiting with her favourite son. Tas was as usual working and didn't appear to be interested in women.*

*Her husband-to-be spent a lot of time in his workshop. She went in several times and watched while he melted lead in his little furnace and poured the molten metal into the moulds that formed the legions of lead soldiers. He had moulds not only of soldiers, but also Red Indians, cowboys and others. He was engrossed in his hobby and in bursts of surprisingly boyish enthusiasm would try to tell her about the games that could be played and the battles that could be refought. She considered it to be little more than a small boy's pastime and didn't really take much notice.*

*Tas never entered the workshop much, if at all. He was very fond of his mother and spent considerable time with her in the front room, talking with her at length and reading to her. Her eyesight was starting to fade and she was also getting very forgetful. Helen read to her a lot too, something she found very satisfying. Meanwhile she endeavoured to satisfy her lover's quest for her flesh, hating the violence and the haste in which it was accomplished. She wondered when they would make the engagement official.*

Harry raced into the shop and changed into his overalls as quickly as he could. He wanted to get back to his welding. The more practice he could get the better, even if it was only for ten minutes a day, at most.

Dinky came into the section. Harry had not seen much of him at all since the new apprentice had started work. 'The boss wants to see you. In a hurry.'Dinky had decided to add that last bit for spite. He had still not forgiven Harry for being a smoko kid for only just under a fortnight. Here he was already welding and obviously enjoying himself. He and Pug would sort something out. They both had a score to settle with Harry. Time, thought Dinky. He had plenty of time.

Harry knocked on the boss's door. 'Come in. Sit down. Won't be a minute, Harry.' Harry waited patiently. 'Right. How did it all go last night with the Trade Board, Harry?'

Harry recounted the previous night's events, at the conclusion of which the boss nodded and said, 'Well, that's a relief anyway. Now just a word of warning, Harry. You've got to go like a cut cat and prove yourself. I'll be right behind you of course but it's up to you. Blot your copybook and it's curtains. Do I make myself clear?'

Harry nodded and added, 'Thanks for your support. It certainly is pretty kind of you to put in that report.'

'Get out of my office, Harry, and don't forget to get stuck in.'

Harry left with a light heart. Everything was turning up trumps. He couldn't be luckier.

In the afternoon he managed to get time off to go to the Technical School to enrol. To his consternation he found there were already three evenings per week allocated to night school classes for motor apprentices; this meant he would have to attend at least four nights a week!

Just how was he going to cope with this? he wondered. Things once again were proceeding for him at a breakneck pace.

The problem of what to say to Helen when he arrived home after work had been niggling at him all day. Tas most probably wouldn't be home by then. In fact Tas's absences from the house had become more and more noticeable. He was drinking heavily and though he didn't show it by being bad tempered he was very taciturn in his conversations with both Harry and Helen. He took no notice of the work that Harry had carried out around the house, expressing neither praise nor condemnation for all of Harry's efforts. To be quite honest Harry wasn't really fussed, though he had to admit it always seemed to stir him on to greater things when he received the occasional pat on the back. Praise from Helen would be more than sufficient at this stage. Besides, he consoled himself, it was actually her that he was doing all this for. The drive up to the garage area was now clear and one could actually see the back fence once more. Harry had even found a gazebo in one corner of the section. Helen told him Mrs Mann and she used to have afternoon tea out there. It would have been lovely and cool in the summertime, he thought.

He took his boots off and entered the kitchen. Helen was standing at the sink peeling potatoes.

'Hello,' she said. Had she deliberately averted her face?

'Hello,' he replied awkwardly.

'Have a nice day?' No, she seemed unfazed.

'Pretty busy one.' He wanted to reach out and touch her, run his fingers through her hair. He resisted the impulse.

'Anything exciting happen?' She wasn't making a very neat job of her peeling.

'Yes but that was *before* I got to work.' A bit daring, he thought.

'Oh.' She allowed herself a half smile and hoped that her voice wouldn't crack.

'How did yours go?'

'Much the same as yours, I suppose. At least the thinking part of it was.' The peeling job had slowed down considerably.

Nothing more was said. He went outside, worked for half an hour then brought the wood in and set the front-room fire and washed up for tea. It was getting to be a bit of a ritual. They completed tea with a desultory sort of conversation that skirted round the subject on both of their minds. Washing and drying the dishes together as usual they were very careful not to touch each other as they worked, and an unusual degree of politeness was displayed by both. It was ridiculous really.

Tas arrived and sat down at the table to have his tea, which Helen always seemed to have in the oven, whether he wanted it or not. Helen went into the front room and Harry decided to remain at the table to see whether he could induce Tas to converse with him.

He would have preferred to have joined Helen but imagined it would have been awkward. They seemed to be at a stalemate position. He hoped it would improve.

'How was work today Tas?'

'Very busy, Harry. Very busy. The cold weather is really keeping the gasworks working flat tack." He finished what was in his mouth. 'Ever been into the gasworks?'

'No, I haven't, Tas. Strath said he would show me around some time but seeing I shifted in here I haven't managed to do it. Sounds an exciting place.'

'Ever seen that picture, Harry – *Dante's Inferno*?'

'Yes, I've got it in one of my old school books. Why?'

'Looks just like that Harry. Just like that. When I start at five in the morning I go down into the clinker bays and what with the steam coming off the coke and the heat, it's just like hell, Harry. I reckon I know what hell is like so I guess when I do go I'll be quite comfortable." He gave a laugh that sent a tiny shiver down Harry's spine.

'Who says you're going to hell, Tas?' Harry was trying to make light of it.

'Oh, I'll be going to hell all right. Maybe I'm going through another sort of hell here on earth before I get there but I'll be going down to the depths. I have to pay for what I've done. A debt has to be squared away. An eye for an eye, Harry lad.'

'Is that why you work so hard, Tas?'

'Aye. That amongst other things, and that's why maybe I drink so hard – to forget. One must be able to forget. And if one can't forget unaided then one must seek help. The booze helps me to forget, Harry. Works very well at times. Then again, sometimes it doesn't.'

His voice was slurred and for a moment Harry wondered whether Tas was talking to him or himself.

'I suppose Helen has told you all about me, Harry?'

'Helen has told me nothing about you. She's only interested in getting her gardens and the grounds cleaned up.'

'Noticed that, Harry. Noticed that and it looks good too. Seen the car in the stables, Harry? Used to belong to George, my brother. You can have it if you want it, Harry. Take it. I don't drive any more since I lost mine.'

'Tas. Thanks all the same but I couldn't afford to buy it off you. I'm only an apprentice.'

'No, no. I mean it. You have it. Take Helen out for a drive. She never gets out at all. Do her the world of good. Hasn't been out for ages. In fact I don't think she's been out since… ' he hesitated '… since then.'

'Since when?' Harry asked.

'Since the accident. That seems a long time ago.' He slipped into a reverie. 'A very, very long time ago it seems now.'

He got up abruptly. 'Enough talk – I'm going to bed. Sleep sometimes lets you forget. Then again, sometimes it seems to make it worse.'

He walked along the passage to his room and closed the door.

Well, thought Harry, that's the longest conversation I've had with him ever. He cleared Tas's dishes away and put them in the sink.

The front-room fire was blazing cheerfully when he walked in. 'Tas all right?' Helen asked. She was as usual reading again.

'Yes, we talked a bit. Or rather he did. Best chat we've had in ages.'

'I'm glad.'

To make conversation he said 'I went to the school and enrolled today. There are already classes three evenings a week and now I'll have to go four nights, from seven till nine.'

'So I won't have your company at night now then,' she replied rather wistfully.

'Oh, it will only be for a couple of hours each night, though I suppose I'll have to do more study now. The boss said I had to keep my nose to the grindstone.'

They sat there in the room like a couple of strangers in a railway waiting room, neither of them game enough to bring up the subject closest to their minds. They played a couple of hands of euchre before Harry finally said, 'Well, I better be off. Long day tomorrow. G'night, Helen.'

'Good night, Harry.'

He undressed and lay in his bed. He imagined he could smell the faintest trace of her cologne on his pillow. He could hear her in the kitchen and as he lay there in the darkness he tried to visualise what she was doing out there. His door slowly opened and he could just see the outline of her body as she came up to his bed. She bent over him and kissed him fully on his lips. 'Sorry about this morning, Harry,' she whispered. Before he could reply or hold out his arms to her she was gone. The kitchen light snapped off. Total darkness.

What exactly did she mean by that remark? he thought. Sorry that it *had* happened or that it hadn't?

As he lay he pondered over Tas's statements. Clearly he was in turmoil over something that had happened long ago. Most probably it had to do with the deaths of his brother and mother. Harry couldn't quite figure out how Helen fitted into the picture. He was puzzled how a young woman like her could be married to a considerably older man like Tas. Did she love Tas? Or was she in love with him? She was obviously starved for company. Perhaps she was just having him on? A hundred and one questions were waiting to be answered. Perhaps in time things would sort themselves out. He slept.

He didn't hear her enter his room. When she spoke she sounded like a totally different person from the night before.

'Good morning, Harry. Here's your breakfast. Sleep well?' She sounded so cheerful.

'Wow! Is that the time already? I didn't even hear you in the kitchen.'

'Tas has already gone.' A statement of finality. Was there a hidden meaning attached to it?

He sat up in the bed and placed another pillow behind his back. 'You certainly know how to spoil me, Helen.' Was this going to be the start of another inane conversation?

He noticed the extra cup on his tray.

'Going to join me?' he asked boldly.

She went to take the cup but with a rapid movement he pulled the other side of the bedclothes back. 'Might as well get in before your leg gets cold.'

She looked at him quite intently for a moment, as though undecided, then moved around to the other side and slid in beside him. He handed her the cup. 'Let's make sure it doesn't end up on the floor like before.'

He could feel her closeness but he wasn't about to push his luck. Let her make the first move. Maybe he had frightened her off with his impetuosity yesterday. She finished her tea and waited till he had completed his breakfast.

Not a word had passed between the two of them. He took the cup from her and placed it on the tray. He then carefully balanced the tray on his bedside table. There wasn't much room. He stretched out his arm and switched off the lamp. It wasn't till he did that, that he became aware the kitchen light was off. She obviously had planned it that way. Or had she?

'You'll have to leave for work in an hour and twenty minutes, Harry,' she stated ever so softly.

'I hope I don't fall asleep.'

'I'll try to keep you awake. Is that okay?'

'Great. What do you want to talk about?'

'Can I finish what I was telling you last night?'

'Fire away.'

She reached over under the blankets and felt for his hand. She then guided it onto her mutilated limb. He explored her stitch marks with gentle strokes of his fingers – they were quite easily identifiable – and when he moved his hand to a warmer place she didn't demur.

'Tas married me. I didn't actually know why he did it. He never told me the reason and I never raised the courage to ask him. I think I was frightened of hearing his answer. That was two years ago. Since that time I have never left this house. I'm almost too scared to think about venturing into the outside world. I have my books – I travel the world with my reading. I have my dreams. My fantasies.'

She had moved closer to him. Her dressing-gown was beginning to create a barrier between them. He slowly slipped the garment from her shoulders and with a shrug of her upper body she freed herself of its encumbrance. Unceremoniously it was tossed to the floor. She snuggled into his body once more. He had half turned so she could again feel his hardness..

She smelled of cologne. She found the tail end of his singlet and ran her hand up his spine. Her maimed stump once again described sensations on his hip.

'What fantasies? Tell me more of your fantasies.'

'I've always dreamed that I would stand and watch my knight in shining armour ride up and carry me away on his chariot. You know, Rapunzel let down your hair sort of situation. I even thought of growing my hair long for that very reason. We women dream these things you know.'

Her hand was tracing patterns on his back. She nuzzled into his neck so hard that he had difficulty understanding her words.

'Do you love Tas?' He couldn't prevent himself from asking. He once again sensed her coolness. Tas was a forbidden word at this point. He immediately regretted the question.

'Why do you always have to bring Tas into it?' she asked.

'Sorry. Just curious. How do you feel about me?'

'How do you feel about me?' she countered.

'You are a woman. A very lovely young woman. Anyone would give his right arm to be here in bed with you.'

'Harry, I have given my right leg and I'm in bed with you.'

With that flippant remark she lightened the whole conversation. Sitting up she drew the nightdress over her head, then started to divest him of his pyjamas. He helped in the process. He found himself almost being skinned by the ferocity of her eagerness.

They lay there, devoid of their clothing. He held her close and then slowly knelt over her. She held him at arm length by his shoulders. 'Gently, Harry. Love me gently,' she whispered. 'I'm a stranger to this.'

'But Tas... ' Harry tried to protest.

She held her hand over his mouth to silence him. 'Harry, darling. Don't you understand? Tas has never ever touched me.'

The next hour was lost completely to their passion. He was almost late for work. His welding was terrible.

# CHAPTER SEVEN

Harry lined up with the rest of the new students at the Technical School. He was tidily dressed – Helen had seen to that. He wasn't too sure whether he should have brought overalls or something. He had a sharp pencil – that was a comfort anyway. As he stood outside the enrolment room waiting to be shown where his initial class was to be held, he heard a familiar voice.

'Hey, what have we got here? A newbie of all things.'

It was Dinky who, in company with Pug, was making his way down the main corridor. 'Which class are you in, Harry?' Dinky enquired.

'Not too sure yet. I think it will be tech drawing, by what I've heard.'

'See you later then.'

As he was about to turn away Harry heard a new voice. 'Harry. Harry Evans, isn't it?'

He swung round and confronted Leda. A genuine feeling of warmth came over him. She came towards him and gave him an affectionate hug as though she had just come across a long-lost cousin. Harry was too surprised even to blush. Dinky looked on.

'What are you doing here?' asked Harry.

'Oh, I decided to do something to better myself and take pattern and drafting classes for dressmaking. It's so lovely to see you again.'

They made an arrangement to see each other after class to catch up on things.

Harry's next two hours were spent learning the basics of technical drawing. The teacher was of the old school: a Scottish ex-marine engineer, a product of the Clyde shipyards, who reckoned that freehand drawing was superior to any produced by draughtsmen in flash offices with all the paraphernalia handy to them.

'Och, now how the hell in God's name are you supposed to

communicate what you want fabricated when you're down in an engine room? The ship is rolling at thirty degrees and you're covered in oil and all you've got is a pencil and a dirty bit of paper to write on. Are you supposed to wait for fine weather? Now, lads, draw the idea roughly and you can always improve on it later. Now here is a steam valve. I want you to take it to pieces and draw me a pretty picture of what you think it should look like.'

He had the genuine knack of communicating although his Glaswegian accent was so broad it was almost unintelligible. He also had that rare ability to get the most from his pupils although some of his methods were highly questionable. He encouraged the students to imagine they were sitting inside an engine component such as an oil pump and draw the workings from where they were seated. To be able to do this of course one had to have a working knowledge of the pump and therefore the lesson was twofold: if you didn't know how the damn thing worked then even if you happened to be Michelangelo you just couldn't draw it.

He treated the students to a stroll though the lubrication system of an engine as though they were going for a walk through a park. He referred to a radiator as if it was a sweatbox and to a temperature gauge as if it was a dog's nose. Oil was the lifeblood of an engine. An oil pump was its heart. All very loose connotations but it kept the class's interest and that to him was the most important thing about educating students. He reckoned the silly things in life were more liable to stick in your memory longer. It worked admirably.

The bell rang and class was finished. As Harry came out he noticed Dinky talking to Leda. He was obviously chatting her up because as Harry approached he broke off the conversation and walked away.

'Your friend is pretty quick on introductions,' she said.

'He's not exactly my best friend,' replied Harry.

'Well, he gave me the impression that you and he were the best of mates.'

'That was probably his idea of a way to get to know you. I think he fancies himself somewhat with the girls.'

'He's asked me to go out to the pictures with him.' She looked closely to see what sort of reaction was forthcoming. She was slightly disappointed by his reply.

'Why not? Real great film on just now at the Empire – *Goodbye Mr Chips*. A real tear-jerker. Tracy, my cousin's wife, couldn't stop howling for days.'

Harry hurried home and found Helen reading a book by the fire.

'Tas home yet?' he asked.

'I'm expecting him any minute. Tell me how did your first night at school go?'

He started to tell her but at that moment Tas walked in. As he sat down and had his tea Harry tried to get him to talk a little more. It was hard going.

'Is it all right if I use some of the tools in the stables, Tas? I'll be extra careful with them.'

'Sure, help yourself. Could do with a clean up too, I bet.'

'Anything you want done specially?'

'Not a thing. How are you and Helen getting along?'

Harry felt a sudden twinge of guilt. 'Oh fine. Just fine.'

'That's good. Now, I'm off to bed.'

Harry thought to himself that Tas seemed to do nothing but work, eat, drink and sleep. No other interests at all by all accounts. Not a very stimulating existence. He was still curious regarding Helen and how she fitted into the scheme of things. He would have to be patient.

Next morning the door had hardly closed behind Tas when Helen had his breakfast ready at the bedside. She didn't bother about her cup of tea – just undressed and lay beside him while he manfully tried to finish his breakfast and be dead nonchalant about things. They were gradually becoming used to each other's body language. He didn't rush things but let her decide the pace and that seemed to please her.

She was still lying in his bed when he left for work. She said it was warmer there. He kissed her as though he had been leaving for work like that for ages. She lay there thinking once again of past events.

*She didn't quite know whether to be pleased or frightened when the doctor informed her she was pregnant. She wondered what Mrs Mann would have to say, and waited impatiently for the chance to tell George. He appeared pleased at first, yet she was puzzled when he suggested later that they should delay telling his mother. He said he would break it to her gently as soon as the time was ripe, but that they should ease the way by telling the family that they were engaged first. It had been almost a month and he had not let on to anyone. He still wanted to have his way with her and was almost brutally insistent at times. She wondered if he was trying to back out of the arrangement. She was feeling frightened of him more and more. His mood swings seemed to be getting worse and she wondered whether the scar on his head had anything to do with it. Too late now. The die was cast, well and truly. Her unease grew day by day.*

Harry had just begun work on his track welding work when Reg came and said, 'Harry, me lad, we've got to get you sorted out with your truck licence as quick as possible. Let's go for a drive, shall we?'

Frank had been giving Harry a few lessons during lunch breaks and Harry was expecting this summons so was fairly well prepared. He handled the Bedford five-tonner quite confidently and Reg appeared satisfied with the results of his impromptu test. When they got back to the workshop he informed Harry that he would suggest to the foreman that he was ready to take his test.

A week later Harry's erstwhile Irish traffic officer strolled into the section. 'And how's Harry today? All set for the big one, eh?'

Harry felt quite at ease, as he knew the cop slightly. He tried to appear nonchalant. 'All set to go,' he said.

'Are you sure the brakes are okay on this machine?' asked the cop in a conspiratorial whisper. 'We sure as hell don't want to go through that rigmarole again, do we now?'

Harry laughed and replied, 'It was the first thing I checked.'

'Now, Harry, which machine have you picked for us to ride in?'

Harry pointed to the five-tonner.

'Big enough? To be sure it's a lovely looking truck if ever there was one. Right, let's be goin.'

They climbed in and once more Harry adjusted the rear vision mirror and suchlike to impress the examiner, who nonetheless failed to notice.

Bloody wasted effort, thought Harry.

They swung out into the traffic. 'Where to?' Harry asked.

'Up here and turn left. My word, you sure can handle this machine, Harry.'

Harry decided he wasn't going to get swollen-headed about a remark like that.

'Now, Harry, do you know where Herbert's Hardware is? It's right in the middle of town and quite difficult to get to. Know it?'

'Yes, I know it.'

Harry didn't find the driving that difficult and in no time they drew up outside the shop. He waited expectantly.

'Now, Harry, see that little wee driveway up the side there?'

Harry nodded.

'Well, be very careful as it's just about on limits for a truck this size and it would take a very experienced fellow to back up there. And this being a new truck and all. T'would be a crying shame to scratch it now, wouldn't it?'

The cop looked rearwards. 'Now, Harry, do you think you can be managing it now?'

Harry, to be quite frank, couldn't see it as any sort of problem and once again nodded. He reversed up the drive easily and with tons of room to spare. The Irishman climbed out of the cab and called out to the yard storeman. 'Hey Fred, which bay for the cement?'

Fred signalled that it was the end shed and Harry, without any further ado, backed up to it. Fred opened the sliding doors and with the aid of a trolley soon had six bags of cement and two sheets of reinforcing mesh on the back of the truck. The traffic cop gave

Fred a docket, signed the other one, and once more pupil and instructor hit the road.

'Where to now?' asked Harry, rather enjoying himself.

'Well now, Harry, this is what you might call the navigating part. You've now got to find 23 Acacia Avenue. I'll give you a wee clue. It's about two miles from here.'

'It's just off Grey Street, right?'

'Excellent! Well done, son. You're good, no doubt about it. Carry on.'

Harry was lucky he had been to that neighbourhood with Strath when he was having lessons. He drove there confidently and found the street without difficulty.

'Great going, Harry. I've never seen so much skill. Really incredible.'

Harry wondered if this fellow was for real. He hadn't heard so much blarney in a long time.

'Now, Harry, can you be backing this big truck up this narrow drive?'

'Oh, I think so,' said Harry, once again very nonchalantly. He was getting rather used to acting nonchalant.

'Okay, but watch out for my geraniums,' said the Irishman as he climbed out of the cab.

Harry reversed carefully up to the garage door and was waved to a halt. He remained sitting in the cab with the engine ticking over while the cop unfastened the padlock and opened the double doors, then waved the truck back even further. Harry came to a halt.

'Give us a bit of a hand now, would you Harry?'

Harry jumped up onto the deck and helped the cop unload the goods. They both stacked the cement bags in the garage and after closing and padlocking the building they drove out of the gate and up the road, the Irishman busy whistling 'The Wearin' o'the Green' in a tuneless sort of way.

'Well now, Harry. That would be about the best bit of driving I've had the honour of seeing in a long while. Better take us back to yer work place now.'

Harry carefully ran the truck back into its parking spot on the lot and climbed out. 'How did I go?' he asked.

'Sweet as a nut, Harry. Sweet as a nut.' The cop proceeded to write out the heavy-traffic endorsement on Harry's licence and handing it back said, 'Congratulations, thanks, and drive safely, Harry lad.'

At the end of that day's work Harry found himself hurrying home to Helen. She caught him in the porch as he was removing his boots.

'I want you.' she said in a put-on sultry Mae West way.

'You've got me,' he replied. She was getting more and more exciting.

'Not while you're all oily and stinky with diesel. I've run your bath for you. I thought we might have one together,' she added, with a girlish giggle.

'Bit risky, isn't it? How do you know Tas isn't going to walk in?'

'How do you know he is?'

'Helen, I'm not too sure that we should take a risk like that. It's a bit too much. We could lose everything.'

She sobered instantly. 'Quite right. I shouldn't have suggested it. Silly of me. It just seemed so exciting to do it with the thought that he might arrive at any moment. But no, you're quite correct. Sorry.'

Harry breathed a sigh of relief. One could push one's luck just so far.

He had just finished soaping himself and was lying there in the water when the door opened suddenly and Helen literally threw herself into the room. Dropping her crutches, she knelt down awkwardly beside the bath. She was out of breath and as she leaned over the bath to kiss him on the lips she gasped, 'I've just been down to the gate and looked and he's not in sight. God Harry, you're lovely. I could eat you all up.' Just as awkwardly she rose and, grabbing her crutches, left the room, her face flushed.

Tas arrived about five minutes later.

Close call, thought Harry.

He dressed and went into the kitchen. Tas was sitting at the table and seemed sober for a change. In fact it was the most sober Harry had seen him so far.

'Had a good day, Harry?' asked Tas.

'Bit of fun,' Harry replied, and told Tas about how he had just sat his so-called test for his heavy trade licence. The three of them had a good laugh over it.

Suddenly Tas got up and instead of saying he was going down to the pub as usual, said, 'Right Harry, let's go and see what you've been up to out the back.'

Both of them went up into the back garden. Harry had done considerable work up there and was secretly pleased when Tas showed astonishment at his efforts. They went up to the stables. Tas couldn't even remember where the key was. Harry retrieved it and they went inside. Tas looked around. 'You know, Harry, I haven't been in here for about... since the accident.'

Harry was rather bewildered by this statement, but then realised that with all the shrubbery that had invaded the area it sort of figured.

They went into the workshop and Tas sat down on a nail box and looked at all the cobwebs and dust. 'George was always working out here,' he said. 'He reckoned it was his most comfortable seat. We had some great conversations in this very spot. He had so many wonderful ideas and so many projects on the go all the time. He was a very clever engineer – always inventing things. We were awfully close as kids. He was my younger brother and I was always called upon by Mum to be looking after him. When the war broke out I couldn't go because of a heart problem. I had a funny feeling when he left that I should still be taking care of him, which was nonsense really. You can't look after a fellow all his life now can you?'

Harry, who by this time had found himself another nail box and had sat down, just nodded and kept his mouth shut. He had long ago learned that if a person starts reminiscing the idea is not to break the flow.

Tas went on in a low voice. 'When we got word he had been wounded I felt as though it was my fault and I must admit I was pretty upset. When he finally got home from England he spent a lot of time at the Kew Convalescent Home out South Dunedin. The doctors and nurses were marvellous.. You know, Harry, it took him about five months to get himself together again. Everybody thought he was fine, but I knew that the old George was missing. I couldn't quite put my finger on it but he had changed and I didn't like it one bit. We tried hard to ignore it but to be honest we felt that it just was not working."

Harry was dying to ask questions and found it difficult to sit there and play dumb, but he did just that. The fact that he had said all this to Harry seemed to spur Tas on to greater efforts to unload much that was on his mind, and he continued with what seemed to Harry greater confidence.

'Mum was terribly shocked by all this and as she had been starting to lose some of her faculties this caused another problem. She had managed to get Helen to come and be her companion help about three years previous, thank goodness. She was a great asset. I hadn't known what to do and Helen seemed to fit in just marvellously. She gradually took over running the house and I just carried on working. She and George became sweethearts. They were a really happy couple. I was so pleased for George, then he was called overseas. Some people can manage these sorts of situations. I couldn't. I've always liked my drink and to be quite honest it seems to give me a bit of confidence.

Since you've come to this house, Harry, I've noticed how Helen has perked up and I was thinking about what I'd said about the car. It used to be George's. And it hasn't been driven since the… since George died, and I reckon the idea would be to get it going and take Helen out a bit. Get her out of the house. I don't think she's been out much since… the accident.'

Harry noticed Tas always had difficulty when he came to mentioning 'the accident'.

'Yes, Harry,' he continued, 'I think that would be just the ticket.

You're a mechanic. Just fix it and take her out. Any parts that are required – just buy them and I'll pay. What do you think of that idea? Good, eh?'

Harry was flabbergasted by this suggestion. First of all he wasn't a mechanic. He didn't have a clue as to what was wrong with the car. He could think of a hundred reasons why he shouldn't accept this task but instead of refusing point-blank he found himself nodding his head in agreement with Tas and saying, 'Yes. Good idea. All right, Tas, I'll see what I can do.'

'Right,' said Tas, 'that's settled then. I'm off. Probably see you tomorrow then. Good luck.'

Harry remained sitting rather stunned on the nail box after Tas had departed. He heard Helen ring the little bell for tea and, after locking the garage, went down to the house. He took off his boots and went into the kitchen.

'Tea's ready,' Helen said, with a lightness in her voice. 'Tas has gone out again.'

'Yes I know. He said he was going back to the pub. Doesn't he ever eat?'

'Not very much. In fact he seems to eat at home less and less. He worries me. He gets very depressed at times.'

She moved around behind his chair and put her arms around Harry's neck.

'What were you two talking about up there tonight?'

'Well, for a start off, it's been the most Tas has talked to me since I met him. He told me all about his brother, George – sounds as though he was pretty fond of him.'

'Yes. They were very close to each other. Tas always looked after George. He took it very badly when he died.'

'How did it happen?'

'Tell you what, what say we finish up tea and I'll try to tell you as much as I can in the front room where it's more comfy, and I can get the weight off my leg. It's starting to ache again.'

'Okay.'

The fire was burning cheerfully when the couple finally settled down on the big sofa in the front room. Harry sat down and Helen came and put her arms round him.

'Hold me, Harry. It seems to stop my ghost from playing up.'

They laughed and she snuggled closer to him.

'Now start from the start,' Harry said.

'Well, once upon a time there was a little girl and her name was Helen. She had so many dreams about what she was going to do when she grew up and became a woman. She would lie in her bed at night and imagine that she was Helen of Troy and had all those lovely young men in their metal clothes running after her. She wondered if they made a clanking noise as they walked. Her mother would read to her and she would go off to sleep with all these silly thoughts running through her head.

She loved her father very much. He was a handsome, smiling-all-the-time man. He would sit her on his shoulders and carry her everywhere. He stood a mile high and she could see to the end of the earth from his shoulders. She knew she would marry a man that would be just like her father and laugh a lot. They would have about ten children and would spoil them rotten. But then the war came and her father had to go away. He would come home now and then in his uniform. It was a dull colour and the cloth was rough and chafed her when she rode on his shoulders. He wore a big hat with a very wide brim. He called it a lemon squeezer and Helen often wondered where he would get such big lemons and what he would do with all that lemon drink when he didn't have a cold.'

She snuggled even closer into Harry's neck.

'Not sending you to sleep am I?'

'No. I'm all ears.'

'Okay, well, one evening Helen's mother burst out crying and told Helen that her father wasn't coming back and that he was dead.'

Harry could see Helen's eyes were brimming with tears. He tried to comfort her. 'I know how you felt. It's pretty sad when you lose someone close to you.' Somehow it didn't sound right but Helen understood anyway. She continued.

'Helen tried to make it all up to her mum by working harder at school and helping her as much as she could, but the laughter and the sparkle had gone out of her mother's eyes and she kept on saying that life held nothing for her now that her husband had gone.'

Helen got up and said in a dull voice, 'I was fifteen when Mum took her own life. I came home from school one afternoon and found her lying with her head in the gas oven.'

Harry was shocked by Helen's matter-of-factness. Suddenly she sounded completely lifeless. It was as though there was another person talking to him.

'Now I'm going to bed to try to get some sleep. No, Harry, please don't follow me. Just leave me alone. Please dear. Good night Harry.'

He woke next morning. The kitchen sounds were normal. Should he get up? Would she be in that strange mood still? He heard Tas go to the toilet. He knew it was Tas: Tas always farted. He decided to lay there and just sweat it out. Better to wait till Tas had left and find out then if things were on the mend. He had done nothing to upset Helen and would always try to avoid doing so. She was a very mixed-up woman and quite frankly he could see that she had a lot on her plate. He ran over the things that Tas had said the previous evening. He had come to the conclusion that Tas was a basically gentle sort of person who seemed to be handicapped with a guilty conscience. It was definitely something to do with George. What Tas considered himself to be guilty of was anybody's guess. Harry still had to find out what the strange relationship was between Tas and Helen. It was all very mystifying. He lay there in the darkness listening to the pair talking. He could not hear them clearly enough to make anything of their conversation but at least it didn't seem to be heated. That was a relief. Tas could go very cold in his conversations with Helen. She, on the other hand, took it all on the chin and it didn't seem to bother her much.

He heard Tas leave and almost immediately his door opened and she slipped into his room. She had extinguished the kitchen light and all was in darkness. She didn't even enquire as to whether he was awake or not.

He heard the rustle of her nightdress and felt her tugging the bedclothes back. A moment's pause and she was slipping in between the sheets. He lay there in suspense, his heart pace up. She ran her hand over his chest. He replied by placing his hand over her naked breast. Nothing – she was wearing absolutely nothing. His hands ran the length of her body, from her neck to her poor mutilated stump. There his hands paused in their explorations and rested for a fleeting moment before moving on further. He heard her quick intake of breath as his fingers explored her intimate region. As she pressed herself closely against him her body language signalled that she was totally acquiescent. Her hands were clutching at his clothing, urgently trying to dispense with them. They helped each other till both were locked in each other's naked embrace.

Only then did she speak. 'Harry, I am so sorry about my behaviour last night.'

It was his turn to hold his fingers across her lips.

'It must have taken a lot of courage to tell me what you did. Don't say a word. Let me make you feel good.'

He held her close and she could feel herself stirring to his insistent stroking. She lay there and found herself surrendering easily to his advances. She closed her eyes and smelled the rising heat of his young body.

Thirty minutes later she still lay there, though by now she was exhausted. He lay beside her, his breathing deep and measured. She felt entirely satiated.

His voice interrupted her thoughts. 'One thing puzzles me. Just why did you allow yourself to be married to Tas?'

She sighed. 'It all seems so long ago. When my mother died I was devastated – not only by the manner of her death but because I felt that she had rejected me. Abandoned me. Taken me from the warm, loving world that I knew and suddenly thrust me into an unfriendly, dark place that was totally foreign. I really had only one person I could confide in and that was Mrs Mann. When she found I had no next of kin she immediately took steps to become my guardian. It was her last year as principal at the school. Then she had to retire. She hired me as her companion and it worked out very well. She was a warm and lovely lady and I know she loved me. Maybe I was the girl child she had never managed to have. She was very good to me. She brought me home and I was finally introduced to her sons who I had heard a lot about: George and Terence.'

'Terence?' Harry interrupted her. 'Who's Terence?'

'Didn't you know? That's Tas's first name. Tas is only his nickname. Terence Albert Spencer Mann… Tasman. Get it?'

Harry got it.

Helen continued. 'George was a good-looking fellow and we got on great together. He was a lot of fun. We would go to dances and Mrs Mann would wait up for us and scold George if he was the slightest bit late. I had an idea he might fit the picture of my knight in shining armour and I thought that I might be in love with him, only I wasn't that certain. I think Mrs Mann approved of us going together. We weren't engaged or anything like that. He asked me to marry him so many times I treated it as a sort of a joke. He was gentle, polite, and very sweet.'

'Did he make love to you?'

Harry just couldn't stop himself from asking that question. He bit his lip, expecting her now to do the freeze act.

Helen paused for a moment then replied, 'No, he didn't. I had always said I would keep that for the man I was going to marry, and I did.'

'Tas. But you said… '

'You're jumping the gun, Harry. Do you want to hear the rest?'

'Sorry.' He ran his hand over her breast to reassure her. She didn't resist.

'The next thing we knew George had been called up and was in training camp at Trentham Army Base near Wellington. It all happened that fast. Next moment it seemed he was in Egypt. He wrote me a lot of letters telling me how much he missed me and I replied, trying to keep my letters as low key as I could. After a year of writing, however, I decided that I must have been in love with him and told him I would wait. There seems to be some truth in the saying, "Absence makes the heart grow fonder". Then the telegram arrived from the War Department saying that he had been wounded in action and had been moved to a neurological hospital in England for more operations and convalescence. He had sustained terrible head wounds but was recovering splendidly by all accounts. Both Mrs Mann and I would cry together at nights and Tas was very upset. When George had recovered sufficiently to write he kept on asking me about marriage. I said I would give him my answer after he had arrived home. I still had doubts about loving him, I suppose, and I didn't want to rush in.'

She paused and listened to the hall clock striking.

'Harry, dear, you'll have to go. It's almost time for work. Don't want you to be late now, do we?'

Harry rose and dressed. It wasn't till he leaned over to kiss her good bye that both of them simultaneously remembered she hadn't given him his breakfast. Helen panicked and was going to rush out and rustle something up for him but he laughingly shoved her back onto the pillows and said he now knew what living on the fruits of love really meant. They were both in high spirits as he left.

Helen lay back, and the memories returned.

*George came into her bedroom in the middle of the night. 'You asleep?'*

*'George, what are you doing in here? Your mother will hear you.'*

*'Move over.'*

*'No.'*

*'Don't bloody say no to me. Now move over, y'hear?' He slipped in between the sheets. 'Now for a bit of fun,' he whispered.*

*'Please don't spoil things, George. Your mum wouldn't like to think that we… '*

*'To hell with what Mum thinks. You're going to be my wife so don't start getting cold feet now, okay?'*

*She lay still while he satisfied himself on her. After what seemed an interminably long time he rolled off and said, 'Enjoy that, didya?'*

*She just rolled over the other way and hid her head in the pillow. She wished she had her Dad's safe open arms to run to. Where were her dreams that she once had? She couldn't even shelter in those any more. Her knight in shining armour? He appeared to be fading into the distance. Why did she have to be so unhappy? And now to make matters worse she was going to have George's baby, which once she would have considered to be a precious gift from God to love and nurture but now she wasn't so sure how she felt about it. The manner in which it had been conceived was enough to make her feel that she had an unwelcome intruder in her body. She buried her head deeper into the pillow and wept.*

# CHAPTER EIGHT

Jim Schultz called Harry into his office as he went to clock in.

'Harry, I've just spoken to Ted and he's okayed you to help us out with the stored vehicles as long as it doesn't interfere with your tractor work.'

He went on to explain that quite a few firms stored their vehicles overnight in the garage for a fee. These were usually firms which did not have parking in their own buildings and did not wish to have staff take the vehicles home. The standard practice was for the vehicles to be left parked outside before quarter to five at night and the apprentices would drive them inside. Next morning the apprentices would park them in the street for them to be picked up. It was a good idea and everyone appeared to be happy with the arrangement. The apprentices liked this job as they were able to drive all sorts of different vehicles and besides, it was all good practice. Harry soon became adept at starting the various cars, trucks and vans.

It was such a car that he was driving inside one Friday night when he happened to notice that the speedo was just about to turn over. He would have normally never given it a thought but 9999.9 on the instrument just caught his eye. He drove into the garage and parked the car, a Vauxhall Velox, and was a bit disappointed that the numeral drum had not turned over. He heard Dinky call out his name.

'What's up?' Harry asked.

'Better park that Velox next to the back door. The owner might be picking it up early on Tuesday morning. He can get out first thing,' said Dinky. He watched as Harry started the car up and drove it out and backed it into the rear door as requested.

As Harry climbed out he noticed that the tumblers were on the point of change. Silly really, he thought. Fancy hoping that they were going to fall over just because he was watching!

Knock-off time at last. It was going to be a long weekend with three days off. Harry had been asked if he would like to go to a rugby match but declined: he wanted to get on with his jobs at home. He had decided that he would resist taking a look at George's car as he knew very well he might become distracted and that would be the finish of Helen's garden. He knew she was looking forward to making the place more presentable. No wonder she had been getting a bit down in the dumps: the way the place looked was enough to make any one feel depressed. No, he thought firmly, no car... Well, not yet anyway.

Saturday morning. Tas didn't go to work. Helen had a lie-in for a change so it was Harry who was first into the kitchen and he got the fire going so it would be nice and warm for her when she arose.

Just as he was making a cup of tea Tas came out and joined him. He was quite decently dressed and looked the best Harry had seen him for a long time.

'Wrong day for church, Tas,' said Harry jokingly.

'No church, Harry – just going to have a flutter on the horses. Dunedin Cup today. Wouldn't miss it for the world. Like to come along?'

'No thanks. I was listening to the boys talking and they thought that Captain Cargill might have a chance in the third.'

'Know a bit about horses then, Harry?'

'Only that they eat heaps of hay and run bloody slow according to my uncle.'

'I can give you a good tip if you want, Harry. Coral's Choice in the third.'

'All right then, for a bit of fun put five bob on that one for me.'

He went into his room and dug five shillings out of his pocket. He could ill afford it but what the hell?

Tas finished his cup and with the usual 'Well, I'm off' left and walked down the road. Harry stood at the front door watching him disappear. He turned and on impulse knocked on Helen's door. No answer. He gently turned the handle and went in. She was sound asleep and looked beautiful. He went over to her bedside and kissed her on the lips. She suddenly wrapped her arms around him. 'Gotcha!'

'You were awake all the time,' he said sternly. 'And here was I going to pay you back for waking me the other morning. What do you want to do today?'

'I am going to play Lady Muck and spend all day in the garden with my lover.'

'Oh,' said Harry. 'I thought you might have spent it with me. Just lie there and I'll make you a cup of tea. It'll be the first time I've managed to give you breakfast in *your* bed.'

'No,' she replied, 'I'm getting up. We've got things to do today. I'm the boss, remember.'

He sat on the bed and watched her get dressed. He had difficulty restraining himself from touching her. She too was well aware of his presence. She managed to pass the danger point and started combing her long hair.

'Anybody told you you're lovely, Helen?' he said.

'I wish I could dance for you, Harry. I used to love to dance. Now I'm just an old crock.'

'No you're not. Anyway, you're my Dresden lady crock and you dance for me every time we get into bed. That does me.'

'Harry, we laugh and we joke, but I wish things were different.'

'Come on now, we've got to attack your garden – there's no time for getting down in the dumps.'

Harry slaved till just before lunch and managed to get through a heck of a lot of the rubbish. It was while they were sitting just outside the stables that Helen said, 'Harry, would you like to have a look at the car?'

'Well,' Harry said, 'I had promised myself that I would stay away from it till I'd sorted out the garden. But if you insist… '

'Of course I insist. I know very well that you've been breaking your neck to have a look. Come on, give me a hand with the cover.'

Harry rolled back the cover and stood admiring a lovely 1926 Chevrolet. It was lettuce green and in immaculate condition. The tyres were flat but that was only to be expected. He opened the door and there it was, fastened to the step: the silver plate stamped:

*Superior K*
*Body by Fisher*

'Boy! What a beauty!' he exclaimed.

He held open the door. It smelled quite musty inside. 'Your carriage awaits you, madam. It's not a chariot and I haven't got my chain mail on but it will have to do, sorry, my lady.' He bowed low.

'Why thank you, sire. Looks pretty smart to me,' Helen replied, and stepped into the rear. She sat down and looked around. 'Still looks as though it just came out of the factory.'

Harry looked at her. 'Look, you just sit there and I'll go and finish this job. Won't take more than half an hour. You've done enough out there and you look a bit tired. Won't be long. Okay?'

She leaned forward and drew him to her, kissed him on the lips and said, 'Why are you so good to me, Harry?'

'Nonsense. You're just trying to put me off my work.' He boldly placed his hand under her dress and his exploring fingers stroked her stump. Somehow it fascinated him. 'See! You're distracting me.'

She squealed and said, 'Back to work then this minute, squire. Your reward will have to wait. Then I promise you you'll get your lust deserts.'

He went out of the garage and left her sitting in the car. She felt as though she owned the whole world. Life was good.

She sat back into the seat and looked around her. The interior was in pristine condition. Except… She looked closer. Except for a large rip in the back of the seat lining and suddenly her mind flashed back.

*They were driving back from the pictures. It had been a lovely evening. They both agreed Fred Astaire and Ginger Rogers were the greatest. They had sat holding hands, fascinated by the speed and poetry of the couple's intricate dance scenes.*

*'Wish I could dance like him,' he had said.*

*'Wish I could dance like her,' she had said, and they had both burst out laughing. She had really enjoyed herself. He had been so debonair and courteous and sweet. It had been the best she had felt in his company for days. As he seemed to be in such good humour it was without thinking that she blurted out the question uppermost in her mind: 'George, when are we going to tell your mother about the baby?'*

*He didn't reply immediately but continued to drive in silence. She began to think that perhaps he had not heard her. He swung the wheel and drove along a street that she knew was not on their usual way home. She didn't say anything further. She knew she had said something to annoy him. She recognised the signs and was beginning to feel afraid. Why couldn't she have kept her mouth shut?*

*He pulled up in a secluded cul-de-sac. It was an area much used by lovers. Tonight though it was deserted. He got out, went round to her side door and roughly opened it. 'Get out,' he ordered, and leaned in and wrenched her arm. It was as though he was an entirely different person. She emerged reluctantly. It was dark and there were only two street lamps dimly illuminating the area. He slammed her door and opened the rear one. 'Get in.'*

*She tried to pass it off as a joke. 'Ah, George, you've thought up a new game for us?' It didn't sound like a joke and fell very flat as she couldn't disguise the fear in her voice.*

*'No joke. Get in,' he grunted, bundling her inside.*

*She swung round and half fell on the seat. 'What's wrong, George?'*

*'Know why I haven't told Mum?'*

*'No, George.'*

*'Because I bloody choose not to. That's why.'*

*Trying to placate him once more she said, 'Well, that's quite all right, George. You know best.'*

*He put his arms around her. 'You know why I brought you here?'*

*'No.'*

*He raised his voice. 'You know bloody well why. You were moaning last time that Mum would hear us. Well, she can't hear us now so let's get into it.'*

*With that he started to tear at the top of her dress. He ripped it quite fiercely.*

*'Why do you have to do it this way, George? You don't have to be so rough. I'm going to have your baby, George, and you know you can have me. But why in God's name do you have to be so cruel?'*

*'Well that's the way I like it, so lay back and let me enjoy it now.'*

*She struggled vainly and in doing so felt her high heel catch in the back of the lining – a tearing noise which echoed the ripping in her soul.*

*'You bitch!' He dragged her out and completed his invasion of her in the long grass beside the car.*

Harry was just finishing stacking the pile of rubbish in the yard when he saw Helen making her way back to the house. 'Hey, wait for me. I'm almost there. Won't be a minute and then we can take a look at the car.'

He went to her and realised by her body language that all was not well. He ran towards her. She stopped and looked at him, the tears streaming down her face.

'Oh Harry, why does the world have to be so cruel?'

He put his arms around her and held her tight and together they moved down to the big house. Harry was more confused than ever.

Tuesday morning. Work. It had been a very quiet weekend for Harry. Helen had not said anything more about the tears on that day in the garage and was still not talking as she brought in his breakfast.

'Join me?' asked Harry lightly, trying to break down the barrier that he sensed between them.

'No, not today. I've got my… it's my off day.' And she went back out to the kitchen. Women, Harry thought to himself. They certainly keep you guessing!

He arrived at work early, changed, and went to drive the stored cars outside to the street. He hopped into the one that he had parked at the rear door. It looked as though the owner hadn't managed to get there early enough to collect it. He wondered whether the speedo would click over this time. He glanced at the instrument and was surprised to see that it had 10065 miles showing. Strange, he thought, the owner must have come and collected it for the weekend. Must have had some urgent business. Funny that he didn't just keep the car at home.

Harry drove the car around to the front just as Wally the lube attendant came out. 'Leave it running, Harry. It's been booked in for a lube and an oil change at eight o'clock and Mrs Hailsham wants it to drive to Christchurch first thing this morning. It was too late to do it on Friday so her husband left it here.'

'But I thought that this was a stored car?' said a puzzled Harry.

'Sorry, Harry, you've got it all fouled up. It belongs to the Dragon.'

'Oh,' said Harry. Life seemed to be full of mysteries these days. Something's a bit fishy, he thought to himself, then dismissed it from his mind.

Tuesday was machine shop night at Tech and Harry looked forward to it. The trouble was that the class was combined and his old pals Dinky and Pug were in the same one as he, even though both of them were a year ahead.

He had just been shown the intricacies of screw cutting and was getting the hang of it nicely. In fact he was in the process of making a small adjustable hand vice. The tool that he was cutting with was set incorrectly and he switched off the lathe and removed the cutting tool and went up to the instructor to check the angle of it.

'What's wrong, Evans?' the instructor asked, and Harry told him the problem. The instructor was just about to advise him when there was a terrific graunching sound from the lathe that Harry had just left. A quick-thinking apprentice near the machine switched it off and when Harry and the teacher reached it they found a severely damaged tool post and of course the work that had been damaged in the chuck jaws. The screw-cutting mechanism had clearly been engaged and had moved the tool post forward into the revolving chuck. This was a capital sin as far as the operation of a lathe was concerned.

'I want to see you in my office when class is finished, Evans.'

Harry hung his head. He could not for the life of him see how he could have made a mistake like that. One of the other boys came over to him and said, 'Bad luck, Harry.'

Harry looked around, finding to his discomfort that most of the eyes of the class were upon him, felt a bloody big chump. He noticed that both Dinky and Pug were smirking like crazy on the other side of the room. Trust them to treat it as a huge joke!

Class finished and everyone sloped off home. Harry remained and as instructed waited outside the tutor's office. He was called in and told in no uncertain terms that the cost of the damage would be given to him as soon as it was worked out and Harry would have to pay for it. He tried to be as polite as he could and didn't make an effort to defend himself. What else could he do?

He walked outside into the cool air. He had just about finished that job and he was sure it would have taken top marks. As it was now it looked like a heap of shit. As he approached the school gates a shadowy figure detached itself from the gloom and came up to him. Pat Thorpe was an apprentice at the nearby foundry and he and Harry knew each other slightly.

'Bit of bad luck tonight, Harry?'

'Oh, hello, Pat. Yes, a bloody stupid mistake on my part. The thing is I'm sure I turned the damned machine off before I moved away from it.'

'You must be pretty thick to make a mistake like that, eh?'

'Yeah, but you don't have to rub it in, Pat.'

'Okay, so you think you're thick. What say if I told you weren't thick. Eh? How would you feel about that now?'

'I would say that's very nice of you to try and cheer me up. And it was very nice of you to wait for me but there's no need to make fun of me, Pat. That's the last thing I need tonight.'

'Okay then, Harry, what say if I said I know exactly how it happened?'

'Shoot.'

'I just so happened to be looking over in your direction when I saw Dawson walk past your machine and turn it on. Then right behind him came Pugh and I spotted him engaging the threading control lever. I didn't have time to do anything about it but that's why I waited to tell you. Still think you're thick?'

Harry was so overjoyed he could have kissed him. 'Well that clears me. All we've got to do is for you to tell the teacher and I'm in the clear. Thanks a million, Pat. You're a brick.'

'Hold on, Harry. There's only one drawback.'

'What's that?'

'I'm not going to tell anybody.'

'Why not, Pat?'

'For the simple reason that if I tell the instructor the truth then I'm a nark as far as the rest of the class goes. I only told you so you can do your own dirty work. Fair enough?'

Harry thought for a moment. Then his face brightened. 'Pat, that's fair enough by me. You just don't know what it means for me to know that it was somebody else and not me that made a stupid mistake.'

'You sure you're not all pissed off about me not dobbing them in?'

'No way. You made my day. My Nana was a great believer in an eye for an eye and I'm now going to get four of them at once.'

He shook hands with a very puzzled Pat and almost waltzed down the lamp-lit street. He returned home to find a rather sombre Helen. She retired early to her room claiming a headache. He was unaware of her last hour spent dazing into the fire and remembering little things back in those bad days.

*His behaviour had been getting progressively worse. It all seemed to have come to a head about a fortnight before when she found him actually crying. He was sitting on his favourite nail box in the workshop. He was holding a letter in his hand and silently held it out to her. It was a moving letter from the sister of a very good friend who had served in the same engineers corps that George had been in.*

*'Best mate I ever had,' he had said simply. 'We were going into partnership when the war's over and planned to start up a mobile workshop with welders, lathes and everything. We were going to repair all those implements that have been neglected during the last few years. And now it's all turned to shit.' He added 'I've just posted a letter to him too.'*

*But the real question regarding his sanity had arisen the previous weekend when he arrived back from up the Taieri River. He had been prospecting, or rock hunting as he called it, and drove straight into the garage and didn't emerge for two days. She had tried to get him to come down but he yelled out from behind the locked doors that he was busy. Even Tas failed to budge him. She left a plate of sandwiches beside the door, called out to him, and left him to it. They were gone next time she went up there.*

*Two days later she went up for the fourth time to see if he would listen to reason and found the door unlocked. He swung round upon her entering and said sharply, 'What do you want?' He looked like a little boy who had been caught raiding the pantry.*

*'I just wanted to see whether you would like something to eat.' She looked at his work. He was pouring molten metal into the little soldier moulds. 'That's pretty,' she said. 'Just like gold.'*

*'Well it's not gold,' he said hastily, 'it's bronze. Any idiot can tell the difference. A new process I've thought up – makes the toys last longer.'*

*'Sorry, I was only asking.'*

*He had seemed perturbed by her presence.*

*As if to make up for it he handed her a box with brass bindings. 'I'm presenting that to the Settlers Museum. Found it on my last trip up the Hindon Gorge. Going to tell them I found it at Lawrence, up at Gabriel's,' he announced proudly.*

*'Why the difference?' she asked.*

*He looked cunningly at her. 'Why? To put them off the scent of course.'*

*She had left him to it. At times she could not make him out at all.*

Thursday. Night school. This was the extracurricular night Harry had to take up for the year. The tutor, unfortunately for all, was more interested in his own inflated ego than teaching, and was trying to impress the class with an exhibition of his so-called skill at maths. He had started off straight away with no examination of his pupils' knowledge and levels of mathematical ability. Harry was not impressed and it was with the utmost difficulty that he managed to concentrate on the lesson. There were looks of incomprehension on the faces of his surrounding classmates. The class had twenty-four pupils in it and Harry couldn't see them all lasting the pace. He hoped that he could. It was going to be a bloody steep learning curve, he thought.

'Righto class, our first little problem. We have an aluminium rivet with a shank length of seven-eighths of an inch; diameter of the shank is one-eighth of an inch. The head is a perfect half sphere measuring three-eighths of an inch in diameter. How many rivets can we manufacture out of a rod of aluminium seventeen and a half by four inches and if the rod has cost us fifty-six pounds eighteen shillings what will the cost of each rivet be? Right, get to it. Should take about ten minutes to work it out.'

Harry scratched his head and looked around him. All he could see was a sea of glazed expressions. Maybe I'm as dumb as the rest of them, he thought to himself. At the end of fifteen minutes only one person was anywhere near the solution. The teacher explained with lightning rapidity how to solve the problem and then went on to the next one, which was just as bad, if not worse. At the end of the session Harry's head was spinning and he felt quite sick in his stomach. He had always thought he was bright enough at school but with this idiot teacher he was never going to get anywhere.

He walked along the corridor and ran into Leda.

She greeted him once again with a hug which he found slightly disconcerting and enquired how he was doing. He didn't impress her with his lack of enthusiasm. She decided to change the subject.

'How did your weekend go?'

'I worked in the garden on a job I'm doing just now to help defray my board expenses. Didn't manage to go anywhere exciting. How about you?'

'Oh, I went to a dance with Dinky at Milton. Great night. He picked me up in his nice car and Pug had his girlfriend, Doreen, with him. The four of us had a good night. I must say Dinky is a lot of fun when he gets going. Bit of a show off all the same.' She was once again disappointed by the lack of response from Harry. If he was jealous or anything she couldn't detect it.

'Sounds as though it was a good night all right. I didn't know Dinky owned a car though.'

'He said it was his just to impress me. I have an idea it was his dad's Velox.'

Harry didn't say anything. He knew very well that Dinky's dad owned a Dodge. He had seen him pick Dinky up several times after work.

'Well, I better be getting along. Got a bit of homework to do tonight. See you next week. Bye.'

Leda would have liked to have drawn the conversation out but obviously Harry had other things on his mind.

As usual Helen was sitting on the sofa reading when Harry got home. 'Tas back yet?' he asked and on receiving a reply in the negative gave her a nice friendly kiss. They were acting like a long married couple, he thought. He sat down beside her and gave her a run down on his disastrous introduction to night school mathematics. She listened to what he had to say and then asked, 'So what are you going to do about it?'

He snorted. 'There's only one thing I *can* do and that's pull my finger out and try to catch up on the basics. Maybe I didn't pay enough attention at school and it's certainly coming home to roost now, Helen.'

He sat there in silence. Finally he looked at her and noticing a little smile on her face, burst out, 'Hey! This isn't funny you know. This is bloody serious.'

She couldn't contain herself. She burst out laughing, much to his discomfort. He thought that she might have been a bit more sensitive about his problem.

'Okay, what's the joke?' He failed to see any reason for hilarity.

'Okay Harry. Remember me telling you all about Mr Drake and how he used to teach us maths?'

'Yes.'

'Well, he always said I was his star pupil and I was. He reckoned I was a natural. Maybe if things had turned out different I might have become a maths teacher. I reached the stage of being able to work out problems even better than he could. That problem that you were given by your teacher tonight was a piece of cake as far as I'm concerned. Don't forget too that Mrs Mann was amongst other things an exceptional school teacher and she has a library here second to none that nobody uses any more. It's chock-a-block with textbooks. Harry, darling, I guarantee by the time I'm finished with you you'll be able to beat the pants off anyone in that class.'

Again she smiled and added, 'So, Harry Evans, what's your problem?'

It was Harry's turn to smile. 'So when do we start, preceptor?'

'Preceptor?'

'You're one. You tell me.'

'Right now. Get me a pencil and paper.'

Friday. The weeks were certainly flying. Word had leaked out at the garage that Harry had made a stuff-up at the tech machine class and that he had been responsible for the damage. Harry heard it from Frank. He let on that he didn't know how the accident had happened and kept the fact that the machine had been tampered with to himself. When he asked Frank who had told him about the incident he knew before hearing the answer who would have spread the news around. He gritted his teeth and it was with the greatest difficulty that he restrained himself from going up to Dinky and planting him one. That of course would have proved nothing and indeed would have blotted his copybook. No, there were other ways of skinning a cat than sucking its brains out, he thought. He had quite an experienced mind as far as revenge was concerned and wondered whether Dinky would be comfortable knowing what kind of retaliation he'd been capable of regarding a certain person by the name of Jake. But that was another story altogether. Fortunately there was no need to go to those lengths with Dinky and Pug. Harry made up his mind that their actions were going to cost them their jobs with the firm. Good riddance to them – now to make it happen. A certain degree of planning would be required, starting from today.

Lunchtime came and he managed to use the phone to ring Bagleys and ask for Miss Lamb. She seemed surprised that he had taken the trouble to contact her. He asked her if she would like to come to the pictures on Saturday night and could sense the disappointment in her voice as she said she had already made arrangements to go out. Acting very nonchalant about the whole affair he cheekily said, 'Aha, so Dinky did ask first, after all?'

'You knew that he had asked me?'

'Of course I did. (Nana always said white lies were okay.) I was just checking. Never mind, I'm sure there'll be other times. You just enjoy yourselves. Going to Milton again?'

No, Balclutha. There's a harvest dance down there. Should be a lot of fun. I'm so sorry, Harry.'

'Oh, don't worry, silly,' he said. He was slightly concerned that she would become involved but it was a risk he would have to take.

Just prior to knockoff time everyone started to drive the vehicles into the garage and it was Pug this time who managed to manoeuvre a car into the space next to the rear door. Harry was fairly sure that this would be the car they would use. He saw Dinky go over to the car and stand talking to his friend. After being tagged the keys to each vehicle were hung in a glass-fronted key cabinet in Jim's office. That was supposed to prevent any cars from being stolen. What a laugh, thought Harry. Obviously the pair had simply removed the ignition keys, pocketed them and hung another tagged set up on the hook. He slipped into the office to check and chortled to himself as he discovered that the substitute keys weren't even the correct kind for that type of vehicle. He congratulated himself and wrote down the registration number and colour of the vehicle, which again was a late model Vauxhall Velox.

Now came the tricky bit. Were they going to take the car for the whole weekend or just Saturday night? Pretty risky trying the former but then again they were liable to be stupid enough to attempt it. He decided to take a gamble on the Saturday night. Dinky was to pick Lee up at nine o'clock. That was reasonable, Harry thought – it would have to be dark for them to open the garage. That part was simple because all the staff knew that a spare key to the side door was hidden on the third petrol pump on the left.

Harry went home quite elated. After eating and doing all the chores he played several hands of euchre with Helen who, after winning six games in a row, decided that Harry's mind was definitely not on the game. Tas arrived home full as a tick and hiccupped his way to bed. Said he would be working overtime again early. They heard him snoring through the wall. He played another hand of Euchre and lost, much to the disgust of Helen who finally said, 'Now look here, Harry. You've been on tenterhooks all evening. What's the matter? Is there something I should know or what? Don't keep it to yourself.'

'Does it show that much? I thought I was being smart. Well I'm not going to tell you anything till tomorrow morning. I'll say this much, though – it's highly exciting. There, that'll torment you all night won't it now?'

'Aw, don't be mean.' She got up and kissed him. They were both getting daring these days.

'See you tomorrow morning.'

'Meanie.'

Harry went to bed that night without bothering to put pyjamas on. He had a fair idea he would have to entertain a visitor on the morrow.

The back door had barely closed when his visitor arrived, doffed her night gear and literally flung herself into his bed. She bit his ear and whispered 'Harry Evans, if you don't tell me what's going on I'll bite this, or something more precious, right off. I've not had a wink of sleep all night trying to figure out what you're up to. Now come on out with it.'

Harry just lay there and grinned. 'Okay,' he sighed resignedly, trying to sound as though she was dragging it out of him. He recounted the events leading up to the plan he had thought out and as he did so Helen could tell that he was enjoying himself immensely. He finally concluded the narrative and asked, 'Well, what do you think of it?'

She lay back with her fingers describing sensuous circles on his chest and thought the whole thing through. 'Boy, Harry, I don't think I'd like to be on the wrong side of you.'

'Well, I've always said that I make a wonderful friend but a piss-poor enemy and that, I'm afraid, is exactly what my so-called friend Dinky and his mate Pug are going to find out. There was no need for both of them to play that trick on me and I'm afraid my old Nana won't sleep soundly in her grave if I don't extract a bit of an eye and a tooth for myself.'

'What was she like, Harry?'

'She brought me up from the time I was knee-high to a grass-hopper. Straight as a die, she was. Called a spade a spade, though usually she would prefer to call it a bloody shovel. She had a host of favourite sayings like, 'She's got more yap than a shepherd's bitch' – that was one to describe a person who talked too much. To tell me off she would "give me a tonguing" and instead of saying "I remember" she would always say "I mind the time when... " I remember one frosty morning when the sheets were frozen on the clothes-line she happened to remark, "More wrinkles than inches this morning, Harry lad." I was about eight years old and didn't have a clue as to what she was talking about! We could do with a few more like her around the place but I think when God created her he threw away the mould, more's the pity.'

Helen snuggled into him. He recognised the warning signs.

'How's the ghost?'

'Needs laying.'

'There's a special word for it and I can't spell it.'

'What is it?'
'Sexorcism.'
'What a clever fellow you are, Harry Evans. Let's see if it works.'
It did. Her leg didn't hurt one iota.

# CHAPTER NINE

Harry walked into the Dunedin police station and enquired at the front counter for the whereabouts of a Detective Sergeant Maury Fletcher. As luck would have it he was in the building even though it was the weekend. He came down the stairs and recognised Harry immediately.

'Harry Evans. By all that's wonderful. You've finally come to see me. Are you going to join the police and become a "D" like me or what's the story? I must say it's great to see you again. Come into my office.' Harry was even offered a cup of coffee, which he accepted. It seemed strange to be once more in the company of the man who was once going to charge him for being the father of Kathy's unborn child. He was a good cop but he would never know the full story, Harry thought to himself. Still, that was a completely different matter and now he was requiring the cop's help. He put the other business out of his mind completely.

'Well, Detective Sergeant... '

'Call me Maury, Harry. I think we know each other enough by now.'

'Well, Maury, I'm in a bit of a pickle. I've got a real great job as an apprentice motor mechanic and I'm doing all right. Only trouble is I've found out that a couple of apprentices at the works are pinching cars on the weekends and taking them for joy rides. I'd like to get the works handed to both of them. It's a great firm and I think I owe them my loyalty. In actual fact I can honestly say I'd like to see this pair hung by the ears. Only trouble is, if I nark on them to the boss I could get it in the neck from my fellow workers. I thought I'd put it in your hands and you can do the dirty on them.' He paused. 'For me.'

Maury smiled. 'I take it, Harry, you want revenge, amongst other things.'

Harry smiled. 'Too bloody right I do. They've done some bloody awful things to me and I don't mind if they swing for it, Maury.'

'Only too happy to oblige, Harry. We'll see what we can do.' He picked up the phone. 'Send in Tom and Henry. Got a little job for them.'

'Righto, Harry, I'm going to hand you over to two policemen who handle traffic stuff. They'll sort this out, no sweat.'

The two detectives were very interested in Harry's story. They were curious as to why he hadn't reported it earlier. When he explained he hadn't been quite certain that a crime was being committed at all they seemed satisfied with his answer. They wanted to contact Mr Brooks about the whole affair but Harry tried to make them see that once it was known he had dobbed in Dinky and Pug then he would be marked down as a nark. He desperately did not want to be called one of those, yet by the same token he knew he was going to have to stick his neck out to nail these two. He decided to abide by their decision.

A swift telephone call was made to Mr Brooks and the two policemen arranged to meet him at the garage. They had decided to put a surveillance car outside the firm and nab the culprits when they went to pick up the car or as soon as they broke into the building.

Mr Brooks was waiting at the garage when they arrived and to Harry's surprise the car had already gone.

'Did you have any idea where they were going tonight?' asked the cop named Tom.

Harry thought swiftly. If they knew that Dinky and Pug were off to Balclutha to a dance they would intercept them there and most probably Leda would be involved. She would be arrested as an accomplice and Harry just didn't want that to happen.

'No, not a clue,' he lied.

'Well, in that case we'll just have to wait till they come back.'

They dropped Harry off at his home and said they would arrange whatever had to be done. Mr Brooks was fuming and he hardly acknowledged Harry's presence. Harry could see that he was in a hell of a mood.

Helen wanted to hear the whole story and, after she had been filled in on all the details, exclaimed, 'This is really exciting stuff! Much better than a detective story.'

Dinky was in a foul mood. He hadn't really wanted to take the car as early as they had but Pug had kept hammering on about picking up some crows down in the city centre. They hadn't had any success and finally Pug had capitulated and the pair had driven around to collect Doreen from her folk's place. From there they had cruised the city, visiting a couple of milk bars, till the appointed time to pick up Leda.

Leda climbed into the vehicle and made a few complimentary remarks about it, and nine o'clock saw them all heading in the direction of Balclutha. Dinky wanted to stop for a while on the way, but Leda sensed he wanted to have a snogging session and insisted they get to the dance first. To her surprise Pug's girlfriend backed her up on this suggestion.

The dance itself was quite enjoyable. Dinky was a good dancer and took pains to show that he was. He kept on trying to entice her out to the car for a few 'wets' but she said she didn't drink beer. That didn't stop him and Pug from frequent visits to the car, which was parked well away from the dance hall.

The last dance finally came and they were on their way home when Dinky decided the time was ripe to park up. That's when the trouble started. Dinky began getting too insistent with Leda, who wanted to go home. Pug by this time had almost succeeded in partially undressing Doreen, who was quite aware of Pug's little foibles and proved a willing partner. Dinky thought that this would apply to the new girl, Leda, but he could not have been more mistaken. Leda was not at all impressed. When he was finally hit over the face with her shoe he decided that that was enough for the night.

Leda was dropped off at her place and the others went to return the car. Dinky was simmering with rage. He had lost face and wanted to do something about it. As they approached the back entrance he switched off the headlights. Pug got out and, using the hidden key, opened the big side door. It seemed to make an awful noise. Maybe it was because of their guilty consciences, thought Dinky. He eased the Velox carefully into its previous position and with the aid of a flashlight checked that nothing incriminating had been left in the vehicle. The three of them were just leaving the building when the headlights of one of the cars parked at the kerb outside the garage were switched on. The three stood transfixed in the glare. The garage floodlights came on next and to Dinky's dismay there stood his boss, Mr Brooks. Before they could move a uniformed constable strode from behind one of the cars.

'Don't move. Just stay where you are. You're all under arrest.'

Monday morning. The garage was abuzz with the news of the break-in. Dinky and Pug failed to arrive for work. Harry was sweating over the fact that his name hadn't been mentioned. How long that would last was anybody's business.

Mr Brooks called the staff together at smoko time. He stood in the middle of the smoko room. 'I have an announcement to make. To scotch any rumours that are bound to get around I'd like you all to know that last Saturday night two staff members, namely Dawson and Pugh, were apprehended by the police when they were caught red-handed returning one of our customer's vehicles that they had stolen earlier in the day. Let me tell you that I have been painfully aware for some time now that there have been mileage discrepancies on vehicles that have been stored here in the garage overnight. Following advice from the police it was decided to – stake out is I believe the term they use – this garage on Saturday evening. Sad to say, Dawson and Pugh are no longer in this company's employment. They will be duly charged sometime today. I have arranged for their lockers to be cleared out and they are no longer allowed anywhere near this building. Thank you.' With that he walked out of the room.

Harry sat there with a great sense of relief in his heart. Mr Brooks had for some reason completely cleared him of any involvement.

An hour later he was summoned into the boss's office. 'Come in, Harry, and close the door behind you.'

Jim pressed the intercom button. 'Christine, don't accept any calls or visitors for me until I inform you otherwise. Please sit down, Harry.'

He thought for a long moment and then began. 'Harry, first of all I'd like to thank you for the information you gave the police the other night. I know it's easier sometimes to look the other way. I happen to know Maury Fletcher quite well and he rang me not only about your wish not to be involved but he also informed me of other events in your life which have been rather tragic. I presume you noticed I came out with that stuff about mileages and so on just to stop the tongues from wagging. I hope I was successful with my red herring.

'Harry, I am deeply in your debt. As they say, I owe you one. And now I'd like to show my gratitude towards you. This will be strictly between you and me. I would like you to tell me how best I can help you – in some sort of tangible manner. You can go away and think about it if you wish. But I repeat, this is just between you and me. Now, what do you have to say, Harry?'

Harry sat there thunderstruck. He finally gathered his thoughts together and said, 'Thanks, Mr Brooks. All I wanted really was not to be named as being involved and you certainly fixed that.'

His mind was racing. This was too good an opportunity to pass up. He drew a deep breath and plunged on in.

'There is one thing I would really like if it's not too much. My landlady is crippled and she has a car which has been stored at her place since her fiancee was killed. It's been covered for four years or so and I now have the use of it to drive her around if I like. But as you know I'm not a mechanic yet and it would take me a month of Sundays to get it up and going. I was thinking of paying for it to be fixed here but maybe your offer would be just the ticket. Would that be asking too much do you think?'

'Sounds fair enough to me, Harry. What sort of condition is it in? Is it an old bomb or something?'

'Heck no. It's just the fact that it hasn't been used for so long.'

'Where's the car now, Harry?'

'Stored in a garage at the place where I board.'

'Okay Harry,' said Mr Brooks, warmly enthusiastic. 'Sounds like a great scheme. Is there anything else you require?'

'Nothing at all, Mr Brooks. That will do just fine. Just that,' Harry replied simply.

As he closed the door behind him he left a rather surprised boss sitting there. Boys like Harry usually asked for money. He shook his head. Wonders would never cease.

Tas stayed at home that evening and Harry managed to tell him and Helen all about the way Dinky and Pugh's plans had been foiled.

'Real cops and robbers stuff,' laughed Tas, who seemed in a rather jovial mood for a change. About time too, thought Harry.

He went up to the rear section and did some more rubbish burning. He didn't want to get the neighbours too upset with excess smoke. The area was being cleared nicely. He went into the garage and couldn't resist taking a further gander at the Chev. He hadn't told either Helen or Tas about his plans.

He was busy working on his lathe at Tech next night when his instructor came up to him in the class and said, 'A word with you, Evans. Come with me.' He led Harry up to the little instruction podium. 'Stand there.'

He brought out his whistle. He used this to signal that the machinery was to stop while he talked to the class. It was a nuisance in a way but this was his method and that was that. He blew it. Harry felt a real idiot standing there at the front. He was obviously going to get balled out again. Once silence had been established and the instructor had everyone's attention, he addressed the class: 'Some time ago I chewed Harry Evans's ear very hard for making the stupid mistake of leaving the lathe in a dangerous condition – mainly by leaving the screw-cutting mechanism engaged without supervision. Thanks to an honest class member who had the intestinal fortitude to step forward I can now say that it was not

Evans's fault at all and I would like to offer my sincerest apologies to Harry in front of this class.'

With that he turned around and shook Harry by the hand. To Harry's complete surprise the whole class clapped. It was very embarrassing but, thought Harry, it was also very, very nice.

Helen and Harry lay together next morning, her long hair draped over his arm. They had finished making love and were wrapped up in their own thoughts.

'Tell me again what the instructor said last night, Harry,' Helen whispered. 'It makes me feel good all over.'

'I've all ready told you three times or more, I'm sure, but I must admit it gives me a nice feeling too,' said Harry. 'The thing that really got me was what Pat said when he walked out the gate with me at the end of class. I'd asked him what had made him change his mind and do it, and he said, "Well Harry, I heard about the business of the garage and all that and I remembered your words to the effect that you were going to get not only an eye for an eye but four of them in one go and I guessed you must have had something to do with it. Good on you." Then he went on to say that if snitching on Dinky was good enough for me, then it was for him too, and that he's sworn the instructor to secrecy. Now don't you think that was really nice of him?' Harry asked.

'He sounds a nice chap. You must bring him around some time. You also better get going or you'll be late for work.'

*She had been weeding in the garden behind the shed when the first signs of an argument became apparent. Both men's voices were raised and she heard her name mentioned. She had never ever heard them shouting at each other before. She heard George mention something about not giving two hoots if the child was a bastard and that he definitely wasn't going to tell his mother. Then he went on to say that both she and Tas had been spying on him and he knew they were talking about him behind his back. At that stage Tas managed to quieten George down. Minutes later they both appeared from within the shed and she could tell that George had been crying again. Tas was patting his brother's head and saying, 'There, there, Georgie. No need to cry. Tas will fix it. Dry your tears and cheer up. We'll all go for a nice ride in the car and take Mum and Helen out for a spin just like we used to do. Everything will be okay.'*

*She had crouched down in the bushes and they had passed within feet of her. Now Tas knew, what would he say to her? She felt terrible and decided to return to the house and have it out finally with George and his mother. Something had to be done and the quicker the better. She felt an inner strength and held her head up in anticipation of an ugly encounter with some unpleasant business. She walked into the kitchen and found Tas, George and their mother coming out into the sunlight. She was about to tackle them all together when 'Grab your hat, Helen,' George had said gaily. 'Tas is going to take us all for a ride in the car. Won't that be nice? Hurry along now.' He sounded like a little boy going out on a Sunday school outing. Totally unlike the man with a single purpose on his mind last time he had ripped her clothes off her.*

*It was not the right moment to bring the subject up. She combed her hair and went outside to Tas's car in the drive. Tas and Mum sat in the front while Tas avoided her eyes, she noticed. It was almost as though he had a guilty conscience. George kept up a running inconsequential conversation with her in the rear. They stopped at a little tearoom for afternoon tea. Mrs Mann was enjoying herself and on this day was more lucid than normal. George on the other hand was at times talking like a ten-year-old. It was late in the afternoon as they were driving back on the homeward journey when it happened…*

Harry was working at his welding once more. He found it relaxing and was getting quite proficient at it. Frank came along and said, 'Harry, just had a funny request from Mr Brooks. It's been okayed by Jim. I'm to go with you and bring in a car that's at your place. Know anything about it? He said you would be able to shed some light on it.'

'Gee, that was quick,' said Harry. 'Mr Brooks is jacking up a surprise for my landlady. She wants the car fixed so I can take her out in it. The tyres are flat so I guess it might be an idea if I let you take a look and see what's got to be done to it first.'

Frank allowed Harry to drive the van home and they both went up the drive. Harry didn't go inside the house. He unlocked the garage and uncovered the car.

'What a beaut!' Frank exclaimed. 'It's in mint condition. How long has it been sitting here?' he asked.

'Oh, about four years.'

Frank set about looking over the car. It didn't take long for him to decide that it would be easier in the long run to come back and take the wheels off and fit new tyres just to be on the safe side. They could then tow the Chev back to the garage and work on it there.

Just at that moment Helen appeared. 'What's going on, Harry?' she asked.

'Oh, now you've spoiled it,' said Harry. 'We were going to pinch the car and fix it up.'

'Really?' she was astonished. 'Is it going to take much?'

'Well, we happen to have the best mechanic in the firm working on it,' grinned Harry, and he introduced Frank who actually blushed.

'How do you do, Mrs Mann,' said Frank. It wasn't until they were driving back to the workshop that Frank said, 'That's your landlady? She seems pretty young to be a landlady.'

'I suppose she does,' agreed Harry."

'Awfully nice looking,' said Frank.

'You think so? Hadn't really noticed myself.'

'You're a bit young yet,' said nineteen-year-old Frank wisely.

Driving back to the garage, Harry was pleased as punch the way things had turned out. Frank went and had a talk to Jim and it was decided to remove the wheels from the Chev and bring them back to the garage to check them over. Frank said, 'Look Harry, we may as well do that now. Bring the four stands and we'll put the old girl on blocks and then when we've sorted that out we can tow her in here and give her the works.'

Harry went and checked with Ted who it appeared was in the

know and readily gave his permission. 'Seeing it's your landlady's car and you'll be driving it you might as well learn a bit about it while you're at it.'

Back they went to the Chev and found Helen to be very excited about getting it back on the road. They refused her offer of morning tea.

Mr Brooks came down to the garage while they were checking the tyres and said, 'Don't bother wasting time on them. Put new ones on. And tubes too,' he added. He patted the bonnet rather patronisingly and left with a smug look on his face.

Frank looked at Harry and with a puzzled look on his face said, 'The boss seems to think a lot of your landlady. Nothing too good for her, eh?'

Harry shrugged his shoulders. 'Must be in a good mood, I guess.'

Back to the Chev. Frank said that seeing the car had not run for so long it would be best to start from scratch and do the whole thing properly. The brake drums were rusty and they grabbed a bit, but with Harry towing and Frank in the Chev the car was brought to the garage without incident.

Once more Mr Brooks appeared on the scene. He seemed to have taken a somewhat personal interest in the machine. He ran his hand over the paint. 'Nice condition, Frank. What's got to be done to it?'

'I haven't checked it over yet, Mr Brooks, but I'll let you know as soon as I get into it a bit more.'

The boss smiled at both of them. 'Tell you what, I might just go and rake up a set of overalls and get my hands dirty for a bit. Haven't worked on one of these for years. Used to own one myself.' He was behaving like a cat that had just discovered it had ten tails.

Word had travelled fast that the boss had decided to come and work in the shop. He was an excellent mechanic and a perfectionist. It was obvious that the Chev was going to get the full treatment.

Harry arrived home that night and the first thing Helen asked was, 'How's the car going?'

'It's not.'

‘What’s gone wrong?’

‘Oh, nothing wrong. It’s just that Mr Brooks isn’t satisfied with the engine Says it was idle too long and the cylinder bores could have glazed over, and although Frank reckons it doesn’t need it, insisted that it be re-honed and have new piston rings fitted, and God knows what else has to be done to it. It sounds like it’ll be a brand new car if he has anything to do with it. And he will because he’s working on it himself. And I have the grand job of cleaning every last nut and bolt of it.”

‘Oh, Harry. Isn’t it exciting?’

‘Certainly is.’

At that moment Tas walked in and Harry had to repeat the good news. ‘Sounds a bit expensive, Harry, said Tas. ‘How much is it going to cost me?’

‘Not a brass razoo, Tas. The boss is picking up the tab. Now what do you think about that? It gave me a bit of a shock, I must say.’

Harry then of course had to divulge how all this came about and at the end of the tale Tas admitted it certainly was something. ‘Just goes to show what results can come out of a good action. Just make sure those two don’t hang one on you.’

‘They’ll never know. There’s only about four people including yourselves that have any idea that I dropped them in it.’

‘By the way, that’s not all,’ Tas said, pulling out his wallet. ‘I meant to give you this the other day too.’ He pulled out five one pound notes and some silver. ‘You were right about Coral’s Choice. I happened to have a tenner on it myself. Paid just over twenty quid. Nice going, eh? Right then, I’m off. Might just celebrate tonight.’

Once again he was gone and Harry and Helen were alone.

Helen came over and kissed Harry gently on the lips. ‘Thank you, Harry, for doing all this for me. You’re really too much.’

Harry grinned. ‘Aw, c’mon, Helen. You’ll have me blushing.’

‘No, Harry, I mean it. Truly.’

He felt a little uncomfortable. ‘I guess I’d better get ready for night school.’

He ran into Pat as he was going into class. 'Everything hunky-dory again, Harry?'

Pat asked.

'Couldn't be better, thanks to you, Pat.'

'No problem.'

'Tell me, Pat. You work in a foundry. I guess you must know a fair bit about forges, furnaces and things? I'm mainly interested in lead pouring. There's a lot of gear in the workshop at home that belonged to the owner's late brother. He used to make lead soldiers and the like. I thought that perhaps I might have a go at it for a bit of fun. It looks like everything necessary is there – I just don't know how to go about it.'

'Sounds interesting. Perhaps I could come round some time and take a look at it. Might be able to help you out a bit.'

They went into class and were soon involved in maths. It stank.

Harry came home with a stinking headache. Helen, on his arrival, sensed that he was out of sorts. Harry was not usually given to bad moods and he sat at the table with his head in his hands. 'Boy! This is getting worse. This fellow we've got just can't get through to the class. Everybody's grumbling about him. We need a completely new teacher. He's hopeless.'

'Hey, Harry. Harry. Don't let it get you down. I've been busy going over these lessons of yours and I've worked out a method of teaching you, starting tonight or any time you want we can get into this stuff – it's not that hard. It's just that you need to look at it in a different way. Lateral thinking is the requirement here. I'm sure of it.'

He looked at her and gave her one of his best smiles. She immediately felt a thrill go up her spine. Then his face dropped. 'No, I'm afraid we can't Helen.'

'Why not?' she asked, alarmed at his attitude.

Because I think it states somewhere that teachers should not have love affairs with their pupils. So there, that puts a stop to that, doesn't it now?'

Helen threw back her head and laughed with relief. 'Tell you what, I won't say anything if you don't say anything. Bargain?'

'Okay. Where's me pencil?'

Harry was busy having a nosy around the workshop, looking at all the tools and gadgets that had belonged to George. The more he found, the clearer it was, even to his untrained eyes, that the previous owner had been a very talented engineer. There were a tremendous number of what seemed to be unfinished projects lying about, only some of which Harry could figure out the purpose of – others were incomprehensible. In his rummaging he came across a small wooden box. The lid was very stiff and it was with some difficulty that Harry managed to carefully prise it open. It was empty but its attraction for Harry was that it was beautifully bound with brass, and for its size quite solid. It had a Chinese inscription on the lid which didn't mean anything to Harry. He had discovered quite by accident that it was Helen's birthday the following week and he decided that he would refurbish the box and give it to her.

It took him all week working in his spare time to carefully buff the brass until it shone. He had also managed to obtain a piece of purple velvet cloth and he meticulously lined the box with it. The lid, after a bit of work, opened and closed nicely and by the time Harry had finished the box he was very satisfied with his handiwork. He bought a small but heavy brass padlock and key from a second-hand shop to complete the surprise.

The pair of them by this time had settled into a pattern of lovemaking which had not by any means cooled the eagerness and frequency of their morning trysts, but if anything had developed into a more caring attitude.

The morning of her birthday arrived and so did she into his bed. They made love and as they both stretched out, luxuriating in the diestrum, Harry reached under the bed and at the same time said, 'This is your second present from me this morning. Happy birthday, darling.' He handed her the present.

She squealed and sat up in bed. 'How did you know it was... '

'That will teach you to skite about your driving licence. I spotted the date on it.'

Helen carefully unwrapped the box and was delighted with it. She expressed her gratitude further and as a result Harry was almost late for work that day.

She lay there with the box in her hands, studying it closely.

*Yes, it was definitely the same box that George had said he had donated to the museum. Why on earth would he lie over a little thing like that? George was an unwelcome memory – maybe one way to stop him appearing constantly in her thoughts would be to rid the house of all those things that once belonged to him. She would have to do it gradually and be careful that Tas didn't take exception to what she was up to. Would she ever be able to stamp the bad, recurring thoughts of him out of her mind? she wondered. Of course, she tried to remember the good times that they had shared and forcefully fix them in her mind, but it was difficult to stop the disturbing flashbacks that kept being triggered by a phrase, a place, or an object. The mystery of the brass box nagged her. Why had he lied?*

# CHAPTER TEN

The Chev refurbishment was proceeding apace. Mr Brooks, as owner of the firm, of course had first call on all the help he required. Jim Schultz considered his boss's intrusion onto the workshop floor a bloody pain in the neck and his only recourse was to try and get rid of him. To successfully accomplish this he decided to extend as much aid as he could so that the job on the Chev was completed as quickly as possible. Mr Brooks could then return upstairs to his office, peace would again reign down in the workshop, and everyone could relax.

Mr Brooks couldn't have had a more willing foreman in his employ if he tried. Jim even amazed himself at the effort he put into the job. He even ground the valves himself after work, telling the boss that the machine was going to be used all next day and he didn't want the Chev delayed. Mr Brooks, as can be expected, was delighted in the extreme and the whole exercise was completed in two days. The car had been virtually reconditioned throughout.

Mr Brooks called Harry into his office just prior to knock-off time and, when Harry went to thank him, said, 'Don't thank me, Harry. To be quite frank I haven't had so much fun in a long time. Did me the world of good and it was a bit of fun down at the coalface again. Keep it just between you and me though, okay?' He tapped his nose with his finger. 'Now, scoot out of my office, d'you hear?'

It was a very proud Harry who drove home that night. The front doorbell rang and Helen went to answer it. She received an awful shock as she opened the door. There standing on the step was a figure, obviously human, wearing two square sheets of tin, one in front and the other behind. On its head she recognized a welding helmet obscuring its features. The wearer of this outlandish-looking creation flicked the visor up and she heard Harry say in sepulchral tones, 'Let down your hair, Rapunzel. Let down your hair and come away with me.'

He whipped off his helmet and bowed deeply, rattling a bit as he did so. 'Well, Helen, I had to improvise slightly. I couldn't get a knight's helmet and my tin suit doesn't fit too well. I couldn't get a shine on my rusty armour and it's not a chariot, it's a Chevrolet, but it's got horses under the bonnet to drag you away.' He threw the helmet and the tin onto the steps and lifted her up easily and carried her down to the car. 'What about my crutches?' she cried.

'I'm afraid there's no room in this chariot for crutches,' he said, and gave her a kiss on her cheek.

She giggled and lay back in his arms. 'My hero.'

She climbed in and as an afterthought Harry went back, closed the door and picked up her crutches, placed them in the back seat and eased himself into the driver's seat.

'Where to, my lady?' he asked.

'To the moon and back, squire,' she said.

They drove down the drive and as they breezed along she sighed and said. 'Do you know, Harry, not counting medical trips, this is the very first time I've been out of the house since the accident.'

'I find that hard to believe but I can understand why you didn't want to come out. But you're out of the house now and you haven't answered my question. Where do you want to go?'

'Down to the beach, please.'

Harry drove down to St Kilda and helped her out of the car. They sat on a sand dune and held hands, and she took her shoe off and wiggled her foot in the sand. 'You know, I haven't done this for a long, long time. This is just wonderful, Harry,' she said.

*They had sat on a sand dune and held hands, watching the ships out to sea. 'I'd love to be a captain of a big ship out there. Master of all I surveyed, with my own crew who loved me and thought I was just the cat's pyjamas. I wouldn't take any nonsense from anyone and I would be in complete control of all that went on. I would pick up survivors in lifeboats and all that romantic sort of stuff and I would come back home and be treated like a hero. I would fight heroic battles with dive-bombers and guide my badly crippled ship into a harbour to deliver badly needed food supplies and return once more to a hero's welcome.*

*'You're going to be a bit worn out after all that sort of carry-on, don't you think?' She had said, trying to be a bit lighthearted about it all.*

*He abruptly rose. 'You know the trouble with you? You just haven't got a sense of purpose. You've probably never dreamed about anything in your bloody life, Helen. You don't have any imagination like I have. You just wouldn't bloody understand just what I'm talking about. Trust you to spoil things. C'mon, we're going home.'*

*That was her last day at the beach.*

Driving home from the beach Helen seemed to be rather subdued and Harry wondered why. She cheered up once they had returned home and Harry had put the car away, and after tea they had an hour of maths. Harry, under the tutelage of Helen, was feeling more at home with the subject. She had sorted out books from Mrs Mann's extensive library and told him to carry at least one with him to work, and if he had time just to go over it without trying to swot his guts out. Learning, she reckoned, should be a matter of absorbing things, not shoving them into your brain. If they don't get sorted out before you down them, you definitely won't be able to bring them out in the correct way.

Harry paid heed, as he knew very well he was listening to a person who knew her onions.

He had tried all sorts of ways to disprove her idea about the magic figure nine but he couldn't. It was certainly a fascinating numeral.

They had their ritual game or two of euchre, then Harry went to bed. Tas still hadn't arrived home. He was just about to fall into the arms of Morpheus when his door opened and Helen slipped in. 'God, Helen!' He said. Don't you know it's dangerous to come in here at night? Tas could arrive at any time and there would be hell to pay. I do wish you wouldn't push your luck like this.' He was genuinely worried.

'Sorry, Harry. I only came in to say good night.' She sounded so contrite that he felt sorry for her and immediately apologized. Just at that very moment they heard Tas come through the back door. He switched on the light. The pair froze. There was no way for Helen to return to her bedroom, and Tas sometimes looked in there to see if she was all right. They heard the door open to her room.

'Quickly. Into the toilet! Harry whispered. She leapt out of bed and as silently as she could, crept into the toilet. The light switch clicked on in her room and they heard Tas say in a thick voice, 'Hey, Helen. Where the hell are you?'

Harry saw her come past his door. 'Here I am, Tas. Are you all right?'

'Yeah. Just checking. You been in bed long?'

'No. Why? I was helping Harry with his maths.'

'Did he get the car going today?'

'Yes. We even went for a little drive in it.'

'Good. I'm off to bed.' He closed his door and within ten minutes his snores were reverberating around the house.

*What a wonderful person her Harry had turned out to be. Her father always said that you make your own luck and things had changed so much since her youthful cavalier had come into her life. Her thoughts went back to Harry arriving at the front door and his silly way of being ever so nice to her. Fancy wearing a welding visor and capturing her in his 'chariot'! She lay in the warm bed and imagined all sorts of romantic situations. These were far, far better than the nebulous dreams she used to conjure up when she was much younger. She could now focus on one person – Harry. And what's more, he was real. Solid flesh. Harry. Her Harry. She curled up in a delightful cocoon of happiness and wiggled her toes. Yes, even the ghost was wiggling its toes. It felt marvellous. No tears tonight, Helen. She slept.*

Ted had taken Harry on another demonstration of his beloved Ferguson tractor. A tremendous amount of his enthusiasm had rubbed off on Harry and to hear both of them extolling the virtues of this machine must have been irritating to some people. Harry was getting rather one-eyed in his obsession with the little grey tractor. Ted, of course, made no effort to stop him. He always maintained that if you really believed in a product then it would sell itself.

It was quite early and not all the local gentry had arrived as yet. There was no hurry, Ted reckoned. They had got there in plenty of time to set everything up and prepare for the forthcoming event and all that was now required was an interested audience. The show wasn't due to go on the road for another hour. In the meantime Ted talked to various farmers regarding the respective merits of their machines. 'One thing to remember, Harry, is that however well you like your product, never ever knock the other fellow's. In other words, it's far better if a joker starts spouting off and beating on about how good his is, to say, "Of course it's a great machine, one of the best – but ours is better. We'll prove it to you." Remember that, Harry. Never ever knock the other fellow's product.'

With Ted's words still ringing in his ears he joined a group of farmers talking about the forthcoming demonstration. Nobody seemed to take any notice of him and he listened intently as a rather florid-faced fellow with a very loud voice held forth on how he had paid the best money for the best machine and it certainly wasn't a Ferguson. He had gone into the specifications in depth and it was drawbar horsepower that counted and not these fancy gadgets that got the work done. His own tractor, which he had driven over from his nearby farm, could make a big mess of anyone's in the district. He actually was wasting his time by being here but as he was an open-minded person he felt that it was his duty to keep everyone informed as to the mistakes people could make when buying machines. The little group he had gathered together seemed to be listening and agreeing with him. It was just too much for Harry to stand, and in a quiet voice which the group could hear, he said, 'Excuse me, but is that your machine there? The one you're talking about?'

'Certainly is, son,' replied the farmer in a condescending tone. 'Beauty, isn't she?'

'She certainly is all right. Pity that the Fergy can outdo it though.'

'Like hell it can,' blustered Farmer Red Face. 'You don't know what you're talking about.'

'Bet the Fergy can out-pull it.'

'You must be out of your head saying things like that.'

'Want to have a bet on it?' asked Harry.

'There's one born every minute,' laughed Red Face. 'Just how much are you prepared to risk?'

'Say a week's wages?'

'How much do you get paid?'

'Two pounds fifteen shillings. You?' Harry was pushing his luck but there was now an audience and he reckoned he had Farmer Florid well and truly cornered. 'What's a week of your wages?'

'None of your business.'

'Well, what would you like to bet?'

'Go on, Rube. Put up or shut up. The lad's made a play. Going to make a go of it?' asked one of the farmers.

'All right then, I'll bet ten pounds against your wages that my machine can out-pull yours.' He had regained some face. He knew he was onto a good thing so he wasn't overly worried.

Harry climbed up on the tractor and backed it up to the other machine and dropped a pin through the drawbars. At that moment Ted walked up and said, 'What's going on, Harry?'

'Just a little contest, Ted. I should have asked you first.'

'What's the story then?'

Florid interrupted at that moment and said 'This smart-arse apprentice of yours, Ted, reckons he can out-pull my tractor.' He smirked. 'You haven't taught him much about horsepower. Mine's got over fifty more than him.'

Ted looked at Harry and said quietly, 'I wish you had spoken to me first, Harry. However, on your own head be it. How much have you bet him?'

'My week's wages against ten pounds.'

Ted looked at Harry very closely. 'I see. Good luck.' A smile came over his face. 'Wait on, Harry. Are you going to do what I think you're going to do?'

Harry looked into Ted's eye. 'I think you know what I'm going to do, Ted.'

One of the farmers paced out ten steps in front of each tractor and placed a stick down on the mark. 'First one to get the other's front wheel clear across wins. One pull only. Start your engines, gentlemen.'

It sounded as though it was the start of the Le Mans races.

He dropped a handkerchief and Florid's tractor started to drag the little Ferguson backward. Harry looked a bit anxious. His wheels were skidding, he was using only his brakes and hadn't even put the tractor in gear.

Florid was letting out little war whoops.

When the big tractor reached the line and all that was required was one more effort, Harry reached down and gently pulled the hydraulic control up. His drawbar rose up and with it raised the rear wheels of the large machine. Harry then engaged a low gear and drove forward across his line with Florid's wheels spinning helplessly in the air. He dragged him clean across, stopped, switched off his machine and shouted to the judge, 'Far enough?'

The crowd was laughing and a couple of farmers came over and slapped his back.

Florid was fortunately gracious in defeat and handed Harry a tenner with a flourish.

Afterwards a farmer who had been watching from the sideline came up to Harry and said, 'I heard you only get two pounds fifteen a week. Would you like some weekend work?'

'I certainly would,' replied Harry.

'Right, I'll pop into your workplace next week and talk to you then.'

Ted came up later and said to Harry, 'Because of that little bit of showing off by you today it looks like I could have an order for two tractors from two farmers who were all against buying a Fergy last month. Thanks, Harry. Bloody good work. By the way, you were taking an awful risk betting a week's wages, weren't you?'

Harry looked at Ted and winked. 'Reg and I tried it out last week at work. Think I'm *that* stupid?'

'Well, Harry, thank goodness it turned out to be a piece of cake,' said Ted. It was to his intense satisfaction, however, that a fortnight later he found Florid in his office waving a cheque around and demanding immediate delivery of a new Ferguson tractor complete with a plough and several other expensive accessories. That was definitely the icing on his cake.

It was Saturday and Harry had promised Tas he would meet him at the gasworks and have a look around the show. He might even get the chance to see Strath. In any case he would call in and visit Tracy on his way home. It would be a superb idea to take Helen round sometime to introduce them. He was confident that they would take to each other.

He made his way into the main office. The man on the gate said it was okay to go down to the big coke-houses at the end. There was an overpowering smell of Jeyes fluid in the air. Harry made his way down and heard a shout from above his head. There was Tas waving to him. He climbed up the vertical steel ladder until he seemed to be a long way up. He wasn't really, but he was unused to heights like this. He was a little out of breath when he reached the platform Tas was standing on.

'Bit high up here, eh Tas?'

'Well, Harry, it'll give you some idea of how the whole works are set out.' He explained in detail to Harry where everything was and what it did. Harry managed to keep up with the concept of the works. They then went down a different set of steel stairs and found themselves in an area which Tas had once referred to as 'Dante's Inferno.'

Harry watched, fascinated, while a man controlled a machine that literally spewed coal into fiery ovens. There must have been at least thirty of them and the smoke came out as fast as the coal went in. The ovens were then shut and the coal was cooked and the gases which were released were extracted by pumping the chambers empty. The end result was that the gas finished up in great big tanks that floated on water. You could see at a glance how much gas was stored in the tank by how high the tank was. The water was used as a seal and, depending on the season and the requirements of the city, the tanks could be towering above one's head or be quite low in the ground. Harry found the whole thing extremely interesting.

He watched in awe as one of the kilns had to be emptied. A power-operated steel hoe arrangement was inserted into the kiln in order to pull the white-hot coke out of the hole. The coke built up into a huge heap as it fell from the oven. Another worker, wearing heavy protective clothing, stood and sprayed copious amounts of water on the heap, producing clouds of scalding steam. Finally, when the temperature had been sufficiently reduced, the coke was shifted to storage bays outside the building. This residue from the kilns would eventually find its way to city coke yards and be sold for fuel. It was clean burning and didn't smoke as much as coal.

To Harry, working in the gasworks looked to be a highly dangerous sort of job, but nobody seemed to worry about it too much.

'Now you know what I was talking about when I said the fires of hell, Harry,' Tas shouted above the noise. Harry didn't think he would have remembered their talk and was slightly surprised.

Tas asked, 'Are you going to take Helen for another drive?'

'Now that's a great idea. I'll do that when I get home. When are you coming out to see how the old girl runs?' Harry said.

'I don't think so. Sorry. A few too many memories locked up in that machine, Harry. I'll give it a miss. Before you go you better come down and have a look at the boiler-room.'

Tas took him into the boiler-room where the fires for the steam side of the works were. The fires were fed by brown-skinned sweating stokers who seemed to shovel coal as though their lives depended on it. Harry mentioned this to Tas as they walked out of the room, and said he wondered just how they kept that sort of pace up. Tas just laughed. 'Oh, don't you worry yourself about them. They always put on a show when they know somebody's watching them. Take a look back in there, but don't let them see you.' Harry looked around the door and could see the sweating stokers sitting down laughing their heads off. Somehow he felt a little better about the slave labour he thought he had just witnessed.

Tas introduced Harry to the engineer in charge of the pumping station and was shown over the engine room. There were two massive flywheels about twenty-five feet in diameter turning slowly and these in turn drove great big rods that operated the gas pumps. The area was so spotless one could have eaten off the floor. Harry remarked that he thought steam engines were supposed to be noisy. All he could hear was a slight hissing sound from a valve above his head. The engineer laughed and said, 'When you come in here, Harry, it's lovely to listen to the sound of silence.' The area was warm and totally different to the noisy, smelly works outside. He shook the engineer's hand and left to find Tas again.

After thanking Tas, Harry went on to Tracy's place and had morning tea with her. Strath was in the city somewhere so Harry played with the girls for a while then went home to do some more damage to the back section.

As it was Saturday Helen had already jumped the gun and was ready to go. 'I've been waiting as patiently as I could,' she said. 'But I'm dying to out into the big world again. What say we go to the pictures? My shout.'

Harry said, 'Okay. Your wish is my command. Let's get a paper and find out what's on.' He didn't have to get changed so they were off with a hiss and a roar, as Harry described it. They had a look in the paper and the film they wanted to see wasn't on for another three hours.

'Let's just kill some time in the Early Settlers Museum,' said Harry. 'It's easy to get parking and it will help to fill in a couple of hours.'

They paid to get in and had a wonderful afternoon wandering

through the place and discussing various objects. It wasn't until they went into the goldmining section that Harry exclaimed, 'Helen! That's almost the twin of your box lying there in that cabinet.' Helen took a close look and a shiver ran up her spine. The Chinese lettering was in the same place and it wasn't till they read the inscription that she said, 'That's strange. This is the box that George said he had presented to the museum. So he didn't lie to me after all. I wonder why he didn't tell me there were two of them? Very strange.'

It was all rather confusing to Harry and it took some explaining on her part. She remembered then that George had said 'to put them off the scent' and neither she nor Harry could make head nor tale of this strange remark. But then of course they realised that George's behaviour was getting rather strange at that stage anyway. They discussed it at length and decided to forget about it in the meantime and just enjoy each other's company and go to the pictures. They were about to turn away when an ancient attendant who happened to be standing next to them said, 'You two seem to be more than just rather interested in that box.'

'Yes, as a matter of fact we think we have a bit of a mystery on our hands,' replied Harry. 'We have an almost identical one at home in our workshop.'

'The curator had to go to a lot of trouble to get a translation of the writing on the box. It wasn't until I called in my Chinese friend who runs a fish and chip shop next door to where I live that the writing was sorted out. Trouble was someone failed to include the woman's name when they wrote out the label. It's written in tiny letters under her picture. You can only read it with the aid of a magnifying glass. 'But we managed,' he stated importantly. He waited.

'She's beautiful,' said Helen. 'And her name... ?'

'Yen Mu Len. It translates into... Now let me see... Lotus Flower... Yes... Beautiful Lotus Flower, or something like that.' He gave a deep sigh and looked at the tiny painting. 'Yes, you've got to admit she was beautiful all right.'

They left him still standing there. A wintry old man gazing at an aged box.

The movie was a real tear-jerker. It was *Goodbye Mr Chips* and Helen cried all the way through it. On the journey home Harry remarked dryly that as far as a cheerful afternoon's entertainment went it had proved to be an absolute disaster. However Helen, who had not stopped crying, said it was the most beautiful picture she had ever been to and that she loved every minute of it... Women! thought Harry.

Helen had decided she would make a determined effort to start to clear George's belongings out of the house. She realised she couldn't move everything but even if she succeeded in getting some out it might help to prevent further disturbing flashbacks. One of the rooms in the house was full of his personal paraphernalia. Though the door was not locked she never went in there and Tas seemed to keep well away from it too. She went in and gazed around. There was a small writing desk positioned in one corner. She sat down at the desk and looked at the dusty pile of papers stacked in a heap. She wondered if Tas had bothered to go through them. There was even some unopened mail addressed to George. She wondered why it had never been seen to. Funny, until this moment she hadn't even thought about it. Surely she must have seen it before?. She sat there, bracing herself for the task ahead. She would have to approach the job with a certain amount of caution, though at the same time it had to be carried out methodically. Should she obtain Harry's help? She was still unsure of Tas's approval. Still, it had to be done sometime.

Standing on the writing desk was a framed picture of two soldiers – George and his great friend Len. They had been very close mates and had joined up simultaneously, done their basic training together and to their great satisfaction were posted overseas in the same company. The picture had obviously been posed as the two laughing soldiers were standing in the same pair of woollen underpants, each with both their legs in only one leg of the undergarment. George had mentioned that some of the clothes they were initially issued with were quite ridiculous sizes. The picture was captioned 'Two legs are better than one' and signed by both of them.

*She, Tas, and Mrs Mann had gone down to the railway station to farewell them. The station was packed. Bands played patriotic tunes and plenty of oom pah pah stuff, and there were little patriotic flags galore. Len, who had no relatives, had been to stay with George on his final leave. They were both good-looking, gallant, good-humoured, and were treating the whole thing as a sort of Boy's Own exercise. They had read about the Fuzzy Wuzzies in the Sudan as lads and it seemed as though all they had to do was to go over, fire a few shots and the enemy, whoever they were, would turn tail and run. They would then come home as heroes.*

*Anyway, they were in the Engineers regiment and seemed disappointed that they would not be up in the thick of things. How wrong they proved to be, as Helen found out later. Len kissed her on the cheek and gave Mrs Mann a surprise big hug. George, on the other hand, instead of the big-brotherly kiss on the cheek that Helen always had been used to, took her in his arms and, disregarding the fact that his mother was in the vicinity, kissed her in a manner that she had never in her life experienced. He held her very close and his hands pressed her spine to him. His tongue explored her mouth in a manner she was totally unused to. She was too surprised even to resist and found herself responding in a fashion that made her blush later. She was quite sure proper young ladies didn't kiss in that manner. When he finally released her he whispered in her ear, 'Been wanting to do that for a long time now. Pity I left it this late.' She was shaking and almost felt like approaching him for a repeat performance but Mum Mann was standing there. The moment had passed. But she remembered that burning kiss for many long nights afterwards.*

Helen stood up and moved towards the door. She felt both soldiers' eyes on her back. Somehow she didn't feel so enthusiastic about cleaning the room up. Damn! Why did he always have to come out of the shadows and upset her? She went into the kitchen and began preparing dinner.

Harry arrived home, changed, and went up to the workshop. He came back about half an hour later, washed his hands, and they both sat down to tea.

They talked about how their day had gone and then, both at the same time, said, 'I've been thinking.' Their combined outburst was so beautifully simultaneous that one would have thought they had been practising it for weeks. The pair sat there for several minutes laughing their heads off.

'Boy, we certainly know how to make our own fun,' giggled Helen. 'Okay, you go first.'

'I was wondering if it would be okay to clean out some of George's stuff in the workshop. Reason being, I'd like to have a go at pouring some of his moulds. That Pat Thorpe I told you about said he'd give me some tips.'

'Well, isn't that strange. I decided I'd like to clean out the room that all of George's personal stuff is in.'

'Well, if you want a hand at all, I'm here. Your squire will handle furniture as well as gardening, slashing, driving, loving, and so forth. It's all in my contract, you know. Just ring your little bell and I'll gladly come arunnin', ma'am.' Two seconds later, 'Hey, that doesn't include chewing my ear off!'

'Sorry, you were just a bit irresistible. But seriously, I'd like to do the room but I really don't know how Tas would feel about it.'

'You'll just have to approach him cautiously and ask.'

They left it at that.

Harry had his head under a tractor bonnet when he felt a tap on his shoulder. It was Reg.

'Harry, you got a visitor.' He looked around and recognised the farmer who had spoken to him the previous week.

'You're Harry Evans, aren't you?' He made it sound like a statement rather than a question.

'That's dead right.'

'My name's Dave. Dave Robbins. Got a few acres out of Dunedin. I want someone with a bit of know-how to do a few jobs on the farm and I certainly don't want to pay the hourly rate that these garages charge. I thought it might help your pocket a bit and me at the same time. Just a bit of mechanical stuff. Nothing too complicated. I'm as mean as cat shit and hate paying for nothing. Get my drift?'

Harry wiped his hands on a piece of rag, paused, then answered, 'Nice to meet you again. I've been wondering what it was all about. Look, Dave, it's almost my lunchtime. Can you wait five minutes and I'll meet you outside and we can talk then. Is that okay? You don't mind?'

'Suits me to a T.' He moved outside and was waiting in his truck when Harry found him.

'Now,' he continued, 'know where Christmas Creek is? Well, I got a farm just up from there. You can either catch the train up or you can come in by road. Got transport of your own.?'

Harry thought swiftly. 'No,' he replied.

'Doesn't matter. Come up by train either Friday night or Saturday morning. One of me boys can run you back Sunday afternoon or evening. When can you start?'

Harry quickly made up his mind. 'This weekend and I'll come by train Friday night. We'll try it out. You may not even like me!'

'Wrong there, Harry lad. I consider meself a good judge of character. You stood up to Reuben Jackson about that tractor business the other day, and that was good enough for me. Anyone that can take him down stands okay. Here are some instructions the wife wrote out on how to get to our place.' He handed Harry a slip of paper with directions on it and drove off. They hadn't even discussed wages or anything.

Harry scratched his head and went inside. He thought to himself that he might have made a sad mistake in accepting the job so eagerly, but he supposed that a person had to take a chance now and again, and anyway, you've got to make your own luck and wasn't he riding a high these days? Time would tell. He crossed his fingers, just in case.

He had a funny feeling that Helen might have been a bit dubious about him being absent for the weekend but to his surprise she seemed to be quite in favour of him getting an extra job.

'Never ever turn down a chance to work. You may not be asked again. Give it a go, Harry.'

He felt happier because of her attitude. Somehow it was very important to him to have her approval. Tas thought it was a good idea, too. Strath, however, cautioned Harry. 'Just watch he doesn't try to diddle you. Some of these cockies think they can get blood from stone. Just be careful. By the same token, as long as you're getting a bit more experience then just go with the flow and have fun at the same time.'

Harry kept his own ideas to himself. He was curious and his mind was made up.

Friday evening found him waiting for the train. It was a goods train and stopped quite frequently at all the little whistle-stops. Finally, after a somewhat tortuous journey along the banks of the Taieri River, its minute tributary, Christmas Creek, came into sight. The train drew to a halt and as soon as Harry stepped down onto the little platform the engine impatiently gave a toot and steamed off, leaving Harry looking rather bereft on the little siding. There was a tiny shed and some cattleyards and nothing else. No welcoming party except two grazing sheep that seemed to have completely ignored the train pulling to a halt only yards from them. A gravel road wandered down from the yards to a creek and Harry could see it then wound its way up a fairly steep incline until finally disappearing over the hill. He wondered whether or not he should start walking.

At that moment he heard the noise of a racing engine and a small Fargo truck came speeding down the hill at breakneck speed and hit the ford with a tremendous splash before climbing up towards the whistle-stop station. The brakes, with a protesting squeal, coaxed the truck to a stop. Dave leaned out of the window. 'Hello, Harry. Sorry I'm a bit late. Had an argument with a bull that got out of the yards. Hop in and we'll be away.'

Harry slung his bag up onto the back and climbed in. The Fargo leapt away up the hill. Looking out of the side window Harry, owing to the speed they were travelling, hoped that Dave knew the road. He wasn't too keen on the way he cut all the blind corners and he was relieved to hear the driver say, 'Well, that's one thing about driving on a road that's only used by one car – you can do this sort of thing.'

The homestead was situated along the top of a ridge with a tremendous view in every direction. They stopped outside and Dave said, 'Bring your gear in, Harry.'

His wife had a late tea ready and after they had finished Harry, despite Daisy's protests, dried the dishes. Later they sat at the big kitchen table and talked. Dave seemed pleased to learn, amongst other things, that Harry could shoot, and he suggested that maybe he would take Harry out for a bit of fun later. Harry slept well and early next morning both of them were out in the woolshed.

Dave explained that a lot of mechanical things just needed 'duffying up' a bit, as he put it, and he hoped Harry could help with these as he himself was too busy. Harry got the strange idea that Dave didn't like things mechanical, especially when they broke down. There was a workshop of sorts next to the woolshed and Harry was delighted to see that it contained, amongst other things, an electric welder. When he commented on this Dave just said, 'I've had it for a year now and I just don't seem to be able to make enough time to use the bloody thing. And God knows there's enough things around here that need welding.'

'Well,' said Harry,' no time like the present.' Before he knew it Dave had collected a pile of broken equipment that needed touching up and mending with the arc welder. Harry was in his element and set to with a will. It was a good machine and with all the practice that he had had in the last few months he was quite confident. Dave just left him to it.

The workshop was sufficiently fitted out with the necessary equipment to make his repair work much easier to carry out. By the time lunch break arrived he had 'hit the straps' and was into it.

Dave came in to watch for a while and tell Harry lunch was ready. He was pleasantly surprised to see what Harry had achieved in the relatively short period that he had been there, and said something to that effect. Harry glowed.

Dave's wife was very keen on horses and that, apparently, was how the pair first met. She had a beautiful hunter standing over sixteen hands high and to see her in the saddle one could see that she was in complete control. It was a high-spirited beast and needed plenty of work. She often joined her husband on a muster and was as good at working dogs as some other shepherds around the district. She reckoned her horse could walk at about twelve miles an hour. Most horses when moving at that pace would usually have to either use a gut-wrenching jog or break into a very slow canter, but this one would hold its head up and go like the wind and all the rider had to do was sit there, quite comfortable in the saddle, with the minimum of body movement. It was comparable to sitting in an armchair. Everyone wanted to ride her horse, of course. Everyone, that is, except the roustabout, Alan, a tousled, red-headed young fellow who loved pig hunting. He had immediately taken a shine to Harry and wanted to show him everything at once. He seemed rather peeved that Harry was staying at the boss's house and not in the shearers' quarters.

Sunday morning found Harry back at his job of repairing the fractured pieces of equipment that Dave had collected. It being Sunday he had to deal with Alan's presence, as it was his day off. Alan followed Harry around like a willing little puppy asking innumerable and inane questions. He wasn't the brightest of lads but his curiosity was insatiable. He considered himself an authority on pig hunting and couldn't see any reason why Harry couldn't come with him there and then to do a bit of shooting. He was about seventeen and had worked for Dave for two years. Willing as hell, but a pain in the neck to Harry, who was determined to try to finish the job in hand.

He was still hard at it late in the afternoon when Dave came into the workshop and ordered a halt.

'Time to finish, Harry,' he said. 'How about tea before we leave?'

'No thanks, Dave. I think I'm ready to hit the road any time now.'

'Okay by me.'

After taking leave of Dave's wife, and Alan of course, they set off back to Dunedin. It was past eight at night when Harry arrived at the house. As he got out of the car Dave handed Harry an envelope and said, 'Thanks, Harry. That was great. I'll ring you at work sometime during the week to let you know about next weekend. See if you can make it. And thanks again.'

Harry went into the house to find Helen was on her own. She kissed Harry.

'I really missed you. Welcome home.'

It felt like home, too, thought Harry. On opening the envelope he was pleasantly surprised to find a five pound note - two weeks wages!

Class had just finished and he heard his name called. It was Leda. 'Harry, what on earth has happened to Dinky? I just heard that he's in deep trouble. Do you know anything about it?'

'I'm sorry, Lee. I meant to come and tell you what had happened but I'm afraid I just got tied up a bit. Come and sit down on this bench.'

He enlightened her as to everything that had happened and what had first led him to suspect what Dinky was up to.

'You mean it was me that first gave you the tip, and you didn't tell me?'

He then had to explain the whole thing right through and the reasons behind not keeping her in the picture. The look of relief on her face was indescribable.

'So you went out of your way to protect me?' she said incredulously.

'I only told a little white lie actually. I had a fair idea that Dinky would have dropped you off home before he returned the car,' said Harry. 'Sorry about that, though. Really I am.'

'The creep. I had to hit him over the head with my shoe.'

'Oh,' said Harry and left it at that.

'I owe you, Harry Evans,' she said, and kissed him on the cheek.

He thought a bit about it on the way home. Steady now, Harry, he thought to himself.

Helen had gone into the room again while Harry was away and cogitated deeply about what she should do. Sitting there at the desk she had pondered a while, then opened his top drawer and pulled out some letters. Some, as she had noticed the other day, were still not opened. She decided that perhaps Tas had put them in there after George had died, though it was strange that he had not even bothered to read them. Two of them were from Egypt and one was a letter that George had obviously written to Len and had been returned unread. She looked at the date and estimated that was about the time that Len had been killed. She checked the date and sliced open the first letter from the war zone. It was from Len and dated Monday January 31st 1944. It read:

*Dear George,*
*Well here I am again with my usual small quota for the week. My word! I sure did have a lovely spread for lunch today. The cooks really excelled themselves. Your two letters arrived okay, also your mum's cable dated 10th December. Nice to hear you are getting over that nasty operation and into your 'rock hounding' again. I don't quite get what you were up to up the Taieri River. I can't quite work out what you were doing there. It doesn't make sense somehow. Remember the times we used to sit with Shirley Atkinson and swap notes with one another? If what you want to tell me is that important why don't you get back to Standard Three again, like the old days? I might be able to decipher the cross words, ha ha. I hope your memory isn't that bad and you can write some sense to me, old pal.*

*Well on to more mundane things. I'm so sorry those snaps didn't arrive. I suppose it's not worth bothering about them now but if I ever come across that officer who censored my mail I'll tell him what I think of him…*

The letter went on in a similar vein for another seven pages but the bit about Shirley Atkinson puzzled Helen and she decided to talk to Harry about it. More mystery, she thought. Her foot started to ache and it was time to start getting tea ready. She didn't read any more letters.

# CHAPTER ELEVEN

Pat met Harry after class and came home with him to have a look see at the lead-melting equipment in the garage. He made a few comments about Harry being so fortunate to have the use of such a workplace. Helen came out and both Harry and she sat while Pat explained the elementary principles of lead pouring. He said he would come on a weekend when Harry wasn't busy on the farm and have a bit of fun casting lead soldiers. It really was pretty simple and Harry could possibly have had more fun working out the pitfalls on his own but he had decided that he liked Pat and they seemed to click okay.

'Can you make some bronze ones too?' asked Helen.

'Not with this sort of equipment here,' replied Pat. 'You have to have some bigger stuff than this to handle the higher temperatures. This is only kid's stuff.'

Helen didn't ask any further questions. Something didn't seem to fit properly, but she couldn't quite put her finger on it. Some words from *Alice in Wonderland* came to mind. How did they go? Something about things getting 'curiouser and curiouser'.

They went inside and after a cup of tea Pat left. It was almost midnight before the couple finally retired to their separate beds. Tas still hadn't arrived home.

The insistent hammering on the door awakened Harry. He pulled his trousers on, went down the large passage to the front of the house and opened the lead-glassed door. At that moment Helen poked her head into the passage and asked sleepily, 'Harry, what's happening?'

Harry opened the door wider. There were two policemen standing on the porch in the rain. One was holding a torch. 'Could we speak to Mrs Mann?' asked the biggest man.

'Certainly,' replied Harry and went to call Helen, but by this time she was standing behind him pulling on her dressing-gown.

'What is it, Harry?' she repeated.

Before he could answer the policeman stepped forward. 'Mrs Mann? May we come in?'

Harry opened the door even wider and stepped back, motioning the couple inside. They all moved into the still warm front room.

'Would you like to sit down, Mrs Mann?' one of the policemen said to Helen. 'I'm afraid we have some bad news.' Helen sat down on the big chair and in a low, controlled voice said, 'What's happened? It's Tas, isn't it?'

'Yes, I'm afraid your husband was involved in a serious accident this evening.'

'Run over?' she said instinctively, thinking of his departure from the pub along the road.

'No, Mrs Mann. This happened at his place of employment at about ten o'clock tonight.'

'But he wasn't working tonight,' both Harry and Helen exclaimed together.

'The circumstances haven't been gone into fully as yet, Mrs Mann. In the meantime he's in the burns department of Dunedin Hospital. He's unconscious at present but if you wish to go down now we can take you.'

'No need to, thank you, Constable. We have a car and Mrs Mann and myself will go down right away. Is there anything else?'

'No, that will be all just for now.' As an afterthought he added, 'I have an idea they will require a signature from you, Mrs Mann.'

The policemen left and within minutes Harry and Helen had dressed and were driving down to the hospital in silence.

Harry helped her up the steps and they soon found themselves outside the small room where Tas lay. The ward sister showed them in and it was immediately obvious that Tas had been in a fire. One side of his face was heavily bandaged and his shoulder and arm were completely swathed in dressings. At that moment a young doctor entered the room and introduced himself.

'What on earth happened to him?' asked Harry impulsively.

'Are you one of the family?' asked the doctor, looking at him.

Helen immediately answered, 'Yes, he is, and I'm Mrs Mann.' The doctor glanced at her and it was plain to see by the momentary look on his face that he was puzzled by the marked disparity of the patient's and Helen's ages. It showed only for an instant but it was there all the same.

'Apparently, from what I can gather from his workmate who accompanied him here, Mr Mann was at work and fell sideways into a heap of molten coke which had just been taken out of the ovens. He sank into it and badly burned his left arm and fingers. There are also extensive burns to his face on the left side and we may have to amputate his hand, and as a last resort his arm. He's heavily sedated now and we'll operate as soon as the necessary papers have been signed. Mrs Mann, will you give us approval to go ahead with any remedial surgery we consider necessary?'

'Of course,' replied Helen in a low voice. 'When will you operate, Doctor?'

'As soon as you've signed the forms. Mrs Mann,' said the doctor patiently. He was quite used to dealing with relatives in shock. 'I suggest you go home in the meantime. He won't be out of the anaesthetic till at least ten o'clock tomorrow morning. You may remain if you wish, but really there is no point in it. Do you understand, Mrs Mann?'

She nodded.

'We will certainly contact you as soon as there is information.'

They drove home in silence. Harry made Helen a cup of tea. 'I wonder why he was at work?' he remarked.

'I'm curious about that too,' she said.

'I think it's about time you turned in. It'll be a long day tomorrow.'

'Poor Tas,' Helen said sadly. 'I wonder how it happened? He was usually so careful at work. We'll find out tomorrow most probably. Harry, would it be awful if I slept with you tonight? It seems a bit heartless but I feel lonelier than I've felt for a long time. Will you please let me sleep with you?' She sounded like a small girl frightened of the dark.

'Course you can.'

They undressed and climbed into bed. He cradled her in his arms as she gently sobbed herself to sleep, and for a long time afterwards he just lay there with his eyes open, wondering what was going to happen to her.

First thing in the morning Harry went down to the phone box and rang the hospital. Tas was in a stable condition. He then rang Ted who said he could take time off, no sweat, and Strath, who hadn't heard about the accident. Then he went back and talked to Helen about what they should do that day.

Eleven o'clock found them back at the hospital. They stayed beside Tas's bed all day. His arm had had to be removed just above the wrist but he was doing all right. He finally talked to both of them that afternoon, and though he was heavily dosed, was quite lucid. The police had not been able to get a coherent statement from him earlier but would return the following morning. When they left that evening at about eight o'clock he was resting comfortably.

Two days later he was sitting up in bed, with Helen and Harry once again at his side. The police had taken a statement and were making more enquiries. Helen excused herself to go to the toilet, and as she was absent Tas said in a strange tone, 'I want to see you, Harry, and have a talk to you on your own. Is there any chance of visiting me without Helen's knowledge?'

Puzzled, Harry replied, 'I can come in at lunch time tomorrow. Would that be all right?'

'Good.'

Helen returned and sat at the bedside while Harry and Tas talked on about mundane matters. She looked around the ward. Things hadn't changed. Clean. Clinical. Antiseptic smells. Starched uniforms, making that sound that only smartly moving nurses can produce, always moving with a purpose.

*She lay there inert, her mind overwhelmed by the painkilling drugs. The nurse had come in with the young doctor and she felt a prick in her arm and the doctor was talking to her in soft tones. The lights assumed a different hue and she watched the ceiling pass over her head at varying speeds. Three masked faces peered at her from above. A mask thing was placed over her face. She heard a voice, talking, calling her name. 'Now, Helen,' it said. She was told to count down from twelve. That was easy because she was good at figures, wasn't she? From twelve. Why didn't they give her something harder? Twelve… eleven… ten… easy meat, she could whiz through this test… nine… the magic number nine… no silly, you've said that… eight… then nine… no, wrong way. No, it was SO nine… Nine… nine… Damn! Somebody's shifted the ni…*

'Okay to go home now, Helen?'

She kissed Tas on the cheek and they set off for home. 'He's looking a bit better, don't you think, Harry?'

It was late when they got home and she fell asleep almost immediately. Harry was there. She felt safe.

Harry lay there in the dark for ages wondering just exactly what it was that Tas had to tell him tomorrow.

*He lay there in the clinically clean bed, staring up at the off-grey ward ceiling and wondering just exactly what he was going to tell Harry the next day. The pain had reduced itself to a deep throbbing ache which he could endure without too much of a problem. The pain in his heart, however, was of a completely different nature. There was no medicine in the night sister's medical cupboard which could alleviate it. The anguish which he had endured since his brother's untimely death somehow seemed to get worse every time he relived the events leading up to that day.*

*The day had started so simply. He remembered asking George to have a look at the front wheel of his 1930 Wentworth, which he seldom drove. He always admitted that he wasn't a mechanic, and anyway, George knew more about such things. George quite happily said he would and it didn't take him long to find the problem. The grinding noise Tas had been experiencing had been caused by the front wheel bearing collapsing. George had walked down to the garage and bought a replacement. He fitted it on and did the necessary adjustment to it.*

*'Still got to have a new split pin put in the castellated nut to lock it, Tas. I'll leave you to do that. Don't want the bloody wheel falling off, do we? I've got a few things to do. I'll see you later.'*

*With a grin he placed the shiny steel split pin on top of the nail box he had been using as a seat. He went to walk out the door.*

*'Hey, hold on a second, George. Just when are you and Helen getting hitched?' he had innocently asked. To his utter dismay he discovered he had said completely the wrong thing to his brother. The change in George's manner was instantaneous and a malevolent, cunning scowl came over his face. 'I knew it! You're both scheming to get me, aren't you? Plotting, I know! Don't think I don't know all about it!' The intense look of hatred was frightening to perceive. He had looked at his brother in sheer disbelief. What on earth had got into him? He watched George stalk out of the building. Springing to his feet, he had followed his brother into the sunlight.*

*The replacement pin lay forgotten on the nail box.*

Visiting hour was two o'clock that afternoon and Harry was waiting in the passage when the bell rang. Everyone charged into the wards supervised by a glowering matron who looked on the invasion as a personal affront to her. Fortunately Tas had no other visitors and as Harry sat down beside him he managed to smile, and said, 'Glad you came, Harry. I've been trying to get my thoughts together to perhaps explain a few things.'

Harry just sat.

'First of all, this stupid accident shouldn't have happened. I'd had a fair bit to drink and decided to visit the works to see a mate of mine on swing shift. It was about a horse, of all things. That's when I tripped. Now, Harry, between you and me things are not too good with this arm and I have a premonition that they're not going to get better. Just that silly feeling. So, I want to tell you a few things that I've never told anyone before. It's about George and myself. I was much older than him and looked after him all my life. I loved him as a brother should. I thought that he was going to marry Helen and I was as happy as hell. But when he returned from that convalescent home he started changing before my eyes almost day by day. I knew somehow he was upsetting Helen but I kept well out of it. Lovers' tiffs and all that. Nothing to do with me. Well, one day while he was doing a small job on my car, he got into a particularly nasty mood and told me that he had got Helen in the family way. I was quite happy because that's what I had been expecting to happen eventually. But when I told him so he flew into a hell of a rage and said that he wasn't going to marry her; the only reason he had proposed was to get into bed with her. I said it was a dirty trick to play on a young, innocent girl. I thought we were going to come to blows.

'All of a sudden he changed again and it was astonishing how quickly his mood had swung. It was as if I was talking to my little brother when he was small and happy and our argument had never happened. A complete sort of Jekyll and Hyde. To cheer him up and to get him calmed down I said the four of us would go for a ride in my car. I can still see Helen looking at me as though I knew something. While we were driving George kept prattling on and on as though he was trying to impress us – just like a little boy vying for attention. Then suddenly the front of the car dropped and it was as if a big hand was pushing us sideways towards the edge. I discovered later that the front wheel had dropped off. The next instant we had gone over a bank and the car came to a crunching halt on a ledge. The car was upside down and Mum was trapped in it, and George underneath. It was the most horrible moment of my life. I tried to get Helen to help but she wouldn't move: she was holding George in her arms. Somehow I remembered that we had passed a farm entrance back up the road. I scrambled up onto the road and ran downhill till I got to the farmer's drive. My luck was in that day as he was actually driving the tractor towards me. He certainly didn't waste any time mucking about – took him no time at all to fasten a wire strop to the car and start pulling the weight of it off George. But then there was a hell of a crack and the rope snapped and hit Helen, and the car started to roll over the cliff edge. This was the worst part. God, it was horrible! I can still see it turning slowly over and over in the river. It was awful to feel so helpless. Worse was to come when I found George was dead and Helen's foot had been severed by the snapped cable. It was then that the coincidences started. He was a medic who had just been discharged from the army. A nice fellow, Jack Armstrong. He saved Helen's life. Knew exactly what to do to stem the bleeding. Not only that but he had been with George in the desert when he had his accident. Didn't find that out till much later. He was too late to save his life a second time. Helen was taken to hospital and the rest was a blur of police and Mum's and George's funeral. One big happy family, and in two minutes it had all changed.

After the funeral I went out and got as tight as a tick for two days solid, then I realised I had to do something for poor Helen. She had looked after the three of us for that long, I had to somehow pay her back. I enlisted the help of the local Registry Office who provided the necessary papers and I can't even remember if I asked Helen if she would marry me. She was so dosed up with painkillers it didn't make any difference. She agreed and we were married. She finally came home and carried on looking after the house. I never forced myself on her and she never asked for any consummation of the marriage. The thing was that I married her to give George's baby a name, so her name wouldn't be dragged around the place and it wasn't till afterwards that I found she had miscarried and there was no need to have done that. I've been scared she would up and leave the house and nobody would look after me. I was being so bloody selfish about it all. That's why I've never asked for a divorce. She seems to be quite happy as she is and since you arrived she has been quite content. I'm asking you, Harry, if I don't come out of this, will you keep an eye on her?"

'All right, Tas. Don't worry about a thing. I'll see that she's all right.'

'Now, Harry, the worst thing is that apart from the demon booze I have another problem. I started gambling after the accident and that's why I work so much overtime – to try to repay my gambling debts. I'm broke, Harry. Dead broke. The house is in my name but it's going to be repossessed in a month's time if I can't keep up the debt repayments. That's what's really worrying me. Helen is going to have nowhere to go at all. I've borrowed sixteen hundred pounds on the house. The papers are in a loan shark's hands and he's told me unless the total amount is in his bank account by the end of the month then it's curtains and he'll repossess.'

Harry just sat there beside the bed. Tas had closed his eyes. The effort seemed to have been too much for him. The nurse came in and beckoned Harry out to let him rest.

'Mr Mann is in a worse way than you think. He seems to have had a very bad shock.' As Harry went to leave Tas opened his eyes. 'Sorry, lad, to foist my troubles on you but I'm glad now I've told you.' With that remark he closed his eyes.

*He felt an enormous sense of relief welling up inside his chest after he had talked to Harry. For his age he was a pretty sensible fellow. There was only one other secret now, but he had decided it was one he would take to his grave. Only he himself knew that he had forgotten to put that split pin in the axle. It was he who was responsible for the death of his mother and brother.*

Harry returned to work, although his mind wasn't on the job. He went and had a long talk to a very sympathetic Ted, filling him in on the details about Tas being in hospital and the fact that Helen was an amputee. Ted told Harry just to play things by ear and the firm would be only too happy to help out with time off.

Harry went home that evening with a heavy heart and although Helen greeted him with a big kiss at the door it was with some difficulty that he kept a cheerful countenance. She told him that she had made a start on the spare room and had sorted out quite a few papers. She was still puzzled over the business of Shirley Atkinson. He was due to go to the farm the next evening and was going to ring up Dave to tell him he couldn't make it but Helen insisted and said she would take a taxi to see Tas. He was not to worry. She would be quite all right here at home in the big house. So that was that.

Dave was there to pick him up at the Christmas Creek whistle-stop and before they went into tea he showed Harry the jobs he had lined up for the weekend. There didn't seem to be very many for him.

'Well, it's Alan's birthday on Sunday and I asked him what he wanted and of all things he said he wanted to take you pig hunting. I told him the other day there was a decent porker up in Chinaman's Gully and he wants you to shoot one. I just happened to mention you were a good shot and he wants to see you prove it. You know how mad keen he is on those damn things. So I decided I would let you go out with him instead of working. Now how's about that, Harry?' Dave said, with a big grin. 'The wife's putting on a cake for him afterwards.'

'But that's going to make you very late for running me home, isn't it?'

'Not at all. We'll both run you back to Dunedin and then we'll stay at my sister's place in Mosgiel.'

Next day Harry worked like a Trojan and was well ahead of himself by the time tea came around. Alan and he took the rifles down to the back paddock so that Harry could zero in his borrowed weapon. He insisted upon this because, as he pointed out to Alan, if you don't know where a weapon is firing, you're just wasting time. His was an old Long Tom that had been cut down and made into a rude sporting gun. A sacrifice of accuracy for lightness. Sufficient for the job, however.

Setting off early next morning through the remains of a light fog the pair walked the two miles into the gully. They had only one horse with them – to cart the trophy home, Alan explained. Harry was quite glad, for although he could ride he certainly was no expert, and he was sure Alan would try to give him a frisky beast just for laughs. Alan tethered the animal to some willows and began climbing the steep hill leading to the gully.

'Better have a breather,' Alan said, when they reached the top. This was for Harry's benefit as it was obvious that he was not as fit as the roustabout. They both lay down on the ground and took a look see at the slopes opposite. Alan was obviously enjoying himself. He had a pair of binoculars slung around his neck and, after sweeping the other side of the gully, he announced, 'The boss was right. There is a pig over there. Right along on the ridge just under the Chinaman's grave. Looks like he's been having a good old dig. Wonder how many sheep he's eaten?'

Harry raised his eyebrows. Although he had been brought up on Nana's little farm, as far as he was concerned pigs had curly tails, went 'oink' and ate cabbages and pea stalks.

'Eating sheep?'

This was Alan's chance to show some superior knowledge to this townie. 'Didn't you know pigs eat sheep?' He went on to inform the new boy about some of the strange habits of wild pigs. About how during lambing time they would smell the afterbirth and the blood on the new lamb; how they would eat the lamb and then perhaps go for the ewe, who would try at first to defend her offspring, and finally how pigs had been known to actually bail up ewes and bowl them over just to eat them. Wild pigs were to be respected. A .303 bullet could ricochet off a pig's forehead. Alan pulled off his boot and peeled down his sock and showed Harry a two-inch scar on his foot. 'That was my first pig. Maybe I was his first victim. I was certainly his last. He got me and I went back three days later and got him. I've got a whole box full of tusks at home.' He looked through the glasses again. 'We'll have to take a bit of a detour around that spur – that will give you about a hundred and fifty yard shot. Should be a doosey for you.'

'Are you sure you don't want to have a go yourself?' asked Harry.

'Hell, no. I'd get just as big a kick out of you knocking a porker off. I can get a pig anytime. No, this is your one. It's your day for a pig, my day for a birthday. Don't stuff it up, that's all I say.' He laughed. 'Now, let's go get him, Harry.'

They took about half an hour to get round to the point Alan

had chosen. They cautiously raised their heads above the rocky outcrop and sure enough, there was their target rooting in the soft ground. 'He's all yours,' whispered Alan, though they were easily 180 yards away. Harry had a good look at the conditions. He had plenty of time and decided to go for a neck shot. If the pig moved forward it would be double insurance for a shoulder hit. Harry always tried for a clean shot. His uncle had always insisted on a clean kill. No need to cause unnecessary pain. Looking around, Harry carefully checked the wind and the light. Breathed in, out, in and held it. Squeezed the trigger gently before his pulse rate went up and started waving the sight. The pig looked up and the shot was on its way.

The target just dropped.

Didn't even have a death shudder.

'Nice one, Harry,' Alan said. 'Clean shot, all right. Right behind the ear?'

'That's where it was supposed to go.'

They both clambered over the rock shelf till they reached the other side. The pig had been in a small grassy sheltered spot below a cliff. Alan pulled out his skinning knife. 'Might as well try to bleed him a little more. And get rid of his nuts at the same time.'

He worked cleanly and swiftly.

He straightened up.

'Now, I'll just go down and get the horse and be back in a flash. That's about one of the quickest pig hunts yet.'

He started to walk back down the hill to where the horse was tethered. Harry sat down on the grass and looked at the pig. It had been rooting around the area and had caused a surprising amount of damage. Quite an interesting sort of a place. It almost looked as though it had been artificially constructed. There were flat rocks placed on top of each other like a wall which had been built by human hands. Harry wondered if Alan knew about it. He moved over and looked more closely. There, leaning hard against the cliff was a small trenching tool and beside it what Harry supposed was a geologist's pick. Somebody must have lost them. Both were quite rusty. He retrieved the pick and could see it was not a mass-manufactured tool but appeared to be handmade. It had a manuka handle and on the blade were stamped the initials G.M.

Harry was standing holding both implements and still examining them when Alan returned.

'Hullo. Whatcha got there?' asked Alan.

'Somebody's fossicking tools. Must have dropped out of their bag when they were resting here, I suppose. Want them?'

'No bloody use to me.' replied Alan. 'Might as well keep them yourself.' They loaded the pig into the saddlebags and were back at the homestead within the hour. Dave was surprised to see them so soon. He thought it was a bit of a giggle to have a visitor go out, shoot a pig, and return so quickly. 'I think I might start catering to tourists and advertise it as a "Thirty-minute safari".' Harry wanted to get back and do some more work but Dave insisted, 'No, not on your *Nelly*, Harry me boy! I'm declaring a public holiday. Relax and have a beer. Then we'll cut the cake and take off for the big smoke.'

Harry just had to enter into the spirit of things. Alan had wrapped a hind leg in newspaper and he was told how to cook it when he got home. They set off and on the way Harry told Dave about what had happened to Tas.

He was pleased to get home, and Helen was pleased to see him. She held him very close and whispered in his ear, 'I've missed you so much. Welcome home. And do you know what? I've just filled the bath.'

They played in the water like a couple of two-year-olds.

'How I'm ever going to clean this mess up tomorrow morning I'll never know,' Helen complained jokingly as they started trying to towel each other down.

'I give up,' said Harry, trying to put on a disgusted stance. He picked her up and carried her into the bedroom.

'What now, squire?'

'Let the jousting commence, my lady.'

'Will you wear my handkerchief as your badge of honour, Lord Evans?' she asked.

'No,' he replied. 'I have visions of you badly bending my coat hook before the night endeth and there is no other place to hang it, my lady.'

'To hell with the handkerchief then, sir,' she said. 'Just joust.'

The tournament part of things finished, they lay there and Harry told her of the events of the past two days. When he came to the part about finding the pick he said, 'You know, Helen, I'm sure there's another just like it in the garage. Must have a look for it tomorrow.'

She then told Harry about visiting Tas and how he seemed to be recovering but there seemed to be something wrong with his spirits. She didn't expect him to take things so hard.

Harry was at a loss as to whether or not he should disclose Tas's financial problems to her. He decided not to spoil her night; she was riding such a terrific high. Helen went on to tell him that on the way back from her visit she had asked the taxi driver to take her to Shirley Atkinson's place. Shirley was at home and had warmly welcomed her inside. She used to visit Mrs Mann before she died and Helen had been round to her place long before. They hadn't seen each other since the funeral.

Helen carried on to say that while they were having afternoon tea she had brought Shirley up to date with all that had happened since George's death. She had then broached the subject of Len's letter and his reference to Standard Three and the cross. She explained about going through the mail and said it just puzzled her a bit. Shirley at first didn't have a clue what she was talking about. Then it dawned on her and she had burst out laughing. Apparently the three were great friends when they were children at school and had developed this silly code for passing messages to each other. They called it 'Cipher', and if one of them received a note with a cross on it then it meant there was a secret message in it.

Shirley had had to have a good think about it before remembering more details about the code. Finally it came to mind that hidden in the message were certain words, which were prefixed by a small cross. In other words, Helen explained to Harry, they could send a message with a lot of gobbledygook in it but the secret message was revealed when those words were joined up. Apparently George and Len had had a lot of fun passing rather salacious messages under the nose of the teacher.

'Len must have been asking George to send him a message in code to get past the censor,' Harry commented.

'Sounds like it, but he died before he got it.'

'Wait a minute!' cried Harry, sitting up in bed. 'The letter that was returned – have you burned it?'

'No. I haven't even opened it,' replied Helen.

'Then where have you put it? That would have been the last letter that George wrote to him.'

'I'll find it. I know exactly where it is.'

She hopped out of bed and out of the room without even bothering to put her nightdress on. As she came back Harry just could not refrain from ogling her bouncing breasts. She glared at him. 'Keep your mind above your belt.'

'I was keeping my mind above *your* belt,' he replied.

She climbed into bed and together they opened George's letter.

*Dear Len,*

*Well, here I am again. Great to get your letter. What luck! Course I remember Shirley! She's with me now! Found her address – she still lives in that big house.*

*Well, I've gone and done it now. Remember I always said I wanted to get into Helen? Well, I finally did. I asked her to marry me and she now thinks it's sort of okay to have a little bit of what's good for the rooster. I was a bit disappointed with her performance though. She generally lies there like a wet sack. Then she tells me she's got a bun the oven. Well that did it! I'm going to strike out on my own and not be tied down by a gold wedding ring. Might settle in the Hindon Gorge area and also see a Chinese market gardener there. Look at my cache of money in the bank. The snows have melted and it's time for me to get down on my knees and thank the Lord for not yet casting you and me into the next world.*

*Come home Len and stop playing at toy soldiers. The sooner I get out of here the better. Both Helen and Tas are spying on me. They are actually after you know what. But we'll beat them at their own game, won't we? My good old mate. Look after yourself and come home safe.*

*Your best friend in the whole world,*

*George*

Helen's cheeks were wet with tears by the time Harry had finished reading the letter.

'I have never been so disgusted and humiliated in my life. Fancy writing to his friend about me like that. And now you've read it too. Oh Harry, I'm so ashamed of myself.'

Harry tried to comfort her. 'Look, he was slowly going mad, Helen. How else do you explain that bit about you and Tas spying on him?' He eased her back on the pillow and stroked her neck. 'C'mon, Helen. It's all over and finished now, so don't let yourself get so upset about it.'

She gradually calmed down. She even allowed herself a small smile when she reminded herself that Harry would look after her and George could no longer touch her. As they lay there Harry decided it was high time that he told her about Tas's financial predicament. She grew more afraid as she listened to him. 'Why was he such a fool as to gamble all that away? How much does he owe? Sixteen hundred pounds? Good God. What's going to happen to me? God only knows.' She started to cry again.

Suddenly Harry exclaimed excitedly, 'Hey! We haven't even tried to see if there is a message in that letter. Let's take a closer look.'

On the second reading they could see the very faint crosses that were interspersed throughout the text. Harry got up and found a pencil. He underlined the words with crosses next to them and the content of the message became clearer. Together they read:

*Great luck! I've Found big strike gold in Hindon Gorge also a Chinese cache have melted down into toy soldiers*

'It looks as though George did find gold after all. Maybe the fact that he had found it turned him a little bit strange in his attitude.

Most probably he found a nugget and thought it was worth a fortune. Gold fevered miners act up that way sometimes. Wonder what he meant by *also* a Chinese cache?'

Harry looked at the clock. It was past midnight.

'Get something warm on. We're going up to the garage to take a look around.'

They both got half-dressed and went up to the stables. Helen held his arm as she clumped up the path. 'People are going to think we're a bit cuckoo roaming around at this hour of the night,' Harry muttered.

Having turned on the light they had a look in the chest where George kept his soldiers. There was no sign of gold there.

'Not here,' said Harry.

'What about the bronze ones I saw him pouring that day?' asked Helen.

'No. Remember Pat said he didn't have the equipment to cast bronze?'

'I know. But I *saw* him doing it.'

Harry looked hard at a box of little castings lying in the chest. Elsewhere in the chest there were brightly painted soldiers, but this box contained only Red Indians, still in their grey undercoat. He picked one up and looked at it carefully. Going over to the workbench he found a chisel and scraped the back of the toy. It shone.

'It wasn't bronze you saw at all. It was gold!' Harry almost shouted. 'He told you it was bronze. How cunning can you get?'

Helen could not stifle her gasp of amazement. 'You mean that George was going to paint all these and keep them a secret?'

'Yes, honey, and that's exactly what we're going to do too,' said Harry.

'Let's go back to bed.'

'And discuss it?'

'Of course, and maybe other things too.'

So they did.

Both were up bright and early next morning to take the wonderful news to Tas. They had to wait till ten o'clock: visiting hours were very strict. As they drove up their street they passed a police car going in the opposite direction, and for a moment Harry thought he saw it turn up their drive. He assumed he was mistaken and carried on to the hospital. They bought a bunch of flowers and some fruit on the way and were bubbling over with excitement. They made their way up to the ward where Tas was and went in. The bed was made but empty. Tas had obviously been shifted.

Harry went to get some information from the sister in charge, who immediately came over to Helen and said, 'Are you Mrs Mann?'

'Yes,' said Helen.

'Could you just wait here, please,' said the sister, 'and I'll get the doctor. He'll want to see you.'

It was the nice young doctor. 'Bad news I'm afraid, Mrs Mann. Your husband passed away this morning. The stress was just too much for him and his heart failed him. I presume you knew he had a weak heart? He passed away peacefully about an hour ago. We actually requested a police car to drive out to your place. It only left here a little while ago, but you must have passed each other. I'm terribly sorry, Mrs Mann, but there was nothing we could do. The combined effects of the burns and the operation were just too much for him. He went quite peacefully though. To be quite frank, it looked to me as though he'd had just about enough of the pain. I'm awfully sorry I couldn't do more.'

They walked into the shaded little room where Tas had been placed. Helen stood by the bed for a long time. She then bent down and kissed Tas on the small area of exposed skin on his forehead. 'He was a good man,' she whispered.

As they walked down the corridor she burst into tears. 'Poor Tas. He didn't even get the chance to hear the good news, did he, Harry?'

They stepped out into the sunshine. It was a nice sunny day though both of them failed to be aware of it. Helen turned and leaned on his shoulder. 'Take me home, Harry. Please. Just take me home.'

Time eventually dims the pain of loss. The tears shed in secret become less, as the memory becomes more opaque. Only the sharpest tinges of regret and guilt surface occasionally but these too become less frequent. These are replaced gradually by the knowledge that there *are* good times to be discovered. Good moments to be explored to their fullest. Good company of a loved one to be enjoyed. Sharing of confidences, sharing of companionship freely given. Deepening trust in the other. Cemetery visits become less as the guilt fades. As these good times go on they gradually blot out the memory of the bad ones. Tides advance and recede. Life goes on.

Harry was sitting at his study desk in the room which George had originally occupied. No trace of him remained. Helen had made sure of that. He started writing:

*Dear Maggs,*
*Well, I just thought I'd better sit down and answer your welcome letter which arrived last Wednesday. I was going to surprise you by replying straight away, but you know me – leave it till the last minute!*

*There's been a heck of a lot of water pass underneath my bridge since I last wrote, which seems ages ago (probably was!). I told you about Tas, the fellow whom I boarded with, and his awful accident. Doesn't actually seem like it but he passed away just over two months ago. Well, after the funeral I sat down with the landlady (his wife, Helen), who has been extremely good to me. Tried to help her sort a few things out. She was very upset about the whole affair because she lost her fiancé and his mother in a bad car crash about four years before. Tas was his brother and now she has no one to look after her. Did I tell you she lost a leg in the same crash? We found letters from his loan company threatening to repossess the house if the debt wasn't paid off by the end of the month. It appeared that Tas had been a heavy gambler and mortgaged the house to the hilt.*

*Helen was very upset and decided she would have to sell everything to pay off part of the debt. Well, we both went through a lot of personal stuff that her mother had put away and you'd never believe it but we came across quite a tidy quantity of rough old jewellery that didn't look like it was worth anything, but turned out to be made of gold. We think that it might have been cast by a member of Mrs Mann's family years ago. Maybe as far back as the early goldrush days. We will never know. We took it down to Stewart Dawsons, the jewellers, and they gave us an excellent price for most of it. There's still some left. Helen has now enough money to pay off the mortgage and has bought herself a car, which has been modified to allow her to drive, even with one leg. I'm so happy for her. She's been a great help to me with my maths and other lessons and has put a lot of night work in with me to get me through. It certainly has paid off as I managed to win the Top Apprentice Cup at Tech this year. The boss was over the moon. Helen wants to go to university and become a teacher. She can afford this now. I'm taking correspondence lessons and would still like to become a pilot. We'll see how I go at the end of this next year.*

*By the way, I've recently found out that Nana left me quite a large sum of money which no one knew about. Fancy keeping it a secret for so long! She left everything to me. But I'm going to make sure Mum gets some. Don't want to be greedy, eh? I'm going to invest the rest. Things are really looking up. Dinky and Pug got put on probation for a year. Serves them right. I hope you're looking after Roy and catching plenty of possums. The landlady has said I can have free board and lodging for all the work I've been doing for her. I'm trying to think how I can show her my appreciation.*

*Almost forgot. Can you come down for my eighteenth birthday next weekend? Helen has promised to bake me a cake. You can doss down in my bed. Just like old times, eh? Hope you've given up snoring!*
*Looking forward to seeing you,*
*Your old friend,*
*Harry*

The writer paused in his efforts, scanned the letter through once again, then signed it with a flourish. He showed it to his companion who, dressed in her bathrobe, had already been reading it over his shoulder while running her fingers through his hair. They both acted as though they were sharing a secret and enjoying it. She skimmed over the letter once more and they burst out laughing in unison.

'You mean I have to sleep all alone in my own bed while Maggot's staying here?' Mock concern scarcely concealed in her serenely happy face.

'I guess so. Have you any better ideas?'

'I certainly have, Harry.' Helen grinned wickedly. 'I certainly have.'

The letter fell to the floor, unnoticed, as they departed from the kitchen in what some people might have considered to be unseemly haste.

# EPILOGUE

The musterer had finished clearing the sheep from the steep gorge side that ran down to the Taieri River just upstream from the Hindon railway station, and had returned to where he had tethered his horse to the boundary fence three hours earlier. With the horse he normally rode he usually only had to drop the reins and the animal would remain in that area, grazing. This horse, however, had a mind of its own and would finish up anywhere. He approached the horse gently, talking to it all the time in a low, comforting tone. The horse's eyes rolled back into its head. It had obviously been badly treated by somebody and if it were approached in too vigorous a manner then it would have no qualms in tearing half the fence out, if the bridle was strong enough. The rider had tied the reins with a piece of string; in the event of the horse snatching it would save the cost of another snapped bridle. This did not, however, prevent the horse from taking off if he was too slow to get to the bridle. It was a good high country horse and apart from this annoying trait it was well worth trying to retrain it. The musterer sighed and kept on talking in his crooning tone.

He fortunately had just untied the horse when around an outcrop of rocks trooped seven uniformed young ladies, rather out of breath. They seemed surprised at the appearance of the horse and rider.

The young lady in front, obviously the leader, came up to him and said, 'Oh, hello.'

'Hello,' replied the musterer.

'I wonder if you can help us. We're doing a field march and apparently there is a Chinaman's grave somewhere around here.'

'Oh, I guess that would have to be Wing Two's grave. It's the only one we have here.' His eyes twinkled. 'Just around the big rock there. Hold on and I'll show you.' He led them down the hill a little way and there, nestled in a sheltered recess in the cliff face, stood a marble headstone. On it was the simple inscription:

*Xio Gung*
*CHINA*
*Drowned in the Three O'Clock*
*He shot better than he swam*
*September 1863*

The girls clustered around the simple stone, strangely silent while viewing this bit of history. 'Did you say he had another name?' one of them asked.

The musterer had taken a shiny crumpled tobacco tin from his pocket, snapped the lid open, and with a tissue paper stuck to his upper lip he selected a suitable amount of the weed between his thumb and forefinger. 'Yeah. My grandfather knew him well. He was only a lad when he first met Wing, as he called him, and it was he that buried him here. Grandad later bought all the land around. He and Wing prospected all this claim. This sheep station is still in my family. Grandad didn't know whether a Chinaman had to be buried facing the sun or which way was correct. He even heard of the idea that they were supposed to be buried standing up. Anyway, Grandad decided that Wing would feel quite comfortable right here. Got to admit it's a nice spot. His name? He got that from Grandad too. They were very good friends. Story goes that he let him have a go with his rifle one day and the Chinaman dropped two ducks with the one shot. Winged two. Get it?'

He finished rolling his durry, expertly slid it along his tongue tip and lit it.

'Story goes that he found enough gold and was booked to go home to marry his sweetheart in China. The night before he left he got into the turps with Grandad and on the way back to his hut he fell into the water, hit his head and drowned right here in the Three O'clock Stream. They found him later, hooked onto a willow branch. He was lucky he didn't get carried out into the Taieri River.

They never found any gold in his belongings. Must have sent it back to China before he left. Grandad felt pretty crook about the whole thing and paid for his headstone. When I was just a kid he used to tell me quite a lot about Wing. He certainly seemed to have a lot of time for him. I can remember him once telling me about his girlfriend. Said she was called a flower or something like a lotus. That's it, I remember now, Beautiful Lotus. Wing had shown him a picture of her one time. Reckoned she was a real looker. Young as I was I had a feeling he had fallen in love with her picture himself. Never found out if she knew Wing died or not.

'A few of the church locals were upset that Grandad had spent money on burying a heathen. Chinamen, as they were called, were not accepted by the run-of-the-mill townspeople. At Lawrence they had to be buried outside the town limits. That didn't faze Grandad one bit! He didn't take any nonsense from anyone and told them it had nothing to do with them. Called them a pack of bloody sanctimonious hypocrites. Funny, I often pop in here to say hello to the old fellow and have a smoke whenever I'm mustering this block. I call him an old fellow but he was the same age as my grandad when he died. Only twenty-five. You pronounce his name Shogun. Bit funny having an 'x' in your name, eh?'

He had finished rolling his durry and having lit it, turned and grasped the horse's mane.

'Well, I must get going or those sheep will be doubling back on me.' With a slight grunt of exertion (he wasn't that young any more) he mounted his horse, saluted them with the butt of his stock whip and rode off at an easy ambling gait that the horse could keep up all day. The seven or so dogs which had been resting in the shade rose as one and followed, occasionally looking up at him as if pleading that they be the next one to be honoured with the task of working the sheep.

The Girl Guide leader jumped to her feet and picked up her staff. 'Well, I must say that was very interesting. Time's marching on, girls, and we can't stand gawking all day now, can we?'

The spell was broken.

She led the group down to the stream where they stopped and had a quick sandwich lunch. As they were leaving, the flag bearer came across a pan resting by the bank. Beside it there was a pile of freshly dug spoil and, putting a small amount of this into the pan, she made a great show of washing the dirt in the water. 'Gold! I've struck gold!' she said. 'I'm rich!' she screeched, jumping up and down in feigned excitement. The leader had to almost scream at her. 'Cynthia Waghorn! If you don't put that down and come at once I'll have to give you at least twenty demerits for this trip. Put it down, I say, and stop acting up! I've just about had enough of your nonsense.'

The would-be goldminer reluctantly placed the pan beside the bank and stood up. She looked across to where the pack leader was. Picking up the banner she checked once more to see that the leader was not looking her way, then surreptitiously gave the pan a vicious kick, sending it skidding onto the surface of the stream. With a backward, baleful look at it she turned and started walking up the track towards the bridge.

The pan with its alluvial cargo floated in erratic patterns for quite some time before suddenly being caught in the current and momentarily gathering speed. A projecting rock hanging low in the water caught its lip and overturned it. Its contents were spilled out, and as they sank the flaky gold pieces cast sparkling, flashing reflections in the murky water. One of these particles caught the attention of the large brown trout lurking in the depths. It darted out, and with a swift movement of its mouth sucked in the glittering yellow morsel, paused for a split second before quite violently spitting it out, then returned to the deep dark safety of the pool and, if fish are capable of doing such a thing… sulked.